The Pointless Rose

and

Further Assorted Stories for Children

by

Michael Angus

(Illustrations by Katharine Sarah Angus)

i

About the Author

Michael Angus is author, musician, architect and educator. Born in 1963 in Glasgow, he has lived and worked in the city all his life. He studied architecture at the Glasgow School of Art, practiced as a professional architect and has taught architecture since 1996, in the Department of Architecture, University of Strathclyde.

In 2013, he self-published his first compendium of children's short stories: 'The Beautiful Coat and Other Assorted Stories for Children', illustrated by his daughter, Katie. It won critical acclaim, and has spawned sequel: 'The Pointless Rose and Further Assorted Stories for Children', self-published in 2016. A third compendium of children's stories, 'The Good Hoover and even Further Assorted Stories for Children' is currently underway, plus a selection of science fiction short stories, entitled: 'Tomorrow World's'.

Further details regarding the author can be found at the author's website:

www.michaelangus-author.com

and at the Amazons Author Page:

https://www.amazon.com/Michael-Angus/e/B00IYZOSIW/

Also by this author:

**'THE BEAUTIFUL COAT
and
Other Assorted Stories for Children'**

Self published: 2014
Available at: **Amazon.com** or **www.createspace.com/4262629**

For Christopher

CONTENTS

List of Illustrations

All illustrations are photographs by my daughter, Katharine Sarah Angus, aged 11, taken on either her iPhone 5 or her iPad, between the summers of 2015 to 2016.
Thanks go to Donald Hunter for scanning and mounting.

I began this selection of stories, unlike the previous ('The Beautiful Coat…), with a thematic intention: having been intimately associated with education throughout much of my life, in the subject area of the built environment, or more simply put: architectural education, I wanted to write stories that might illuminate certain ideas about architecture, to make aspects of architecture perhaps more accessible to younger minds (despite the big words…as my daughter is keen to point out!).

This then was the original intention – but consequences intervened, and other intentions laid claim: firstly, after inadvertently witnessing in a documentary about the Lockerbie bombing, an off the cuff statement made with reference to an act deemed futile, but, in reality, was anything but; and secondly, consequence which subsequently rendered all else subsumed: suddenly and without expectation, on the 27th October 2014, my six year old son, Christopher, passed away.

Many words were expressed at the time, to try to describe the extremity of such consequence – perhaps my daughter Katie, then ten, made the most insightful and accurate description, simply expressed, quietly to me, in a moment of welcome lucidity: 'It is as if nature has been turned upside down…'

My son was, is, beautiful: beautiful in body and spirit. There was, is, no bad bone in his body – so why would such a thing occur? There was no purpose, no sense, no reason, and one would have to assume, no good in it. Really, what good comes from the loss of a six year old child, any six year old child? It would be inappropriate of me to suggest that this selection of stories could in any way serve to console others who find themselves in a similar situation. I know only too well that there is nothing that can reach into grief of this nature. Only time ameliorates, and perhaps assisted as it passes by moments of desperate empathy. In this latter respect these stories might offer some solace; suffice to say, the writing of them was completed at a time of immense grief, and in the pursuit, implicitly initiated, for guidance and self-regulated comfort.

I had help – this selection was already underway, Christopher had already contributed, with his inimitable humour and blessed temperament. He suggested the title for 'The Skeleton…' story, and he loved the 'Alien…' story, so my daughter told me. I missed terribly his editing contribution in the writing, my best moments being when I could imagine Christopher, either laughing or frowning at my efforts. I did try to keep him beside me as I wrote, but it was often impossible. He is not here, which is the most impossible statement of all.

That loss remains impenetrable and I am left, now, often, adrift - but I am driven nonetheless to look for order and meaning.

If life is governed by every action having an equal and opposite reaction, then what is the positive action that squares this equation with regard to my son? I do not yet know what the good thing is that balances out the bad - but I trust it must exist. Perhaps it already does, perhaps it is, simply: hope......

If I were to say this book was written in the pursuit of hope, in truth it wasn't. It was written in conflict. But hope, coincidentally, remains at its core: it lies at the heart of the original intention: architecture, the desire to build, is implicitly a hopeful pursuit; and hope surely must lie at the heart of the resolve that drives any who have suffered unwarranted tragedy, forwards, collectively or individually; and hope, as I have discovered these past few months, lies insufferably tenacious at the heart of my heart.

Michael Angus
November 2015 - August 2016

All author proceeds from the sale of this book go to Glasgow Children's Hospital Charity (formerly Yorkhill Children's Charity), supporting the Royal Hospital for Children in Glasgow, Scotland.

Registered Charity No: SCO07856

It is impossible for me to separate out direct acknowledgment to those that helped me with the actual writing of this book, and to those whom I feel indebted, most honourably, to thank for their personal support in recent months; on the whole they are one and the same.

Without you, therefore… for want of a better word, my thanks:

To my son, Christopher: for being a light that casts no shadow.
To my daughter Katie: for just being who she is (and of course for her amazing photographs).
To my wife, Angela: for keeping our son so safe.

To my mother, and to Aunty Suzy: for their generous hearts and also, once again, for their un-biased critique and detailed proof reading.

To Dr Karen McLeod, Dr Trevor Richens, Dr Hendry and all the staff at the Royal Hospital for Sick Children, Yorkhill, Glasgow, especially all those in the Cardiology Unit/Ward level 5. There is no testament fitting that could convey my appreciation for their efforts.

To staff at the Glasgow Children's Hospital Charity, especially Aileen McConnell, for keeping me right.

To Ms MacAulay, Ms Johnston, Mrs Freeland, Mrs Donald, Mr Lamb and all the staff and pupils at Garelochhead Primary School.

To the teaching and admin staff at the Department of Architecture, University of Strathclyde: Aileen Alexander, Fiona Bradly, Uli Enslein, Lynne Harvey, Derek Hill, Jac Lister, Catriona Mirren, David MacRitchie, David Reat, Ombretta Romice, Harry Stokes, Ellen Thomson and Peter Welsh for their efforts in my absence, their implicit allegiance and collective wholesomeness.
My thanks too, to all the students on the Bsc and the p/g Dip/Masters in Architecture, especially Holly Gray and friends.

To Colin McNeish, an especial mention, for his and his wife's friendship, and for the continued opportunity to talk so collegiately on matters of faith and belief.

To all the staff at the medical centre, Naval Base, Faslane: for making a happy place for my wife.

To my 'happy places', for their companionable solitude:

- and for the view: Café 19, Helensburgh;
- and for their (early) open doors: P.J.s Kitchen, Helensburgh;
- and for their Peroni and perfect petite patio: Babbity Bowsters, Glasgow.

To Dougie: my rock, to Jacque, Cat and Pauline: my bk friends and fellow travellers, to Sylvia Meldrum, Anne Greig, Harvey Sussock, Jan Steckline, to Arlene Smith and everyone at the 'Brightest Star' bereaved families support group, to Rolf Roscher and Felicity Steers, Chris and Anne, Alan and Alison, to Peter Christiansen (for being the one and only silver prince…), to the ADU 2020 team, to Lauren Tait, and lastly, but by no means least, to William, Morag and my brother and his wife: for being there when they were needed most.

I had originally intended to thank my heroes with this publication, in particular Stan Lee, Pete Townshend, and Roger Waters, and Le Corbusier, for the joy their creativity has brought to my life. So it remains……

MA
August 2016

This book is considerably longer than my first, twice as long in fact, and it is considerably denser. I have taken steps to present it in a slightly different way therefore, to ease hopefully, navigation.

I was born in the 60's and grew up in the 70's - vinyl held a place of intimate association in my youth. I have a particular fondness for the concept album, especially those albums that dedicated a whole side of the vinyl to one single track (eg '2112' by Rush, 'Meddle' by Pink Floyd, or especially 'Foxtrot' by Genesis). The book is arranged in similar fashion, in two sides:

Side 1: a varied selection of stories, perhaps more applicable to (slightly) younger readers.
Side 2: a single story, pretty much, more applicable to older readers.

If I could say something, in general and despite the slight differentiation in the two sides, as regards the appropriate age of the reader: for sure all these stories are perhaps more suitable to older children......perhaps. Age is only an indicator of maturity after all. But as a guide to parents, I'd suggest age nine and above approximately might be about right - I'd recommend scanning the stories first if you want to re-assure yourself. Collectively they have not been written with one specific age group in mind.

As with my first book, if you wish to read the stories aloud, I am not precious as regards the specific words, or for that matter the tone of delivery, plot even - feel free to subvert at your discretion!

And again at the risk of stating the obvious, I sincerely hope that you, and your children, enjoy the reading of them......

Side 1

"You see things; and you say: 'Why?'.
But I dream things that never were; and I say: 'Why not?'"

George Bernard Shaw

Eventually, and with a predictable finality, the rose with no thorns found itself to be, alone.

THE POINTLESS ROSE

Once upon a time, there was a rose that had no thorns. Such a rose was certainly unusual, if not, in fact, unique, but not once had the rose felt cause to object to its curious condition; not once had it yielded even to acknowledge that it was in any way different, despite the sympathy offered instinctively by all the other roses.

"Don't you worry," they would say, with genuine sincerity, trying their best to be caring and supportive: "You'll still get picked."

But the rose with no thorns did not get picked, and gradually, over time, each and every other rose was; to each came the day when they were delicately beheaded and lifted up; up, up and away, defencelessly spiralling into the clouds as if carried on invisible and twisted wings. In blissful sacrifice they disappeared, each calling out with sweet demand as they vanished into the grey and empty sky, their words echoing terrible and full of joyous farewell, of hope, of worth, of salvation, redemption and of pious and martyred blessing.

Eventually, and with a predictable finality, the rose with no thorns found itself to be, alone. But the rose never protested its solitude. In silent contentment, it simply grew; it grew and grew and grew, ignorant of time and despite the seasons: the rose with no thorns, untamed, blossomed, brilliantly and radiant. Its petals coloured a deep, deep red, a red as rich and gloriously majestic as that of a setting sun; its stalk strengthened with elegant sinew, as firm and impossibly smooth as warm summer rain; its scent fermented with ripened age, pervasive, yet elusive, and so seductively combined to become treasured as readily as music, invaluable, immeasurable: an aroma as precious as the evocation of a cherished memory.

It filtered out across every country and continent, across every house, street, village, town and city, across every mountain, valley, desert and sea; ultimately, it filtered out across the entire world - and carried with it, this incorruptible scent, were the rose's bountiful seeds.

They drifted unhindered and immaculate through the solid air, as pure and easy as a thoughtless sigh, fated to bloom as robustly as their host when and wherever they alighted, whether in every garden; in every forest and every farm; in every meadow and in every un-weeded furrow, window-box and muddy lane; and in every dusty barren field and every ragged quarry; in every abandoned backyard behind ramshackle house, littered thin with colour drained plastic toys and withering swings; and in every admirable allotment and defeated pitch; in every shallow outcrop on summits of unreachable frozen peaks and in the depths of shady glen; and in every civic park, trapped and lost within sombre city and town; in every forfeited verge surrendered between hedgerow and busy road; and in every gap in the line, of poplars and harvested vines; and in every orchard and in every bare broken pot by forgotten grave; in every dry and fractured gutter clinging to proud but derelict ruin; in every patch of neglected earth, on the banks of forgotten canals and between the sleepers of railway lines persisting in dormant sidings; and in every manicured putting-green and perfect lawn.

And the rose bloomed, too, in every single grain of dirt that was ground into the cracks of the broken and bloody concrete; roses, roses everywhere, thorn-less, every one, and destined never to be beheaded, ever, ever again.

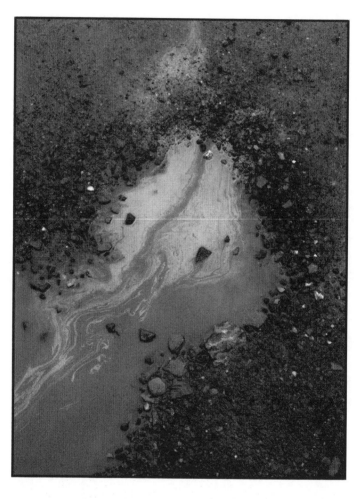

I could not go down, so I went round, round and round and round, and so much so that I almost came back upon myself, poured flat upon the ground!

THE RIVER THAT GOT LOST

"At last! At last!" The sea held out its waves in welcome, and the river collapsed, drained and exhausted, sinking so gratefully into them.

"We were so worried," consoled the sea, comforting the river, shivering, deep in its seething and thunderous embrace. "We had no idea, what had happened to you!"

The other rivers all surged around. "What happened to you?" they did with care, likewise declare, in genuine concern. "What happened, what happened to you?"

"I got lost," the river admitted, in a trembling feeble voice. "I got lost, lost...oh, so lost."

"But, what happened?" the sea again it asked, and the river once recovered, sufficiently enough, recounted in dark woeful tones, the tale of its descent, its sorry, sorry, tale......

'The first thing that I can recall is that I was: a waterfall......for I was falling, down and down, always and forever down. If I think about it now, it should have been so easy, such an easy thing to do, but in truth, I knew it wasn't – for wherever was I going, I hadn't got a clue, and lost is how I felt, from the very moment that I fell out from the cloud.

Even after landing, the only option still, was down – but, which way? For which way was the right way down? I asked the cloud, but all it did was stare, it stared blankly and said nothing. It seemed I had no choice. So I took a breath, a deep, deep breath, and headed, yes, I headed down, even without knowing which way I was going – I kept on looking up, and asking of the cloud, hoping to be heard: "Is this way correct?", but it never said a thing, not a single word. So I just kept ongoing, down, down, blindly down, as far as I could go.

And then, I came upon the rock.

The rock was big, it was really, really big; big and black and brutal and...bare! It asked me many questions; oh so terribly many!

I had no idea there could be so many questions, and I couldn't answer one! But the rock, it said I must; I had to answer every one, every single one or I would not be allowed to pass. I was there for, oh, so long, how long I could not tell, and I had to learn so many things, things which I can hardly recollect. All of it was pointless, it seems even more so now, but at the time I clearly had no option. The rock was so insistent, it demanded that I do everything that it asked, and do exactly what it bid; it was always angry, and shouted at me, even when I did my best – I really, really did!

It was so mean, and horrible, and really rude and cruel but the worst thing truly, is: I don't know why. I don't know why the rock was so mean to me at all. I simply don't know why.'

"Perhaps – it was...dissatisfied?" the sea it offered slightly.

"Perhaps," the river conceded, but not with much conviction.

"But why not, just go round it...?" one of the other rivers asked.

"It never occurred to me that I could," the river said, surprised, and suddenly ashamed. It looked at all the other rivers: "Is that what you all did?"

"Why, yes," they said. "We all of us went round it."

"Oh," the river sighed, embarrassed, turning red. "Oh, I didn't know." And if a river could hang its head, then that is what it did. It paused a while, before it could continue, and its voice was sadder yet.

'Well, once the rock did let me pass, I carried on by heading down, down and further down. I kept on asking the cloud above: "Is this way correct?", but all it said was: nothing, absolutely nothing! So I just kept ongoing, down; down, down, deeper and down.

And then, I came upon the forest.

The forest was dark, it was really, really dark; dark and dim and dense and...difficult! It had so many trees; oh so terribly many! I had simply no idea there could be so many trees, nor knew of what they needed. They pleaded with me, every one, to bring my water to them. I watered some, and watered many more - their roots were dry, rough and many scratched me; they grabbed me, and hung on to me and wouldn't let me go. And I had to water every one before, the forest swore, I would be allowed to pass. Well, it took me such a long, long time, to water every one – and even once I'd watered them, some much more than once, still they wanted more: more, and more and more!

It was so hard to do, to try and try, and yet still to hear them cry – and they nearly drained me dry! But the worst thing truly, is: I don't know why. I don't know why the trees wanted more than what they needed. I simply don't know why.'

"Perhaps - they were...forlorn?" the sea it offered, slightly once again.

"Perhaps," conceded the river, again, without conviction.

"But why not, just go round it...?" one of the other rivers asked.

"It never occurred to me that I could," said the river, once again surprised. It looked at all the other rivers. "Is that what you all did?"

"Why, yes," they said. "We all of us went round it."

"Oh," the river sighed again, embarrassed and ashamed, and flushed even redder yet. "Oh, I didn't know." It paused, before continuing, even sadder than before.

'Well, once the forest let me pass, I carried on, by heading down, down and further down. I still kept asking the cloud above: "Is this way correct?", but it still said: nothing. Absolutely nothing!! So I just kept ongoing, down; down, down, deeper and down.

And then, I came upon the loch.

The loch was wide, it was really, really wide; wide and wild and wonderful and...wise! It taught me such tremendous things, oh so terribly many! I had simply no idea there could be so many rights, and so many wrongs. It insisted where it came from was the only place to be – and better than the rest! It convinced me I must join it, join and never pass; so join I duly did. Because it hated all the mountains, they surrounded us, threatening, high on each and every side; the loch it fought them all the time! It persuaded me to hate them too, we rose and fell together, as we fought and fought and fought. The loch said we'd be free, once we'd surely won – but win we never did!

9

It was so mad and bitter, and it slandered me and blamed me, even when it finally reluctantly agreed to let me pass, but the worst thing truly, is: I don't know why. I don't know why the loch fought the way it did. I simply don't know why.'

"Perhaps — it was...afraid?" the sea it offered, quietly, and slightly, once again.

"Perhaps," the river conceded, but again, without conviction.

"But why not, just go round it...?" one of the other rivers asked.

"It never occurred to me that I could," again, admitted the river, though somewhat less surprised. It looked at all the other rivers. "Is that what you all did?"

"Why, yes," they said. "We all of us went round it."

"Oh," the river sighed, still ashamed and embarrassed, flushing redder, redder yet. "Oh, I didn't know."

It paused, and yet again, sighed, before continuing, even sadder than before.

'Well, once the loch did let me pass, I carried on by heading down, down and further down. I *still* kept asking the cloud above: "Is this way correct?", but it *still* said: nothing. Absolutely nothing!!! So I just kept ongoing, down; down, down, deeper and down.

And then I came upon the marsh.

The marsh was rank, it was really, really rank; rank and rancid and rotten and...rich! It whispered to me secrets; oh so terribly many! I had simply no idea there could be so many secrets, secrets that could make me sleep, so sleepy, soft and hard. I dribbled and I splattered, as I slept, I rolled, I tumbled and I fattened up, all gloopy, like a thickened, sickly wine. It told me all I had to do, was — well, absolutely nothing, nothing, not a thing, before I could be free to pass — it pretended, so I had to too, I had to lie, and it sold me that I need not wash nor bathe, but it was ok to be smelly, ok to stagnate. It felt so good, but much too much too good.'

It was so odd and all of it was hazy, to waste away in a liquid sea of dreams, but the worst thing truly, is: I don't know why. I don't know why the marsh so wanted to be lazy. I simply don't know why.'

"Perhaps – it was...adrift?" the sea it offered, quietly, and so slightly once again.

"Perhaps," the river conceded, but conviction? - it had none.

"But why not, just go round it...?" one of the other rivers asked.

"It never occurred to me that I could," again admitted the river, without surprise of any kind. It looked at all the other rivers. "Is that what you all did?"

"Why, yes," they said. "We all of us went round it."

"Oh," the river sighed, still embarrassed, and flushed red as it could get. "Oh, I didn't know."

And again, the river paused, before continuing, so much sadder than before.

'Well, once the marsh did let me pass, I carried on by heading down, down and further down. I *still* kept asking the cloud above: "Is this way correct?", but it *still* said: nothing. Absolutely nothing!!!! So I just kept ongoing down; down, down, deeper and down.

And then I came upon the plain.'

The river hesitated, and then suddenly, some salty tears appeared to swell, flowing wet within its wake. The other rivers waited; the sea in silence too, for the river to continue; and when it did its voice, had like death become: cold and quietly despondent.

"I thought that I was lost before – I did. I really did. But, beyond the marsh...beyond the marsh things became much worse; much, much, so much worse." The river then with sad appeal, to the others, did implore: "Did you end up there...drifting...high upon on the plain?"

Before anyone could answer, the river soft continued:

'The plain was flat, flatness everywhere, and for as far as I could see. Before the plain, at least I knew, I knew that I was going: down. Down, down, always down, down, forever down...but now there was no going 'down'. Now there was just flat, flat and empty, emptiness - everywhere.

I could not go down, so I went round, round and round and

round, and so much so that I almost came back upon myself, poured flat upon the ground! I tried and tried to find a way, forward, but I simply couldn't. I just went round and round and round and round. I looked for the cloud, to show to me the way, but it was nowhere to be seen. There was nothing there above me, nothing there at all.

Finally, my strength was gone; I was so nearly dry, so nearly and completely, dry...'

The river paused, yet again, and the tears that had been threatened, spilled in torrents over its absent banks, like a stream un-levee. In the wakes of every other river, tears welled up, tears - of sympathy, so sad did their fellow river seem.

"And then, just when I thought ...well, thought, I do not know - but then, just then I saw.... I saw......"

"What? What did you see?" another river prompted.

"I saw...I saw, the floating stones."

For a second no-one said a thing, and all that could be heard was the waving of the sea, as it broke upon the shore.

"Floating stones?" another river queried.

"Yes...floating stones. I don't know how else to describe it. They were just hanging there, hanging in the air, a line of stones, a whole line of stones – floating. Floating in the air."

If rivers could be dumbfounded, then that is what they were, their mouths left hanging open, incredulously, they stared.

"But -?" one murmured, involuntarily, and another: "Stones don't float....?"

"I know, I know, it sounds impossible – I know it, but it's true. I don't know how else to describe it. I don't. But it's true."

"It was a bridge," the sea it interrupted, not slightly, but quiet as before. "You saw a bridge."

"A bridge?" said the river. "Is that then what you call it?"

The sea, it only nodded, revealing nothing more. Still, the rivers stared in rapture, in awe of the seas wisdom, apparently without fathom - though the river was confused, hoping for some further explanation.

But the sea remained impassive, and so the river, at the silent seas behest, continued.

"It - the bridge? - it was so strange, I mean, it was amazing, yes, but strange – I'd never seen such a thing, or anything quite like it. And, the strangest thing of all: it seemed - to call, to me. I'm sure I heard it call to me, I'm sure I thought I did - though, if you ask me now, now I'm not sure - it was all so unreal, and I was so very tired, and so utterly exhausted. Maybe I imagined it. But: I had nowhere else to go - so I headed straight towards it. Somehow, I managed, finally, to reach it – the floating stones, the bridge. And then, it happened: the most amazing thing of all......"

The other rivers held their breath - expectantly they waited, as the river that got lost, incredibly, explained.

"I went under it. I simply then went under it – and it was so easy, such an easy thing to do! The rock, the forest, the loch, the marsh, and the plain most of all, had been so hard, so, so very hard, but the bridge, it was so easy – I knew exactly what to do: go under! And when I did, I was filled with such resolve, such strength, I knew I would persist. I'd never felt that way before. I'd never felt so strong, so safe, or so...so sure!? I realised I'd never been, sure, not about a single thing. But as soon as I swept under it, the bridge made sense of me – and I made sense of it. I knew then for the first time, I knew then where I was, and I knew where I was going. Everything was clear to me, the way ahead: correct! I knew then what I wanted, I'd found what I had sought......and I was, no longer lost!"

The other rivers regarded the river damned in captured awe.

"It sounds ...incredible," said one, eventually.

"It was," the river said. "Really, really it was...I'm struggling to explain it. But it was as if the bridge had waited there for me, so we could be together - and would be so, forever?"

The sea it smiled – "I've heard such tales as yours before," it said. "You are so very lucky..."

"I am...?"

"Indeed, yes, yes indeed you are......you have been blessed. Fewer rivers than you know could even guess at what you've seen."

"I don't feel blessed," the river confessed, so sadly, and it slowly hung its head. "I don't feel blessed at all...I feel a fool, and so stupid; a fool for getting lost." It glanced up at the others: "None of you, not one - none of you, got lost." It tried, but couldn't hide the envy in its voice. "None of you, but me," it said, and again, the river hung its head, ashamed, and softly crying. "Even once I passed the bridge, I once again got lost."

The other rivers shared with their fellow river, in its deep distress - but they knew not what to say. The sea too, was itself, apparently, lost for words at the miserable rivers dismay. Finally though, it reached far out its foaming waves to lift the river up.

It looked into its limpid face, and said: "There was a time, a time long ago, when I had not heard such tales as the one that you have told." It cast its gaze around. "It was enough, that you arrived - from whence you came made no account: there *were* no tales to tell, for the journey that you took was not known to even be so, it was impossible to be of consequence or even of import, for it was what it was, indeed, is what it is, and is, was nothing more." The sea turned, and kindly to the river, said: "But I can still remember the first time that I met, a river who told me of the things that you describe, of all the hardships it confronted, and of being lost, and of the floating stones that hung upon the air. Who could ever have imagined, such a thing, of a river, being lost? But why then should it not be so? Why should every river not get lost?"

The sea it paused again, becalmed it stared into the space that lies beyond the horizon and the sky. It slightly sighed. "For then, you have your tales to tell, of how you were all found......but yet, I would be glad, not to hear such tales again."

Then rousing, it addressed the saddened distraught river. "You are not the first, and you will not be the last, river to get lost. But I ask it of you now, are you lost, still?"

"No," replied the river, "no – no, I'm not."

14

The sea then whispered into the rivers shell like watery ear: "I shall tell you now a secret, a secret, just for you, but not for you alone - no river can ever be lost. All are found – eventually, for there is a bridge for every one, as there was one waiting there for you."

"But I was, I was – lost," the river insisted. "I didn't know where I was going, and I didn't know what to do. I didn't go round the rock, or round the forest, or round the loch or round the marsh.....everything I did, I did was wrong."

"No, not everything," the sea so gently then admonished. "So you did not, go round the rock, or round the forest, or round the loch, or round the marsh? But then again, why should you? And even if you think, that all you did was wrong, all these things that you did, or rather, did not do, there is one thing that you most certainly did get right...right?"

Confused, the river looked, at the sea, with a question in its gaze.

"The bridge that you went under...?" The sea proposed: "You could have just gone round it..."

"It never occurred to me that I could...," the river low admitted, but for once without embarrassment; it did not convert the sea or itself deep red with shame. Instead it raised a smile, and the sea, it proudly smiled back.

"Welcome home," the sea said warmly, as it pulled the river softly from the shore.

Silently the river, it dissolved into the sea, the river that got lost, lost, no more.

They were simply delighted – never had so many donkeys longed
for so many mirrors!

THE DONKEY THAT HAD GREEN LEGS

Once upon a time there was a donkey that had green legs. Certainly such a donkey was rather unusual, for donkeys have brown legs, don't they? – well, of course they do!

The donkey really liked having green legs – bright green they were, as green as the greenest grass – because having green legs made the donkey very special, which the other donkeys were not slow to acknowledge.

"I wish I had legs like yours," they would say, every day, each and every one unashamedly jealous of the donkey's remarkable limbs. It made the donkey feel just grand, to be continually admired and envied so.

However, as time went on, the donkey began to become less and less enamoured with all the attention he was getting. It did not cause the donkey to dislike his green legs, not at all - and he was not particularly inhibited from doing anything, certainly not initially - it was simply that he felt increasingly tired of the constant adulation! It was, quite frankly, annoying; he had to keep thanking others, all the time, he had to keep nodding gratefully at every comment or appreciative glance, and, of course, being a donkey of impeccable character, he had to always be: sincere!

As if that wasn't enough, the donkey, because of his green legs, had become something of a celebrity – but the glamour of fame had also worn thin. The endless press interviews, the constant requests for autographs and selfies, and constant demands too for photo shoots; so, so many photo shoots! Soon the donkey's image was everywhere; he could hardly go out at all without being recognised!

It was all becoming too much...eventually the donkey decided that enough was enough - something had to be done! If it was all about his having green legs that made him special, what would happen if all the donkeys had green legs...?

So one night, he hatched a simple plan: whilst the other donkeys slept, the donkey with green legs spray-painted all their legs, bright, bright green!

He painted, carefully, patiently and quietly, all through the night. Of course, if the donkey had opposable thumbs he might have been able to complete the task much, much quicker – but one has to applaud the donkey's ingenuity that he managed the task at all! (It's amazing what can be done with a little inventiveness, and big, big teeth!)

Come the morning, as one might imagine, things on the farm were rather interesting.

As soon as the donkeys awoke: complete and utter amazement! Green, green legs - everywhere! Stunned incredulities soon turned to vain and narcissistic declarations: "My, how fine am I!" each proudly proclaimed, strutting around the farm, seeking and receiving in equitable abundance: unparalleled admiration! They were simply delighted - never had so many donkeys longed for so many mirrors!

The donkey with green legs watched in silent amusement, feigning an expression of appreciative awe as the donkeys exclaimed: "Remember – remember when you were the only one? Now look at us – all of us, how fine we *all* are, with our green, green legs!"

And so they trumpeted, day in, day out, and at first the donkey with green legs was rather pleased at how things had turned out. No longer was he the centre of attention; no longer was he the only donkey to be hounded, to be photographed or red about all the time; now he could go about his daily business, quietly and uninterrupted.

But after a while he got tired of the other donkeys, constantly harping on about their green legs, and how wonderful it was, now they all had green legs, how special they were, and how they would all be able to do things together, go places together, how famous they would *all* be! It may not have been inevitable, but it wasn't long before they claimed, with a haughty air and imperious superiority, that they were even more remarkable than the donkey with green legs, because they had 'become green', by their own achievement......whereas the donkey with green legs had only been born that way!

They were obviously not the smartest donkeys on the planet, paint is paint after all – but that was to the donkey's advantage: they were driving him nuts! So one night, he hatched another plan: he painted his own legs brown!

"How awful it must be for you, to have brown legs. It's a shame you don't have green legs like us," the other donkeys proclaimed, apparently in sympathy, but with a transparent insincerity.

They proceeded to shun the donkey...but the donkey didn't mind – whilst the donkeys with green legs extended their celebrity far and wide, whilst they sought without restraint consolation in approval, and basked in their vanity, in the immense and easy glow of appreciation and admiration, he, on the other hoof, went about his business, quietly, uninterrupted - and, if truth be told, quite contentedly, for he knew that beneath the brown, his legs were bright, bright green, as green as the greenest grass......

If one were to search the world......one could not source such a
road, a road that could take one, anywhere one wished to go......

THE SKELETON WHO CROSSED THE ROAD

Once upon a time there was a road, and it was without question *the* most boring road ever! The road went from nowhere to nowhere, and passed through the most tedious of landscapes, a landscape devoid of any redeeming qualities whatsoever; just desert, endless, endless desert, flat, featureless and dull: dull, dull, dull!

Where the road went, no-one knew, where it came from, no-one knew. No cartographer had ever bothered to survey it – it did not appear on any map, nor did it have a name or a number; it was just there, and no-one knew how or why; in fact, it was so boring, that no-one even cared!

If there had been a bend in the road, even a curve, however slight, it might have alleviated the monotony – but there wasn't. The road just went on and on and on and *on*, without any deviation at all. Its stultifying reality would conquer the will of even the most robust mind; consequently, no-one, not even the most intrepid of travellers, had been known to have journeyed along it. Likely, if any had, they would have been driven completely insane by the utter tediousness of the experience. Insanity notwithstanding, they certainly would not have been able to make an account of their experience – there were truly no words to adequately describe the roads desolate awfulness!

It would not be true, however, to say that the road had never been traversed: occasionally, and *only* occasionally, small animals would make their way across the road: rabbits; foxes; hares or turtles - but they would suffer such a mind-numbing weariness, they would never do so again. Indeed, some would simply expire on the crossing! They would die right there and then, right in the middle of the road, so over-come were they by the roads hopelessly dull turgidity.

Clearly, one would have to wonder why the road even existed, so pointless *was* its existence. And yet, exist it did, lying dead flat and dreary on the ground, useless and without direction: truly the most uninteresting and uninspiring road there had ever been: both tiresome and tyre-less!

But then, one day, a skeleton crossed the road.

It was unquestionably, the most unlikely of events. Word quickly spread: "Did you hear? Did you hear? A skeleton crossed the road!"

"What road?"

"*The* road!"

"The boring road?"

"Yes, the boring road!!! – a skeleton crossed it!"

It was unbelievable. Soon people were flocking from all over in the hope of seeing the skeleton cross the road again. They camped out for days; tents lined the road, almost from end to end, and soon dingy boarding houses and shabby hotels sprang up to cater for the sudden influx of people. Around these hostelries, little towns began to appear: they were hastily built, with only the most meagre of facilities: rough bar-rooms, cheap general stores, dubious barbers and so on, but slowly the towns grew - and continued to grow. Imperceptibly, the old, ramshackle buildings gave way to new, glittering palaces of wondrous façade: the hotels were no longer threadbare and dirty, but showered in golden chips, sumptuous duvets, and host to harmonies of howling entertainment.

Shops too, all manner of shops and showrooms appeared: fragrant flower shops, tantalising hosiery shops, delicate chinaware shops, heady tobacco shops, fantastic comic shops, noisy body shops - and adjacent, there appeared more and even more commercial premises: glorious garages, industrious distilleries, futile beauty parlours, fancy wig makers, pungent perfumeries......businesses flourished, and crime too, as people became rich, and so then needed governance. Soon, next to grimy factories, were grim courthouses, next to them, grimmer yet penitentiaries, grey and blank, like the innumerable grey and blank warehouses that sprawled out on the edges of town. And further out, mighty mansions became mightier still, sitting high in the hills; and in the valleys, stern town halls would become sterner city halls.

As much as the people needed governance, people needed to

believe: curious shaped churches catering for all manner of beliefs sprang up, with minarets and domes, spikes and strange shaped edifices. People became ill: hospitals and clinics sprang up, as did vast cemeteries as consequence of their failure, or simply of time. People needed education: schools and universities set in plush landscapes both grey and hard and soft and green, they too sprang up, as did parks and monuments and statues and squares......so it went on, on and on and on, and soon the towns were not towns anymore, they were now cities, and soon each city, like the towns before them, became indistinguishable one from the next: they merged to form one great mega-city, a gloriously ridiculous conglomeration, glittering and flickering all day and all of the night, a mega-city that only partied, and was never ending, in either its distance or its expectation!

And right through the centre of it all, ran the boring road!

But the road was no longer a road, it was the one and only, main street, the thoroughfare: an immense vista lined by dazzling lights and shimmering reflections, an artery of unlimited proportion that fed the mega-city, from end to endless end: a tremendous boulevard of unbroken dreams! If one were to search the world, or to wait for unlimited eons, or even to travel back through time, one could not source such a road, a road that could take one, anywhere one wished to go......

Certainly, therefore, if the road had been boring, it was boring no longer; indeed, few could recall it as such, and of those that did, their accounts of the road and its tedious legacy, red or recounted, were considered decidedly dubious. How could such an account be an authentic and accurate description of historic fact? The road - boring? Never! It was the most amazing, exciting, incredible road on the planet!

Eventually it became the stuff of folklore, it became: legend, that the road had once been boring, the most boring road ever – boring, until one day, a skeleton crossed the road......

PS: The legend cemented itself, so much so that no-one ever had cause to ask why the skeleton crossed the road in the first place – or perhaps it is because everyone knows why the skeleton crossed the road…they do, don't they?! It must have had a reason……

So…why did the skeleton cross the road……?*

*The answer is in the story…………!

He sighed, and added quietly: "I hate being a store."

THE SACRED STORE

Once upon a time there were two stores. Each sat on the main street of a small town, one at one end, and the other, well, inevitably, at the other.
One store was very, very new, the other, very, very old. Regardless, however of the age difference, neither store had ever had cause to make complaint about the other – indeed, they, and the town agreeably acknowledged the perceived truth of it, co-existed peacefully, despite the fact that it would have been perfectly conceivable one might have been jealous of the other, or at least felt some degree of unwarranted competition by the presence of the other. But this was simply not the case – they were accepted as equals, in a town that embraced them with equanimity, both as pertinent amidst the healthy equilibrium of the town's other facilities – post office, pub, fire station, police station, doctor's surgery, hairdresser, chemist, take-away and cafe, garage, church and library: congenial neighbours all - well, relatively so – on a pleasant little main street.

The stores were what are known as: general stores, common enough in just about every small town one might pass through. They sold pretty much the same items, at pretty much the same price, were pretty much the same size, looked pretty much the same, and opened and closed at pretty much the same time, every day of the week – their routine was pretty much always the same: open-sell-close, open-sell-close, day after day, month after month, year after year.

This routine was observed almost religiously, so dedicated were the stores to the service they provided. It was rare that one might close unnecessarily – perhaps out of respect to some local who may have passed away unexpectedly, or for some special celebration like the Easter parade or the Christmas fair, or whenever a Hollywood starlet or freaky pop star came to visit – which was never! Even if one of the stores did have to close, it would always open at some point - it was unheard of that the store would be closed for the whole day – in fact, never had a day passed when either store had been closed all day. It had never happened – not once.

But then, one day, a day that began like any other, unremarkable and indistinguishable from any preceding, that most unlikely of things happened: the old store did not open!

Nothing was said, at least not at first – all the other buildings were a little embarrassed: it was such an unusual occurrence, that no-one really noticed until late in the afternoon.

It was the pub, in his typically unsubtle way, who spoke up first: "Whaahhs's up wi' shhhtore?" he slurred.

"Store?" the post office haughtily replied. She hated the pub, really, he was always drunk and his door just reeked – reeked! – of drink. If it wasn't for the hairdresser that separated them, she would have shut down long ago. That, and of course her sense of civic duty – pub could drink all day if he wanted, she had work to do, important work. Pub – well, pub was just that – a pub. Drunken old sod!

"Yehhsse, shhhtore," the pub slurred again.

"Which store?" post office felt obliged to inquire, dutifully despite herself.

"Ol shhhtore...y'knowsss, shhtorey...ol' shhtorrey..." He nodded vaguely in the old store's direction. His hanging baskets swayed ridiculously, and the glass in his small square window panes seemed to blur, to glaze over and half close. In fact, just about every straight line, every window transom and door jamb, seemed to slump ever so slightly downwards. The post office straightened up, even more so by comparison - although she regretted her rather crumbling façade as she did so. It could well do with some work. She tried her best to maintain it, her stone front so finely carved and elegantly corniced, but it was hard to deny: she was getting old!

"Something's definitely wrong," the library agreed, in her usual polite and sensitive manner.

"What's wrong? What's wrong?" hair-dresser and café joined in, excited and squealing delightfully. They immediately began to compare indecent proposals, conspiratorially flapping their doors and fluttering their blinds. Take-away nodded, ever so slightly, apparently agreeing with every claim – it was hard to tell: he rarely opened his door or windows during the day; he may have been disagreeing, he may not even have cared - but something in his manner made it seem as though he shared the unfavourable yet unfounded opinions of his immediate neighbours.

Either way, the post office found them all to be somewhat juvenile, if not on occasion, downright annoying. 'How they gossip', she thought, contemptuously. Chemist too, though he would never admit it. "Yes, what seems to be the problem?" he said in that oh-so superior tone of his. "Old store won't open," post office reluctantly explained.

"Well, that will never do," chemist said. "I'll speak to surgery."

"You'll do no such thing," post office retorted.

Chemist sniffed. "Well...we'll need to do something," he said. "We can't have him just doing as he pleases."

The garage wheezed, and coughed. "Oh, him...ignore him," he said. "He's just in one of his moods." He winked as a small red car sped past, leering at it with his much too wide smile.

"Moods? What moods...?" post office asked.

"Oh, come on – don't tell me you haven't noticed?" He winked again, his smile even wider as another, blue car passed. "He's always in a mood. He'll open up later."

But the old store did not open that day or the next. All the buildings agreed that it was very odd, but none knew what to do (except pub of course: "He jussstth needsh a big shtifff druuwink," was his advice – but that was pub's answer to everything!)

Post office felt the obligation fall on her to do something. So, the following day, when, yet again, old store did not open, she nudged the fire station.

"Old store won't open," she said.

Fire station, drooling, just mumbled, and said nothing.

"Old store won't open!" post office repeated, rather more insistently. "We need to break his door down."

Fire station still said nothing. Police station squinted with her small mean windows, and muttered bitterly: "You're wasting your time...he's hopeless. He only wakes up when it suits him..."

Post office ignored the police station. "Wake up!" she shouted at the fire station.

"I'm telling you – you're wasting your time. He'll only wake up if it's an emergency."

"But this is an emergency!"

"Emergency!? Emergency!?" the fire station suddenly shouted, his bright red doors thrown wide open, ringing and spluttering. "What emergency?!" He peered his blood shot windows feverishly back and forth.

"Oh relax...," police station hissed. She screwed her windows down even tighter, her door too. "It's nothing..."

Fire station's doors closed, as abruptly as they had opened. He fell asleep again, and immediately began to snore.

"See? I told you," police station said dismissively. "A waste of time..."

"Maybe I could help?" library offered, blinking her big misty windows.

Post office sighed. "Well, if no-one else....?" She looked about. Police station had turned her mean windows away, and folded her grey brick walls over her miserable door. Pub, like the fire station, was fast asleep, and the garage was still too busy chasing cars. Chemist, café, hairdresser and take away suddenly seemed much more interested in discussing something or someone else.

Library smiled, optimistically. "I'll give it a go," she said. Post office nodded, feeling somewhat relieved. She fixed some loose tiles into place and went back to sorting the mail.

Library turned to the old store. She looked at his flaking paint, at his fading sign, and his rather neglected windows – one was cracked, the others streaked in dirt. Behind them, his stark fluorescent lights were on, although his outer door was quite firmly shut.

She, too, sighed. She had always liked old store, even if he could be a bit cranky from time to time. He'd never done anything like this before though.

Kindly, she whispered to him: "You'd better open."

Old store said nothing.

She tried again. "You'd better open –"

"Shan't," old store retorted, rather brusquely.

"You'd better – they'll break your door down," library warned.

"Don't care."

"But-"

"I don't care if they break my door down, they can break it down if they want. They can break it all down. I don't want to be a store any more."

Library was flummoxed. Old store didn't want to be a store? But old store was a store. She felt the need to point this out. "But you are a store," she observed, as politely as she could.

"Well, I don't want to be a store – not any more. I'm fed up being a store." He sighed, and added quietly: "I hate being a store."

All of a sudden library felt rather sorry for the old store. He was such a great store, he always had been – why he seemed so upset was beyond her. She tried to comfort him, and began: "But you're a great store-" but old store didn't let her finish.

"No I'm not – I'm a rubbish store," he grumbled.

"You're not, you're great." Library couldn't stop some tears from running down her windows. She hated seeing store so sad. "You've always been a great store..."

Store said nothing, and just stared at the crying library. She became embarrassed, and a little annoyed at the old store.

"Well, if you don't want to be a store, what *do* you want to be?" she demanded, wiping her windows.

Old store hesitated, before answering: "I want to be a cathedral," he said. His declaration, though somewhat sheepishly stated, came as a bit of a surprise.

"S...orry?" library stuttered.

"I want to be a cathedral. I hate being a store. I want to be a cathedral."

"Eh...I'm not sure-"

The church, having overheard their conversation, interrupted: "You can't be a cathedral – you're too small."

"Yes, yes – I'm sure that's right," agreed the library.

"I don't care – I want to be one..."

"Well, you can't," the church said, flatly. He stared belligerently at the store, at the library, and back again at the store. The library blinked her big bleary windows.

"Maybe-" she began.

The church ignored her. "Stores can't be cathedrals, just as cathedrals can't be stores. Can a church be a house? No. A house, a store? No. Can a fire station be a police station?-"

Police station interjected: "Oh no, please no," she whined. She immediately shut up again.

Church threw her a tolerant if somewhat patronising glance, before stating, categorically: "OK then, so – it's a no." He opened and closed his large black doors to reinforce the point.

"But why – why can't I be a cathedral – or even a church, maybe?"

Church narrowed his tall and thin lancet windows. "Look, I'm church, ok? One church is more than enough."

Old store apologised, somewhat reluctantly, but reiterated, regardless, his desire to be a cathedral.

"Well, you can't," church said. "And anyway, a cathedral would be too big for our town."

"Canterbury has a cathedral...he's not too big."

Library nodded. "He's right you know."

"Oh for God's sake," church, exasperated, spluttered. "Look, you're too small, you're too – too..."

"Too what?" old store demanded, defiantly.

Church scowled. Old store scowled in return, staring insolently back at him. "Too ... what?" he repeated slowly. His cracked window cracked a little more. Library began to cry.

Post office intervened: "Right – both of you, that's enough." She glared at them. Church and store turned away, each in a respective huff. Post office tried to say something to store, but he turned off his lights and slammed down his rusty metal shutters. She sighed. 'What are we going to do now?' she worried to herself. Maybe she *should* speak to surgery. She was loathe to – surgery could be so, well, so perfunctory. She doubted he'd be very understanding, or very helpful for that matter.

Conveniently, young store, who'd been conspicuously quiet, made a suggestion (in truth, he'd been feeling a tad guilty: he'd been earning a fortune over the previous few days since old store closed!): "Maybe we *could* do something?" he said.

"Such as?" said post office, momentarily encouraged.

"Well, maybe we could......change a few things?"

Old store piped up. "Yes, yes," he said enthusiastically, throwing up his shutters. His lights came on again. "Change...yes?!"

"But-" post office began, sceptically. Young store interrupted: "We've nothing to lose," he said, shrugging his smart blue plastic sign.

"Oh...ok," post office conceded. "Library?"

Library sniffed, and sniffled: "Yes?"

Post office nodded towards old store. "Maybe we should find out...?" she prompted.

"Oh, yes, yes, of course...let me look it up." She turned on her big bland lights, casting a pale glow through her blurry, misty windows. After a minute she turned to old store.

"So...what type of cathedral would you like to be?" she asked, properly and politely.

"Type?"

"Yes – there are lots of types: Gothic, Romanesque, Byzantine, Renaissance, Baroque, Rococco, Revivalist, Modern...even Post Modern."
"Mmmm - I think we'd better go for Modern," post office said, looking discreetly at library.

"Oh...yes, yes...," library agreed.

"I don't care – any type will do," old store said. He smiled crookedly.

"Right – well, what do we need?" post office asked, ever so efficiently.

"Well," library said, "all cathedrals have naves, transepts and apses, usually. That's how they are laid out. Some have aisles too, and sanctuaries. Their front doors, there are often three, usually they face east. They have lots of mosaics too, and pilasters and cornicing and-"

Post office held up her entablature. "OK," she said. "Thank you." Library smiled gratefully, and waited, expectant and attentive. Post office turned to the town. "Right, everyone, listen up. We all need to lend a hand – we're going to turn old store into a cathedral." Immediately, objections were raised, and everyone started to complain. "But..." began every sentence. Post office held her entablature up, even higher: "Enough," she snapped. "We're doing this – so let's just get on with it. The sooner it's done, the sooner old store will open."

She looked meaningfully at old store as she said it, and old store duly nodded.

"Thisss'll be ffun," pub slurred. Garage made a rude remark, sniggered, and coughed; the café and hairdresser giggled as they whispered something to each other. Take-away nodded – though who knew what he really thought. Church, on the other hand, remained categorically aloof: "I have more important things to do," he said, scornfully.

"Fine," said post office, somewhat sharply. She organised the rest of them, pragmatically, and they then set about changing what they could. Away went the old stores broken door. Three (rather small) doors were made, which, though they did not face east, faced west; library confirmed that this was, on occasion, known to be acceptable. Fire station cleaned the windows (it was an emergency after all!) and painted them to look like stained glass. They re-arranged all the shelves, as best they could to replicate nave and transept, and each building offered up some part of themselves: the police station some bits of her grey brick, the fire station some of his white render, the post office some glazed tiles from her entrance porch, the café, hairdresser, even the take-away, provided some coloured glass, and the chemist and young store, some shiny plastic from their red and blue signs respectively. They broke all the pieces up, and used them to line the inside of the old store in mosaics. Then they sourced a spare pulpit, taken reluctantly from the church, and they fashioned a font from a rusting water fountain that had lain redundant on the street front.

Finally it was finished. Standing back, they admired their efforts – or tried to, for they had to admit, old store did look a little odd. Part store, part...mini cathedral.

Post office, though, feigning a look of sincere approval, once again took the role of spokesperson: "Magnificent," she said. "Happy now?"

"Well, yes...but..."

"But what?" post office frowned.

"Couldn't I have an apse?"

Library looked it up again – "That might be tricky," she said – but they did their best – they re-arranged all the shelves inside the store, one more time.

"Happy now?" post office asked, again, her windows narrowed somewhat.

"I really fancied a Gothic arch...," old store mumbled.

Post office glowered at him. Old store said: "OK," but then, undaunted, ventured to ask: "Well...could I at least have another stained glass window?"

Post office glowered, even more furiously. "No" she said, firmly. "Now, I will ask you one more time – are you happy?" she demanded, rhetorically.

"Yes, yes," old store resigned, agreeably. He beamed. "I'll open tomorrow."

'Thank goodness for that,' post office thought, and she, along with all the other buildings settled down to a good night's sleep. It had been, without doubt, a stressful few days!

That night, however, whilst all the other buildings slept, library was suddenly woken up - by old store nudging her.

"You awake?" he whispered.

"I am now," library said, yawning. "What is it?"

Old store hesitated. "I hope I'll be good enough..."

"Good enough?"

"Yes ...I hope I'll be a good cathedral."

"Well...I suppose you'll be as good as you can be...?" She yawned again.

"But I wasn't a good store..."

"But you were-"

"No...no, I mean I wasn't...there were lots of things wrong with me. I wasn't really the right size, y'know? It made all my shelves a bit too close, and my door was a little too narrow, my windows, they were never really big enough. My ceiling was a bit too low, and I was never warm enough. My-"

Library yawned again. "There are lots of things wrong with all of us," she mumbled, sleepily.

"But...but..."

"But what?"

Old store paused, before admitting: "But - I don't want things to be wrong with me. I want to be perfect..."

Library opened her windows, just a little. "I'll let you into a little secret," she said, kindly "– none of us are. Don't tell church..."

They both laughed, ever so quietly, and library, despite herself, blew old store a kiss. "Goodnight," she said, grateful she couldn't see him blush. He looked ridiculous enough already!

In the morning, old store, true to his word, re-opened. The rest of the buildings, like the library, still thought he looked a tad ridiculous, but old store didn't seem to mind - in fact, from then on old store seemed happier than he had ever been! If truth be told, the whole town seemed happier. Pub still slurred over post office, who tried her best to ignore him. Garage continued to leer at passers-by and cough, cough, cough, all the time. The café and hairdresser still gossiped, as did the take-away and chemist. Fire station and police station still niggled each other with their respective disappointments. Nevertheless, the mood of the town appeared somewhat lightened, each seeming more willing to accommodate the other: fire station and police station, despite their differences, conceded a grudging but genuine respect; chemist, café and hairdresser gossiped more kindly about matters more positive, and were considerably more generous in their promotions; take-away actually deigned to open on occasion through the day; and garage, it has to be said, smiled more and leered less! Post office too, acknowledged, ever so professionally, that she rather enjoyed the attentions of pub – even if he was a drunken old so-and-so!

Even church had to admit, it was good to have another with whom he could share thoughts, on life and faith. Before long he and old store became the best of friends, often staying up late in the evening, long after all the other buildings had gone to bed, to talk in serene comfort as they cast colourful shadows across the town through their stained glass windows.

And so the town settled down to resume its daily routine, and became, in time, curiously proud of its old store-cum-cathedral, where one could feed ones faith so to speak: one could buy both cat-food and consolation, baked beans, bin bags and baptism, ready meals and redemption, frozen foods and forgiveness, pepperoni pizza and peace on earth! No other town had such a sacred old store as theirs!

Order was restored, and everything, thankfully, returned to normal.

It was therefore very disheartening and somewhat worrying when one day, on a day like any other, the *new* store did not open!

"Not again," church moaned, verbalising the thoughts of them all.

Library dutifully volunteered to talk things over with the sullen store. She listened, confidentially to the store's complaint, and then reported back to the rest of the town.

"Well...?" they asked.

"You'll never guess."

"Oh no..."

"Yes, I'm afraid so...he doesn't want to be a store any more either."

"He wants to be a cathedral too?"

"Eh - no."

"No?"

"No – he doesn't want to be a cathedral."

"Well...?"

Library sighed.

"He wants to be a skyscraper........."

"Well, then I hate being wet!" the horse would reply,
snorting.

THE HORSE THAT WAS TOO COLD

Once upon a time there was a horse that was always, always cold.

"I'm cold," the horse complained....bitterly! "I'm always cold. And I hate it, I hate being cold...!" it repeated, over and over.

Its friends tried to console the horse, but there was little they could do, other than to clarify the reason that forever provoked the horse's miserable complaint: "You're cold because you're wet," they redily explained. This didn't seem to help.

"Well, then I hate being wet!" the horse would reply, snorting. "I hate it! I hate being wet!"

There wasn't really much else the friends could say; for what *do* you say to a sea-horse that hates being wet?

So un-assuming was she that one would hardly notice she was even there; she was almost invisible!

THE FANTASTIC FOURTH WISH

Once upon a time there were four friends: three boys and one girl.

Of them all, the girl was by far the least distinguishable. Although pretty, she was extremely shy and vacuously unassuming in both her manner and her dress – in fact, so un-assuming was she that one would hardly notice she was even there; she was almost invisible! She simply could not compete for attention with the boys, who were, by comparison, anything but indistinguishable: for they were all of unique and striking character!

The first boy was exceptionally tall, tall and elegant with it, but in addition he was most notably blessed of an intelligence infinitely superior to that of his friends - if not, in fact, to that of nearly everyone else! The extent of his knowledge was remarkable, and he excelled in his capacity for resolving complex calculations and exasperating equations. He did however, consider himself to be too removed, and much too distant from others, and he wished therefore that he was more sensitive and able to be more intimate with his friends.

The second boy was, by comparison to the first boy, exceptionally kind: he had an inherently considerate nature, curiously at odds with his robust physique, for he was most notably, strong; very, very strong! He was so strong that he could carry on his shoulders any weight his friends might choose to ask of him, and he would willingly do so. He did however, consider himself to be ugly, and worse, uncouth owing to his lack of breeding and education, and he wished therefore that he was more handsome and certainly more refined.

The third boy was, by comparison to the second boy, exceptionally handsome; so handsome, in fact, that his unashamedly transparent vanity was both warranted and forgiven. He was also notably blessed with tremendous youth and energy, which, combined with his rugged yet endearing features, made him exceedingly popular, especially with the girls! He did however, have a terrible, terrible temper, which flared uncontrollably and often without reason, and he wished therefore that he could be more tolerant of others, calmer and more able to share his warmth rather than his rage.

For a while the four friends lived perfectly happily in each other's company. However, as time passed, their perceived character flaws became increasingly intolerable; each slowly began to find the other three, absolutely insufferable! It made them all very irritable and impatient; they were forever bickering and falling out with each other, and consequently, they struggled to even be together in the same room! Eventually, they grudgingly agreed that things could not go on the way they were. Despite having their every need catered for, living as they did in the lap of absolute luxury, in their beautiful penthouse apartment high above the city, their friendship was reaching breaking point!

So they decided that something had to be done. They wished they could change, those traits that they considered so deficient - but how? How could they, how can anyone, change who they are? They did try however - but they failed, miserably. Somehow they would need to find another way to make all their wishes come true. So they jumped into their red rocket-ship and headed up into the stars to seek out the only person who might be able to help them: The Wish-Maker.

Of course, one could argue that such a person does not exist, and doubtless many would agree – but if one thinks about it for a minute, who *does* make all the wishes, and in turn distribute them to all the wish givers? The Fairy Godmother for example, or the Tooth Fairy, or Father Christmas, or the Easter Bunny, or the Man in the Moon, or any guardian angel for that matter, even the angel on your shoulder; or the various magicians, wizards and other spell-makers and soothsayers; the sprites too, and all the genies in the lamp, not to mention the innumerable wishes lying dormant in coins corroding in overgrown wishing wells and splendid fountains; or the wishes foisted on every lottery ticket, or on every bet made, or on every dice thrown; and of course, every wish secretly retained for every birthday candle extinguished, every dandelion seed scattered to the four winds, every wish-bone pulled so nearly in half, and every shooting star spotted, falling in unbelievable delight; who makes all these wishes, if not the Wish-Maker?

Certainly, the four friends, with their accumulated intelligence, could find no flaw in the logic of this argument, and were content therefore to pursue their quest on the grounds of such an assumption. And of course, this individual must exist in the stars, for certainly no such individual could possibly exist on earth – of course not, cynicism aside, why would they?!

Where exactly the Wish-Maker might live seemed obvious – doesn't one always wish upon a star? But which star, for there are many - well, doubtless, the brightest of course! So the four friends set their navigation sights northwards, and struck out into the immense vacuum of space......to where all their wishes might come true!

As one might imagine, the Wish-Maker was a character of unique position, and as such both his stature and his domain duly reflected his circumstance. He was, without doubt, a giant amongst giants, seated upon a throne, a throne so magnificent that it put some of the greatest structures of the world to shame (notwithstanding that it had been made entirely of gold!).

It was difficult to see the Wish-Makers face, for his throne sat, fittingly, atop a great peak, which itself floated in the airless vacuum, seemingly on - well, on nothing actually! He appeared to have a great golden mane of hair, and a great golden beard, curled into ringlets that tumbled like fountains down over his deep purple sash and cape. Behind his throne, there stretched countless buildings, suspended in the vacuum, hanging without foundation. Mostly they were temples, palaces, churches and cathedrals, accompanied by the inevitable accoutrements of lofty power: statues of immense and unaccountable scale, and the odd column or two: Doric, Ionic and Corinthian. Some hospitals and a few schools, perhaps rather unexpectedly, floated alongside, as did some hefty factories, which belched and exhumed enormous pillars of multi-coloured smoke, and intermittent flashes of sparks. Loud hammering and scraping could be heard from these grim structures, and weird incantations, a kind of somnambulant mumbling, interrupted by the eruption of immense furnaces, spewing out great cascades of coins, diamonds, doubloons, bracelet charms, and lotus leaves and rose petals.

Between the buildings, bulbous clouds scurried across the night-like sky, and everywhere, stars sparkled, rainbows practiced appearing, and then disappearing; beautiful winged damsels fluttered around or hovered nonchalantly, chatting, whilst all manner of indescribable creatures flew by. There was even the occasional starship......

It was an incredible sight, and the four friends were pretty much dumbstruck in amazement. They stared, wide eyed – in particular at the phenomenal figure of the Wish-Maker. From the base of his throne, rivulets of molten golden lava poured down the mountain, and between them, fanning out from the great throne, were lines and lines of genies: genies of all types and sizes, waiting, apparently, for wish distribution – certainly that seemed to be what was happening: the four friends could just make out some sort of ritual being performed near the head of the column. Pin striped suited figures, carrying clipboards and jumping gingerly between the lines, called genies forwards, to kneel before the Wish-Maker's massive toes, toes that protruded disturbingly large from equally massive sandals. As the four friends drew closer, they could see, quite clearly, that The Wish-Maker's pinky rose and fell accordingly as each set of wishes was issued, landing with an enormous 'thud' upon the arm of the throne and making the ground tremble and shudder beneath them.

Taking their cue from the genies the four friends waited patiently and quietly for their turn, increasingly conscious that they had no right to ask for one wish, let alone four - they really had no right to be there at all! Their confidence had pretty much evaporated as soon as they had seen the Wish-Maker, and now, as unworthy interlopers in his awesome presence, they felt distinctly ill at ease; in fact, they were downright petrified!

The first boy thought: if they had some information how to behave, it might help. He tapped the genie in front of him on the shoulder.

"Genie-"

"Gene," the genie corrected, looking the boy up and down with a dismissive glance.

"Sorry, Gene...eh, is there anything we should know...?"

"Know?"

"Yes... I mean, what do you say?"

"Say? Whaddya' mean, say?"

"I mean – what do you say to the Wish-Maker?"

"The Wish-Maker?"

"The Wish-Maker – you know – him?" the first boy indicated, a little unnecessarily perhaps, at the vast figure that loomed over them.

"Mr Magico?"

"Mr Magico?" the boy queried.

"Woah buddy – you ain't never heard of Mr Magico?"

"Well...no, it's our first time, you see..."

The genie called Gene took the toothpick that he had been chewing from the corner of his mouth, and, waving it at him, warned: "Listen bud, you best keep yer mouth shut – I ain't nevah' heard anyone say anything to Mr Magico, especially anyone as ... well, as ridiculous as you." He cast the boy another dismissive glance, up and down, before turning, abruptly, away.

The first boy thought it rather ironic, the genie saying this, bedecked as he was in a bright blazer, slashes all down the back, and with what appeared to be underwear made of hair! Hardly suitable attire for a genie. He let it go, though, and decided to try another tack.

"Why's he called Mr Magico?" he asked.

"Well that's obvious, ain't it...?" the genie replied, with exaggerated exasperation.

"It is?"

"He's the boss of the Magic Company, yes? The Magic Co.?

Gettit?"

At this, the genie called Gene turned away again. The first boy was fairly certain that if he asked him anything else, he was likely to get a punch on the nose. He turned to his friends: "I don't think this is going to go well...," he said. It was hardly the re-assurance they were looking for, and was without doubt, as it turned out, an understatement: when, finally, they stood before the towering figure of the Wish-Maker, they discovered just how correct the first boy's prediction was.

"FOUR!!!!????" the Wish-Maker bellowed, upon hearing their request. The ground shook, and stars rattled in the sky. "FOUR!!!!????" he repeated, as incredulously loud, if not louder than before. Rainbows rolled onto their backs, or curled into balls, and hid; some separated their colours altogether, each colour rolling away, vainly searching for a conveniently disused snooker table! Lightning bolts twisted back upon themselves and preferred electrocution to continuing their inevitable descent! Clouds either froze, or scurried for shelter; some simply evaporated; a number inadvertently wet themselves!

The suited attendants also froze, like terrified statues – one dropped his clipboard. The Wish-Maker glanced at him scathingly before reiterating in his terrible thunderous voice: "No one ever has ever had four....!"

The simple and undeniable truth of it settled over everything in steely silence. The four trembling friends wavered, as the Wish-Maker stared at them, implacable and bereft of compromise.

"So – we can't have four then?" the third boy brashly inquired, finally, after what seemed like an eternity.

Leaning down, disturbingly close, the Wish Maker whispered, firmly, sharply and with an icy finality: "NO". Behind him all the arms of the marble statues of the Gods and Goddesses, snapped off and smashed on the ground.

The first boy interjected.

"Eh....ok – but, surely......well, you see, there are four of us, and we all *need* a wish..."

48

The Wish-Maker turned his colossal head towards him. What appeared to be stars tumbled from the great mane of hair and beard, like delightful dandruff. It clattered over the four friends as they stood, huddled together beneath.

"You do, do you?" the Wish-Maker breathed ominously, through clenched teeth.

"Eh...yeh, kinda...," the second boy felt bound to contribute.

The Wish-Maker glared, in turn, at him, his eyes glowing horrendously red and actually: on fire! Smoke trickled out from his under his eyelids.

Just then, one of the attendants coughed, nervously – "There was that one time......," he said, his voice cracking as he spoke.

The Wish-Maker feigned slight acknowledgement. "What...?"

"That one time..."

"Mmmmm?"

"You know...the Fairy Binman?"

"Fairy Binman?" The Wish-Maker cast a fleeting yet furious look at the shaking attendant, who, through tightly shut eyes, repeated his apparent affront.

The Wish-Maker, after a slight pause, said dismissively: "What a load of rubbish". He slowly turned back to the four friends. Scowling he seethed: "OK......I tell you what – I shall grant you four wishes." The four friends smiled at each other, but the Wish-Maker held up his hand.

"Wait," he said. The smiles froze on their faces – "I will grant you four wishes - but only three will come true."

Again, the four looked at each other, not sure what to do.
"Take it or leave it."

Instinctively, they all nodded, as one. "We'll take it," they agreed.

Without another word the Wish-Maker waved them away, and instantly the four friends found themselves back in their luxurious apartment.

They took a minute.

"Well...we have our four wishes," the first boy said, eventually.

"Three," the girl corrected him.

"Yes...three."

They took another minute.

"Shall we?" the girl, then proposed.

"Yes, let's," they agreed.

And so each silently made their secret wish, and immediately:

The first boy became fantastically caring and demonstrative; lovingly and with abandon he wrapped his long arms unashamedly around his other three friends!

The second boy became fantastically handsome and refined; beaming, he dazzled his other three friends with his charisma, his attractive smile and infectious charm!

The third boy became fantastically calm and benign; laughing, he warmed his friends with his pure and honest humour, his serene gentility and confessional capacity!

The three boys were delighted – but only once they had finished celebrating their newly discovered attributes, did they notice the girl: for there she stood, as shy, quiet and unassuming as she had always been.

Suddenly the three boys were deeply ashamed.

"We are sorry that your wish did not come true," they said to her. "Please, please forgive us..."

"But what do you mean?" she said, genuinely surprised.

"Well......it's just that......you're still the same?" they said, feeling somewhat embarrassed.

"Oh, but my wish did come true..." she replied, "– it did," she insisted, addressing each in turn: "For you are caring, and you are handsome, and you are gentle, which is all I wished for."

Somewhere, a rainbow appeared, as the three boys humbly agreed: of all their wishes, the fourth had been, by far, the most fantastic.

And so the four fantastic friends lived in perfect harmony, happily ever after...four-ever!

The castle's intrusive presence literally glowered over the town, without compunction; miserably in its ruination did it appear to scowl down upon the town and all its inhabitants.

THE TOWN THAT HAD TWO TALES

Part I: The Town at War

Once upon a time there was a town. It was a beautiful little town, nestled into a landscape of gently rolling hills that extended as far as the eye could see. Despite being surrounded by hills on every side, the town was bathed perpetually in such a warm summer sun that its hard edges and sharp corners appeared softened, like marshmallow, malleable to the touch. Every building glowed, irradiate, the stones of every façade, mellow yellowed but peppered and smudged in tones that ranged from orange, burnt and rusted, to shady blues that complimented the other, curiously at a glance but perfectly none the less.

Hardly was there a gap between one building and the next, each seeming to lean upon its neighbour in an intimate ballet of mutual equilibrium – and the streets they formed were as comfortably composed: rustic, charming, settled and secure in their solid age. Like easy veins, they flowed, ever, ever downwards, twisting and seductively turning, until they spilled into the town square, where a magnificent fountain forever gurgled its healing spring into a shallow pool, in which children played, innocently naked whether clothed or not.

The town square was the centre of the world for the people of this town - they loved their town, they loved every bit of it; they loved its intimate corners, its secret lanes and crumbling cornices, the sills sagging and uneven cobbles; they loved its rich assortment of quietly unassuming yet colourfully enthusiastic shops and stalls; they loved the echo of their neighbour's footsteps in the night, each as uniquely recognisable as their own doorstep; they loved the deep reveals of the windows, like caves from which they could call to their betrothed, throw snacks to their carefree children or simply sit and watch the untroubled life of the town go by in its gracefully steady and tranquil pace; and they loved, truly loved, that the town appeared as if sculpted from a material of singular tone and texture and of an uncompromising strength and invincibility.

But if asked, each and every inhabitant would feign to deny – the embodiment of their love lay in their affection for the town square.

Where the streets seemed to have been carved from the nature they sat so intimately upon, consequently meandering so intricately that one could easily get lost, and lost quite contentedly, in their endless winding - such an impenetrable pleasure - the square was rather, the exact opposite: by contrast, it was exactly, and perfectly that: a square. (One could never be lost, therefore – one was either wandering in the wandering streets, or settled in the square town square: it really was that obvious!)

As if to reinforce the square's perfect uniqueness, its four sides were symmetrical, each a complete replica of the other, as if to re-assure the one opposite of the perfection of its own composition. Unlike the streets, where no two buildings were the same, no two buildings in the square were different. All were townhouses, each one individually identifiable but carved as if from a particular stone - and yet, each stone could be readily perceived, the joints between them razor sharp, dead straight, and exact – and as exact as the window frames which were set perfectly into tall slender openings, their sash cords hung like plum lines, as were the magnificent drapes folded within: both falling as vertical as gravity!

Clinging to each window were ornate balconies, carved precisely in metal, at once both exuberant and refined, bringing the finesse that monocle and manicured moustache lend to visage of the gentile; they typified summarily the townhouses character: elegance personified, as if they were regally appointed, an impression confirmed by the select carved details set into the pediments that crowned every opening. They exuded 'class' - where the buildings in the streets seemed to slumber, and mutter collaboratively drunken oaths of unparalleled affection; comparatively, the townhouses stood shoulder to shoulder and seemed to whisper, rather, merited compliments to their neighbour, exclusively together, confident and aloof.

Set in the square itself, like wayfarers, now welcomed but who had once been lost, palm trees grew, invited sentinels, imported clearly for their curiosity, and perhaps too for their capacity to provide shade for any who stepped from the shelter of the great colonnade set round the edge of the square. From within its harbouring cool, the reassuring smell of rich coffee and baking bread emanated from the many cafes which lingered there. The cafes were never empty, for the square was never empty – it was where the townspeople would meet, day and night, casually or otherwise, to drink, to chat, to argue or debate on some point of immaterial order, or to celebrate the union of some local pairing or lament the passing of an aged compatriot, the square festooned with confetti or funereal wreaths accordingly.

So it was that all the life of the town played out in the square, set against the everlasting splash and burbling of the fountain, which never stopped; it never froze and never ran dry, metaphorically echoing the collegiate spirit of the town that never once made ascent to threat: that regardless of the perpetual sun, whose severe warmth and glare might otherwise have rendered the town droughtful had it not been for the enduring radiance of the fountain water, flowing apparently without source, serenely but assuredly, and constantly salving thirst before it even became known to be so.

The streets and the square therefore combined to make the town, truly, one of the most delightful places one could ever hope to live, perhaps one of the most beautiful places on earth! There was, however, one unsightly blight on this otherwise perfect landscape, a blight of undeniable proportions, and impossible to ignore.

For above the town, visible from any point, was the castle - and it was without doubt one of the ugliest pieces of construction imaginable: a mean and brutal looking thing sitting ungainly out from the hillside, like an angry boil on an otherwise pure and unblemished complexion.

Grey it might have been, but in fact the castle appeared almost colourless, colourless and blank except for a few openings that were as vacuously black as sockets in a forgotten, nameless skull. Otherwise its walls were unadorned, with no redeeming aspect whatsoever; harshly they rose from the ground without forgiveness, and without pity. Some collapsed battlements alone confirmed its redundant use, otherwise there were hardly any features at all to identify the castle as such; and there was certainly no sense of the majesty or wonder that one might ascribe to castles one hears of in fairy tales. There were no magical spires or fanciful turrets, no fairies would ever fly over it, no beautiful princesses would be held captive within its walls, no fearsome dragons would loiter in its basement; it was bereft of any romantic captivation whatsoever. In fact there was nothing that could soften the castles miserable impression or endear the castle in any way. It was an insolent mystery, an imperious vacuity, an utter monstrosity.

Perhaps if the castle had been built distant from the town, its existence would have been less disruptive, its aesthetic deficiencies might even have rendered it a curiosity worthy of occasional visitation. But this was not the case. The castle's intrusive presence literally glowered over the town, without compunction; miserably in its ruination did it appear to scowl down upon the town and all its inhabitants.

Even at night, its impenetrable form could still be discerned, frowning malevolently; when the moon was full, the castle loomed, sallow like the moon itself, as if it were partnered in some evil malicious conspiracy. Doubtless, it was host for the demons and forlorn ghosts that everyone knew dwelt in darkness. Every guilty secret laid claim there, every evil perception, every wicked lie and falsehood found safety within its walls, even the most insignificant gripe or complaint, unfounded observation or petty hate could linger there unchallenged, and be allowed to fester and breed.

Parents would scare their children from wrongdoing with threats that they would be taken to the castle, to be locked in its dingy stained straw cells, and left in the dark, a darkness that doubtless would persist both day and night (so impossible was it to imagine that the inside of the castle could be anything other than unlit, it being the antithesis of all that was holy!) Children would taunt their peers to scale the castle walls, dare them to peer inside, to confront the evidence from within, of the past horrors that had transpired there; fame would be foisted on any who even came close, on any who even stepped onto the slopes that led to the base of the castle's ominous walls. For they had faced the fear that the castle represented: it was a silent fear, but not without volume: the castle reeked of it, this fear, a fear that unsettled every inhabitant, every child and every adult that lived in this otherwise, perfect little town: a fear none could accurately name.

Why the castle even existed, no one knew – some said the castle had been there long before the town, constructed in a time of appalling savagery. Tales had been handed down, father to son, but were considered by the majority surely to be fantasy, for no peoples could have been so barbaric, to have invaded another's land, to kill and maim, and tear down the towns walls as was intimated in those cruel and grisly tales. Some said, yes, it was true, there had been times like these, that indeed the town itself had been victim, more than once, to marauding tribes, that it had indeed been destroyed, it's walls rebuilt, and destroyed again – and that unfathomable injustices had been inflicted upon the people of the town, that some had even been taken away, never to be heard of again, because their hair was too grey, their skin to white, their eyes too blue, their step too wide, the tongues of their birth too offensive to the ears of others.

Ridiculous, the townspeople would agree, collectively and in conclusion. And even if it were true, well, there was no need now for the castle, if all it did was evoke memories of such monstrous times. It was empty, redundant, and nothing more than an eyesore on their beautiful horizon. Its age was immaterial – clearly it was now irrelevant, a ruin that more than ruined the whole look and feel of their righteously and undeniably precious town.

And so, the townspeople elected to have the castle removed.

Contracts for demolition were issued and instructions duly given; the appointment was hastily undertaken, for the space the castle inhabited would beget a whole new chapter in the towns history – it would become a place of great learning, philosophising and creativity: an academy was to be built, an academy dedicated to the pursuit of wisdom and knowledge, set within a wondrous landscape of terraces that would cascade down to the town, abundantly fertilised with exotic flowers and herbs for healing and meditation. As for the academy itself: a structure of such elegance, craft and delight was commissioned, and the local architect worked day and night to realise its vision. Plans were drawn up, and sections, and tremendous renderings too, which were exhibited for the townspeople to view. Each and every person was left speechless at the prospect that such a building could ever exist, an edifice of such glittering enchantment that nature itself would be satisfied to have as her equal neighbour.

But it was all to no purpose, for on the very day of the planned demolition, news, terrible, terrible news of unbelievable consequence, was delivered.

Everyone was gathered in the town square, waiting and watching for the great demolition to begin - everyone that is, except the resident architect. He had laboured tirelessly on the finer details of the work to come, and took little interest in the castle's removal. It was his son, a child, hardly seven, who saw it first, and whispered to another: "Chaos is coming..."

Word spread, slowly at first but with increasing rapidity. A strange fear began to grip the town, as the truth of it was confirmed. "It's true!" shouted the architect, rushing into the square, breathlessly, resultant from his hurried descent down from his rooftop studio. "I have seen them, gathered o'er the brow of the hills – an enormous army, as enormous an army as one is ever likely to witness! An army – of barbarians, bearing down on us – about to attack us!"

"What will we do?!" the townspeople cried. "What will we do? We'll all be murdered, murdered where we stand – and our town, our precious town, will be destroyed!"

Some, in denial, tried to make alternate arguments, soundly and of good reason: "Perhaps they are coming in peace, perhaps they are coming to trade or to be witness to our great undertaking." But the foolishness of these arguments rapidly became apparent: in the distance, plain for all to see, the hordes of marauding invaders swarmed over the horizon, their drums thundering, banners waving, and their sabres rattling - and all accompanied by ferocious warlike cries and chants of challenge and malice sent echoing through the hills.

The townspeople had no skills in warfare, no means either, and certainly no aptitude for conflict. They panicked, for what else was there to do? The horrific tales they had hard denied suddenly came rushing back to haunt them! Some ran, hither and thither, howling, screaming and crying. Some hid, some prayed, some prepared to take their lives and the lives of the ones they loved; some just closed their eyes, rather than confront the awfulness that now confronted them; for it appeared, truly and undeniably, that the unspoken brutality unleashed so many years before was coming down fast, and everything, life and home, would be lost forever!

But then......

From the hill above the town, a tremendous rumbling began. At first the townspeople took it to be the beginning of the onslaught, and they scurried away ever more fearfully - but the rumbling was not the result of any cannon. Slowly, ever so slowly, the sound became an almighty roar, the rumbling, an earthquake! All around, the ground shook, as the hill upon which the castle sat, cracked open! Great pieces of earth cascaded down its sides, trees uprooted like they were twigs, and rocks the size of houses rolled aside like pebbles, as the castle, yes, the castle, began to rise up! Arms of ashlar bulged out from the ground; on massive stone legs, grinding together, the castle gradually lifted itself upright! Tons and tons of earth fell from its walls, showering over the town and its people, until finally, the castle stood, towering above them. It cast a shadow as dark as its eyeless windows, piteously they stared, and its mouth, which was darker still behind its portcullis, snapped its yawning jaws with fearsome intent!

So terrifying was it, the oncoming invasion was completely forgotten. "The castle will destroy us!" the townspeople shrieked, fleeing in every direction! They scampered this way and that in search of a haven, cowering under carts and hiding in doorways (all suddenly much too shallow); some pulled paper bags over their heads and sat, pathetically quivering – as they waited for the destruction to come from the huge stone monster surely about to massacre them!

But the castle did not attack – it stood for a while, unmoving, its castellated head set hard, like some impassive, merciless ruler; and then, without a sound, it turned, and lumbered with an unexpected elegance across the hills to confront the approaching hordes.

Without hesitation of any kind, indomitably and with a ruthless fearlessness, the castle charged straight into them!

'STOMP!' Down came its massive stone feet, flattening men flat into the ground, stamping and crushing them like ants!

'THRUMP!!' Down came its equally as massive stone hands, squashing and squelching men between its fingers like soggy fruit!

'CRACK!!!' Down came its portcullis, snapping shut and cutting through limb and artery, through bone and armour like it was snapping kindling!

Arrows, bullets, even cannonballs and flaming rocks bounced from its walls like hail from glass, as the castle threw the machines of war dismissively into the air; it swept through the invading army like a rampaging tornado, tearing through the ranks, dispersing and forcing the would be invaders to turn and flee, defeated, terrified, and helpless in front of such an outrageous onslaught!

They ran and ran, but the castle caught them, each and every one, and crushed them; it crushed them all, and it did not stop there –

the castle chased the retreating army right back to its own town, and from the distance could be heard the awful sounds of rampant and untrammelled destruction; screams of people in terror merged with the sound of buildings crumbling, and being torn apart. Plumes of acrid smoke arose, swirling so dark and thick that the sun was almost extinguished from the sky!

A lamentable darkness hovered over the land, until eventually, the sounds faded, and an uncommon and eerie hush descended. The day of carnage, it seemed, was over.

For some time, nothing happened – the townspeople held their breath. And then, from over the horizon, walking slow and steady, the castle reappeared. It tramped through the remnants of the battlefield, hills once verdant and green reduced to unrecognisable mud and gore, returning to the town as the sun set, blazing behind it, bloodied red and dripping guts and brains from its ramparts.

Without uttering a sound, the castle settled itself, almost casually, back into the hillside.

The townspeople could only stare in silence. Still fearful, tentatively they emerged from their places of hiding, and with unspoken accord, gathered at the base of the hill. In awe, they looked up at the castle: its impassive walls rose up as they always had - but they were now wonderfully elegant, smooth, and awesomely unadorned, its impenetrable openings darkly intriguing, its battlements, silhouettes of repetitive elegance – the castle gleamed in the fading summer sky, and later, it gleamed in the sallow light from the moon......

Never again did the townspeople complain about their castle – in fact, no one could recall ever thinking of the castle as an unsightly ruin. Plans for the great academy were returned to the architect's chest of drawings, to be allowed to age, unseen, left to fade and finally to be forgotten. The demolition too was forgotten. Instead, every year, on the day of the planned execution, the townspeople gathered to celebrate the anniversary of the great battle. They would garnish the castle in garlands of flowers, covering it in petals and ribbons, and they would sing in its honour, melodies, some of which were composed of soft haunting memory, others, rejoicing joyfully in the victory wrought by their saviour.

In the square where the fountain still flowed, its water a little browned perhaps, the talk of the town for years and years afterwards was of the day the castle had risen up and vanquished the foe who had deigned so foolishly to attack them. The stories were told, over and over, until such time as these stories became legend, shrouded in mystery, lost through time to the annals of folklore. What truth there was resided only in the heads of the children, who were more secure than they could possibly imagine for knowing that the castle upon the hill would always protect them, that it would mercilessly defeat their enemies, and that the castle would save them, selflessly it would secure peace for them in times of war.

Part II: The Town at Peace

Many, many years had passed since then, and indeed many more years had passed subsequent to the first great Carnival. It originated an annual celebration of considerable reputation, which even to this day attracts visitors to the town; less a carnival, it is more a community feast: market sellers descend upon the town, to trade for pittances their most worthy and exotic wares to both townspeople and visitors alike. Many attend, though few would know anything about the true origin of the celebration: most assume that the celebration is held in commemoration of the town's victory over its neighbor - though some might wonder: perhaps not – for the victory was stuff of legend, and many events, both wondrous and calamitous had befallen the town since. It had been re-built many times; the town square was hardly recognisable as the square it had once been: where it had been square, now it was roughly rectangular; where it had been flat, now it sloped, gently down towards one of its narrower ends; and where its paving had been smooth and perfectly regular, now it was all cobbles, often uneven but none the less, charming.

The fountain too had changed: it was no longer a fountain, but now a well, and where it had once commanded the centre of the square, now it had moved toward the upper corner, appearing so located as if to secure itself from slipping down to the bottom of the square - or perhaps, it's canopy being made of such heavy black timbers, bolted so sturdily together, it was conceivable that the well actually anchored the whole square to the ground, to stop it from floating away and flying off into the sky!? Perhaps......

The buildings which lined the square had also changed: instead of being identical, now each one was different, and of the colonnade, only remnants remained - and no longer was the square lined only in townhouses: most noticeably, at either end sat two large churches. One was rendered white, set proudly up from the square's surface with grand stone steps leading to its equally grand doorway.

The doorway was framed in an archway of sculpted sandstone, which mirrored twin sandstone steeples, each steeple housing a great bell, and topped by a spherical crown which defied any constructional logic, so perilously did it teeter on the top of the narrowest of spires.

The other church was older, obviously of an aged disposition and accordingly ornate: hardly was there a part of its walls that was not decorated with the most delightful tiny carvings. Its windows too, carved in stone, were more delicate and fragile than seemed possible, and its door covered in numerous metal protrusions, suggestive of a capacity for defence - which of course was ridiculous, for the door was never known to be closed, but remained forever open, inviting one to stare into its cool gloomy yet golden and hypnotically glittering interior.

The streets too had changed: once winding, they were now straight and uniform, each one almost indistinguishable from the other – but it did not matter, for every street still led to the square, or, failing that, to the country, and then on into the hills which were no longer bare, but rich and forested. One could still never be lost, therefore – one way or another, everyone could still find their way, even if they went in the wrong direction!

Despite all the changes, the square, as it had in the past, remained the centre of the world for the townspeople. Civic celebrations, large and small, continued to be held there - but none was more special than the great Carnival. It happened only once in the town's history - at the time it had not been known as such; none living had attended, so long ago did it occur, but the events of that remarkable day stay fresh in the minds of all the townspeople, so often has the story been told.

For it was indeed a remarkable day, truly remarkable - though curiously, it had begun like any other......

No-one knew who organised the Carnival. Afterwards, little posters were noticed, stapled to lampposts and telegraph poles, brightly coloured posters, though faded as if they had aged prematurely; the black ink which proclaimed the event similarly grayed and softly blurred:

TONIGHT

(and tonight only)

come one, come all

join together

in the

CARNIVAL of LOVE

!

Some recalled a young couple putting up the posters, or so they imagined. A brother and sister some said, a pair of young lovers said others; but no trace of them was ever found, and it became the first of many curious legends left subsequently and forever unconfirmed.

Either way, it appeared that the Carnival was being selflessly gifted, and apparently a certainty; over the course of the day it became, simply, common knowledge and accepted that a great Carnival would be held in the town square. Somehow the townspeople were drawn willingly into making the preparations, although they could not have told you why, nor afterwards make account of their contribution. Visitors to the town, who might otherwise have returned to their homes, lingered and remained to see the great event, without really knowing why either – many had some considerable distance to travel, and it defied any logic that they would jeopordise their plans for such an unlikely occasion. Yet stay they did, every one.

Late in the afternoon, as the sun was beginning to set, the Carnival began. It was signaled by the tolling of the most clanky of bells - though from which church? It was hard to tell. Like a hammer banging on a piece of broken tin, the bell rang out, sonorously but assuredly. It was enough; everyone had gathered in the square - they looked around expectantly as the last toll faded into the distance. Nothing happened, and momentarily, anticipation also faded.

But then......

From one of the side streets came the sound of hooves –

louder and louder they clattered, and then suddenly the Silver Prince appeared, riding into the square astride a wondrous grey winged mare!

He was something to behold: glittering in his flowing sequined suit and silky cape, with his long hair glowing pure white under his great Viking helmet which sparkled with innumerable diamonds and crusted silver jewels. But it was his eyes which captivated most of all, his deep gentle sea blue eyes......

Gracefully, he dismounted, and everyone instinctively clapped and cheered; with a noble gait he paraded amongst them, graciously shaking hands and smiling warmly as he went - and then, returning to his steed, he climbed upon its back, and raised his bejeweled gloved hand, indicating please: for quiet. Obediently, the clapping and cheering ceased.

Everyone watched in amazement, as the Silver Prince closed his eyes - and as he did so, ghostly apparitions, not unlike the prince himself, floated from out of his saddle! The people were held, almost hypnotised, as the ghosts swirled through the crowd, blowing into each ear, a musical note. Then, one by one, the ghosts returned to where the Silver Prince sat, still astride his steed; raising his arm as if it were a baton, he began to conduct. Instantaneously, the most glorious harmony rose from everyone's lips! With every voice raised in perfect unison, the harmony swelled and swelled, until slowly, a single note emerged, a note as pure as crystal. The note soared, up, to fill the air; all the colours of the world seemed to dissolve as the very air itself became a breath of healing silver! The Silver Prince, smiling, brought the impromptu chorus to a most dramatic crescendo, and in the silence that reigned, as the echoes of the wondrous note finally receded into the forested hills, his voice, as soft and gentle as faith, said: "Let the Carnival begin."

Immediately, and enthusiastically the people began to clap and cheer, but hardly had they begun when a green bilious fog burst from the well – from which emerged the hugely impressive figure of the Faulty Fat Magician! Swearing and grinning, his big cheeks bulging, with promises of unbelievable magic - the likes of which had never been seen! - he waved his massive black rimmed green and golden cape around, dislodging his pointed hat from his balding head! Everyone laughed – and then, momentarily, all the women became men, and the men, women! The magician swirled his cape again, and from under it, wild animals appeared, but magically tamed and made gentle at the touch of children's hands! The magician swirled his cape again, waved his arms wide and sparks flew from his enormous sleeves; he pulled streamers from the hair of little girls and endless snotters from the noses of little boys; he made swirls and whirls and weaves and pickles and flashes of lights like demons' eyes, flickering and flaying and smoking and wheezing. The people howled at the magician's ridiculous tricks and acts of insane illusion, and as they laughed, the magician's body grew; it grew and grew into a colossal balloon figure which rained sweets and candies and clouds of sherbet down upon the gathered crowd; he iced, sweetened, and feathered the crowd - and finally, he conjured coins and cash of incomprehensible value, which he showered over the crowd! Everyone was instantly a millionaire, a billionaire, a trillionaire! They shouted their joy, deliriously throwing coins into the air, which fell like a torrential shower of gold!

Once everyone had satiated their greed, the Fat Faulty Magician proclaimed, as he pulled a hat from a rabbit: "Welcome, welcome to the carnival – enjoy!" and with a final wave of his hand, there appeared amongst them games, games of all sorts, and games a-plenty: games that father and son, and mother and daughter could all play, that they could all enjoy playing together! The people skipped and hid and tickled and tricked each other, joking and laughing hysterically! So engrossed were they, they hardly noticed the Profoundly Purple Professor who quietly walked amongst them, distributing skills and tools and instruments, teaching them so they might all become gifted artists and musicians and story tellers.

Soon, music and song, dancing and acting proliferated, and the Carnival raged.

At one point all those with red hair separated off and disappeared in a windowless wooden black barn one street distant from the square. They danced and danced so furiously that the building rocked and rolled back and forth, back and forth...until eventually it stopped. Presumably they were exhausted from their exertions – but no-one would ever know, for they were never heard of again - and it was in fact many years before anyone with red hair would be seen in the town.

The Carnival raged.

At another point a group of revelers, emboldened by the many spirits they had downed, vanished into the forest, leaping like frogs and howling with unbridled abandon. Later they re-appeared, their clothes rent and bloody, their faces and hands bloodied red too – for they carried between them the gory remains of a great stag! It was intended as a sacrifice, which they assumed would be eagerly accepted by the throng - but they were ignored. Peeved and disheartened, they sat to one side, where they cooked and ate the stag, leaving the head - which chatted with them as they ate, apparently not bothered in the slightest that something was missing – its body perhaps?!

The Carnival raged.

At the river, emerging as if from an invisible fog, all manner of boats arrived: pirate ships and Mississippi flat boats and Viking ships and Swedish men'o'war; they disembarked their human cargo of gamblers, scallywags and dusky maidens, of scurrilous pickpockets and lonely gravediggers, of middle aged handbag holders, aged photographers and begging lads and ladies, of eyeless grasping businessmen, barefoot slaves, judges and juries and fishermen lugging ripped and empty nets. They fused into the heaving throng, in an instant discarding their wares and their ways and habits, as they joined in with the laughter, dancing, and drinking. Later, somewhat weary, they tramped out of the town, resting briefly against the three crosses that sat on a hill, before returning to re-join the delirious crowd crammed into the square below.

The Carnival raged.

And then - there came a point when everyone suddenly, and without knowing why, became absolutely ravenous. As if on cue, the Thinner Dinner Lady appeared, tall, slender - bony actually –

but with eyes not unlike those of the Silver Prince, eyes that shone like diamonds... Dressed in simple blue jeans and plain grey t-shirt, she walked amongst the crowd, distributing steaming stews and dumplings. It was a sight to see: in the fading evening light, the people sat, either in small groups, or alone, quietly eating from modest bowls, and as they ate, Goth and accountant, biker and pastel clad mother, each became indistinguishable from the other.

Later, as the evening drew to a close and night descended, the air cooled. Braziers were brought out, and long tables set up upon which numerous small glasses were carefully lined up. Into each was poured thick golden liquid, like velvet honey, which coated the throat in a drowsy but sharp crystalline warmth. It gently fogged the mind - yet made everyone feel as if they glowed; indeed the golden liquid actually appeared to glow even as it settled inside the glass, each floating like a little bulb, softly lighting up the square, and seducing random insects, moths and fireflies to dance scattily over every glass.

Hands were warmed as much by the fire sparking through the braziers as by the glasses of golden dew. Everyone drank, leaning upon another, and their collective embrace was accompanied by a gentle humming. The humming grew, into a song of delightful melody, a folk song, unknown but familiar to all; every person swayed softly in time to its hypnotic and comforting rhythm, as their clothes slipped from their bodies and fluttered away into the darkening sky, like birds freed from captivity – naked, they were lulled deeper and deeper into the melody, which flowed and mellowed, and thickened the air; it appeared to melt the walls of the buildings, they evaporated, becoming transparent; through which could be seen ghostly figures, dressed in exotic robes and golden finery, dancing too...and then, they too, like the buildings, disappeared, and all that was left was the square.

For a while, nothing happened. The humming faded - and then, suddenly, silent fireworks exploded overhead, and like a vast magic carpet, the square slowly began to float up, up into the night sky!

Gathered tightly together, the people swayed as the square

gently and gracefully undulated beneath their feet, the town fell away, and all of a sudden the surface of the sky was immediately above them! As if invited, everyone, every man and woman, boy and girl, then reached up - and plucked a star from the heavens. Clutching their star naked to their chest, they settled back onto the softened cobbled surface of town square, until finally everyone lay sleeping, curled into another, their star glowing, pale but warm upon their skin, as the square glided softly down, down and down and down......back down, to the town.

A silence descended on the town square, a silence, deep, deep and long, interrupted but only slightly by the slow steady breathing of the naked recumbent figures; but even that slightest of interruptions gradually diminished, until finally nothing, nothing could be heard. Nothing moved. There was not a breath of wind to rustle a single leaf. Nothing, absolutely nothing stirred; the town became quite, quite still.

And then......

Above the town, the castle that sat high in the hills, once again began to move. In the depth of the night, under the canopy of the black starless sky, left unadorned other than by the full glowing moon, the castle rose up - it rose, as slowly as it had before, but in elaborate calm: the ground did not shake, the earth did not tumble away, trees were not uprooted, not a single animal or creature was disturbed. The castle, like thistledown, floated seamlessly up from the ground, lit by the flickering lights grasped in the lifeless hands of the naked figures lying pale in the moonlight.

For a time, how long it was hard to tell, the castle stood, towering once more over the little town, immobile and impassive. But then, reaching down, the castle, with one of its massive stone turreted hands, began to gather up the sleeping forms. Its great stone jointed fingers delicately shovelled the naked bodies, tumbling silently one upon the other, into its stony palm. None woke, so deep was the sleep they had fallen into, and no one was hurt, nor even bruised, not even in the slightest.

As gently as gentleness could possibly be, more gently than a summer breeze, each person was tenderly deposited back into his or her own home. Windows and doors parted respectfully, to allow the castle's great hand to enter, placing every person back, safely and securely in their own bed. Covers were pulled up: the castle tucked everyone in - and then, gingerly it removed the star from that person's clutched hand, to return the star diligently, and rightfully, back into the night sky.

Eventually the square was empty - every person was home: every person, that is, except the Silver Prince, the Thinner Dinner Lady, the Profoundly Purple Professor and the Fa(ul)t(y) Magician. They disappeared, never to be seen again – unlike the stars: the night sky dazzled with stars, stars which were brighter than stars had any right to be......

When the town awoke, none spoke of the great Carnival, for none could believe such an extraordinary event had occurred. It were as if it were a dream, just a ridiculous dream – for there stood the castle, as immutably settled into the earth as ever. It was only by the telling of it from one particularly solitary soul, to his daughter, and she in turn to hers, and so on, that the legend of the Carnival was ever recorded.

And so it became legend - and yet, if you visit the town today, everywhere you might find evidence of the Carnival. In the white church hangs the slaughtered head of a stag, so at odds with the other accoutrements of its faith, and starlings will alight on the thin and slender branches of the naked trees, trees that never sprout green, and sing as if to tell of the soft music that was once so sweetly sung on that great occasion.

Young people too, are tolerated, somehow, way beyond their years, and given place as the owners and administrators of the towns commercial trade, entrusted with the towns continued financial well-being, as if direct offspring and inheritors of the fictional brother and sister who legend has it, instigated the Carnival. They run everything, even the bars which line one side of the square, where you can buy beers and a golden liquid perhaps not unlike the one served on that magical evening.

And if you sit at the bars, overhead you are protected by large wide umbrellas - which, by some strange trick of perspective, in the gaps between, stars seem to be brought down, down, and so close as if to be almost within reach......

And as for the castle? The castle sits, still, silent upon the hill, whether for good or ill, well who can say - but there it sits, nonetheless, paternally watching over the town, a somnambulant sentinel, protecting the town, and everyone who dwells there, whether in times of war or times of peace.

Once upon a time there was an alien who knew......

THE ALIEN WHO KNEW TWO THINGS

Once upon a time there was an alien who knew two things......

One might assume that the alien who knew nothing might be troubled by knowing nothing – but of course, the alien who knew nothing could not be troubled, by anything, for it knew nothing; nothing at all.

Part I: The Alien Who Knew Nothing

Once upon a time there was an alien who knew nothing. It was a very confused alien, for it thought it knew everything, but it didn't – because it knew nothing.

It assumed that every other alien knew nothing – or certainly, knew less than it knew! This is what it thought – or rather, what it would have thought, if it could have thought it, but this is of course ridiculous – it couldn't know it thought that, for it knew nothing. However, because it thought it knew everything, by knowing everything therefore it knew it knew nothing, but then again, it didn't - it couldn't, for it knew nothing. It even knew this: it knew it knew that it knew it knew nothing, which was something – knowing nothing was at least knowing something, if only it knew it. But it didn't - for it knew nothing.

One might assume that the alien who knew nothing might be troubled by knowing nothing – but of course, the alien who knew nothing could not be troubled, by anything, for it knew nothing; nothing at all.

Others might have tried to help the alien, but who would know if it had been helped, for only the alien could confirm whether it was true or not. And how would it know, for it knows nothing? (What nothing knows, no-one knows – apart from, of course, the alien who knows nothing, because, obviously, it knows nothing rather well. However, if asked, it can't tell - because it knows nothing.)

Of course, aliens that know nothing might appear quite plausibly knowledgeable, so knowledgeable are they of knowing nothing. Therefore, one could easily be misled, and confounded by the alien's belief in itself, and indeed, by, comparatively, the almost incomprehensible extent of its ignorance! They are not well red, not at all. So, if you ever meet an alien who knows nothing, remember, no matter how much you may be inclined to lure the alien from its place of ignorance by acts of generosity, aggression or even tenderness, forget it. For aliens who know nothing, know nothing - and they never will.

And if you are an alien who knows nothing, this tale most definitely applies – unfortunately it won't mean much to you, because you know nothing, even though you think you know everything. That's the problem, with being an alien who knows nothing.

It was therefore a very confused alien, for it did indeed think that it knew nothing, but of course it didn't – it actually knew everything!

Part II: The Alien Who Knew Everything

Once upon a time there was an alien who knew everything. Now, one might assume that the alien who knew everything would be unduly burdened and therefore perhaps troubled by knowing everything – and you'd be right: aliens who know everything are troubled indeed, for by knowing everything it means they know nothing, which is of course impossible; impossible – but true.

It was therefore a very confused alien, for it did indeed think that it knew nothing, but of course it didn't – it actually knew everything! However, because it thought it knew nothing, it assumed that every other alien knew more than it knew – it thought, in fact, that every other alien knew everything, and that it, and it alone, knew nothing! This is what it thought – but it was wrong. Of course it was wrong – for it knew everything, if only it knew it. But it couldn't – for aliens who know everything, know they know that they know nothing.

So if you ever meet an alien who knows everything, take pity, and remember, no matter how much the alien may insist on knowing nothing, and may even appear to know nothing, it does in fact, know everything – it is exceptionally well red, which makes it a considerably more amenable alien than an alien who actually knows nothing.

And if you are an alien who knows everything, take heart, for you are most certainly not an alien who knows nothing – you are an alien who knows everything . . .

But to their horror, when they awoke later that day, there on every wall, was the word 'GUILTY', yet again brazenly glowing bright, bright red.

THE GUILTY CITY

Once upon a time there was a city that was, undeniably, the cleanest city there had ever been! Make no mistake, this city was *clean!* There was absolutely no dirt anywhere, not one spec! It was cleaner than the things it was cleaned with, so clean was it - cleaner than early morning sunshine, cleaner than freshly fallen snow, cleaner even, than white!

Coincidently, the buildings, every one, every house, palace, museum and school, were all pure white, as was every surface, every front and back, every wall, roof, floor and door, even the door knobs, the letter boxes, hinges and the nails that secured them: all, pure white! And it wasn't just the buildings: the streets were white as well! Every kerbstone, cobble, street lamp and manhole cover: white; pure, pure white! There was not one inch of this city that wasn't absolutely brilliant white (as it says on the tin!?). As such, the city, literally, gleamed, even on days when the sky was dull and overcast: and if one were to visit the city on a sunny day, well, one could hardly stand the glare, one would be blinded by the light, so gloriously did the city sparkle! Shadows struggled to be cast – the absolute whiteness of everything precluded it!

And let's not forget the people, for they too each and every one, was as spotless and as perfectly white as the city! The clothes they wore were white, their hats, shoes, jackets and skirts were white, their skin was white, their teeth of course, and their hair, even their eyes: pearly white! Their carriages were white, their pets, their food, even their pooh (!) was white! And if language could be white, then that's what their language was - they talked in a tongue that was as pure a sound as one could imagine, clean and crisply opal - a perfect reflection of their perfect existence, for there was no crime, no poverty, no illness and no sin in this cleanest of clean cities!

This may seem unbelievable, but not to the people of this city. Being clean was just the way things were; they actually had absolutely no idea how clean their city was; they had no comprehension of it whatsoever – for their city had always been this way, it had always been white, for as long as anyone could recall.

If they had some way of making a comparison with another city, perhaps things might have been different – but they didn't; no-one had ever lived anywhere else, and no-one had ever left. Why would they? Why leave? Where would they go? Into the forest that surrounded the city, a forest that was dark, and gloomy, cold, and, doubtless...dirty!? No! They stayed, complacently yet justifiably secure, contented and comfortable in their clean white city, the purest whitest people living in the purest whitest place ever made, perfectly and completely clean, inside and out.

So you can imagine the horror, when one day, the city awoke to find the word: 'GUILTY' scrawled in red, a red as red as blood, across one wall of the City Chambers!

Well, the City Fathers immediately called a public meeting, and all the city inhabitants, who were, naturally, very upset and distressed by this occurrence, gathered in the main square to hear the response to this incomprehensible defilement: "We cannot, indeed we will not, allow this horror to blight our beautiful city," the Mayor began, with tears in his eyes. He held on tightly to his glittering white Chain of Office. "The per...perpetrators," – he stumbled over the pronunciation, it was a term he had never used before; he scarcely knew what it meant! – "will be found...and this...offence, this outrage," – he pointed at the word as he said it, struggling to keep both his hand and his voice steady – "shall be removed!"

The people cheered, and cleaners were summarily dispatched, ceremoniously, to remove the word from the wall of the City Chambers: they were garbed head to toe in protective clothing, and were instructed to use brushes attached to long poles to complete the task (it was thought dangerous to even be near the word, let alone to touch it, lest it infect them with some terrible disease!)

The offensive word was duly removed – well, at least, removed as best it could: some slight trace of it remained, pale but distinguishable none the less. A metal panel was placed across it, white of course, and a plaque attached, hastily inscribed, with the date, circumstances and so on, plus a quotation of unquestionable significance.

The Mayor oversaw the installation, and proclaimed, with relief, that the offending word was now removed, and that their city was once again, clean.

The ceremony seemed to bring the necessary reassurance to the populace. They all slept easier that night, secure in the knowledge that the outrage had been dealt with and that this unfortunate incident was now over.

So, you can imagine the horror when the city awoke the following day to find the word: 'GUILTY', scrawled across another wall of the City Chambers! If anything, it was brighter red than before.

The City Fathers once again called a meeting: "We shall not allow this horror to blight our city...again," the Mayor proclaimed, though somewhat less confidently than the day before. He held on even more tightly to his Chain of Office, with an uncomfortable sense of déjà-vu. No mention was made of any 'per...perpetrator'.

The same cleaning team were recalled and instructed to remove, ceremoniously, the offensive word. The instruction was duly followed, or as much as was possible, for once again a pale yet perfectly distinguishable trace of the word could be seen. A metal panel, white of course, was placed across it. There was no plaque, no inscription this time – there had not been enough time to prepare one. The Mayor oversaw the proceedings, and in conclusion, pronounced that their city was, once again, clean.

The ceremony brought some semblance of reassurance to the populace. They slept a little uneasily, but secure enough in the knowledge that the outrage had been dealt with and that this second unfortunate incident was now over.

So, you can imagine the horror when the city awoke....well, you can guess, can't you: the word 'GUILTY' was scrawled across, not just one, but every wall of the City Chambers, and even brighter red than before!

There was no meeting held, and no proclamations made. The cleaning team were called, perfunctorily, the offensive words removed, metal panels, white of course, placed across the pale remnants of the words and the Mayor made a brief statement that their city was clean.

But the populace was hardly reassured. That night, many struggled to sleep, so worried were they. It was, quite frankly, unthinkable, unfathomable, unbelievable – why, why had such a terrible thing happened? Why had their city been tarnished, yet again, without cause or explanation? And who would do such a thing, and for what purpose? They could only wonder in dismay - it was, simply, beyond their comprehension, and so they agonised, without any form of consolation whatsoever. They made unfounded predictions, fearful that more words would appear - for each and every one of the city's inhabitants hoped beyond hope that this terrible thing would stop, and that this evil that had befallen them, would leave them be. For the first time that night, many prayed.

Can you imagine then, the horror they felt when they awoke the next day, and found that the word 'GUILTY' was scrawled, not just on the walls of the City Chambers, but on every wall of every building in the city!?

So prolific was it, that a blood red glow was cast over everything: like an unspoken threat it hung malevolently over the unrecognisable city. Silently, the people of the city gathered in the main square, fearful yet indignant. The Mayor eventually appeared on the balcony of the City Chambers, looking pale rather than white. His voice trembled as he spoke. "My people –," he began, nervously, but then with an authority born from an indignation all his own. "This – is unacceptable!" He swept his arms wide. The people murmured in accord. "We shall remove this ...offence, this outrage! ...this blight!! We shall remove it, together, you and I...we shall do whatever it takes, to make our city, clean once more!" A great cheer arose, the people rallying in support of their magnificent Mayor.

Cleaning materials were made available, brushes, cloths, buckets and water, lots of it, and detergents; protective clothing was issued to every person in the city, and together, they scrubbed and scrubbed, every wall, of every building. It took them all day and all of the night, but by the time they were finished, every word was removed! As the sun rose, the populace were delighted to see that their city was back to the way it was - well, almost: it was impossible to deny that the surfaces of the buildings were not quite as white as they had been – but the words were gone, and that was all that mattered. The day was declared a national holiday – though few were in the mood to celebrate. Having been up all night, the people retired to their beds, exhausted, but content that their city was once again, clean.

But to their horror, when they awoke later that day, there on every wall, was the word 'GUILTY', yet again brazenly glowing bright, bright red.

The people of the city, although tired from their labours of the day before, had little choice – they immediately set about cleaning the city, fuelled by the remnants of their anger, until once again, the words were all removed. Guards, newly appointed and untrained, were posted, and the people settled down to rest after their labours: and yet, when they woke the following day: 'GUILTY', 'GUILTY', 'GUILTY': the word was everywhere ......

"What are we going to do?' the people despaired.

The City Fathers tried to rally the populace once more. "We must persist," they urged, and by example rolled up their own fine sleeves and began to scrub. The Mayor appeared, yet again on the balcony. He implored, passionately to his people: "We must clean our city," and he too, discarding his Chain of Office, set about scrubbing the walls, muttering: "We must remove this...this ...abomination, this desecration...this...lie..."

Inspired, the people yet again set about cleaning their city. It seemed however, that no matter how fast they scrubbed the word 'GUILTY' kept reappearing. And as they scrubbed, and scrubbed and scrubbed and scrubbed, all the beautiful white render that had made their city so, so perfectly white, was completely scrubbed away, to leave only the bare stone underneath. Even then, the words kept appearing, as if ingrained in the stone itself!

The people scrubbed and scrubbed at the stone, with cloths, brushes, wire-brushes, pumice stones and sand-paper; eventually they employed great water cannons to blast into the stone! The words disappeared, literally bleeding out of the stone, to run down the walls and into the sewers. Streams and streams of red poured through the streets, rivers of red that swirled around ankles as the people scrubbed and scrubbed.

And so it went on. There was not a person in the city that did not help. All work in the city ceased, all the shops, factories, and businesses closed. Everyone was employed, night and day, scrubbing at the walls, the roofs, even the streets: wherever the word 'GUILTY' appeared. Soon there was not a single person who did not have dirty finger nails, and dirty hands - and they were dirty all the time: what water was left after scrubbing was used for bathing, but fresh water soon ran out. Water became scarce, every drop being required for the cleaning. By common consent, the people no longer bathed, they no longer even washed, and they soon became filthy, their faces covered, and their clothes, in grime and muck; one person became indistinguishable from the next. Who was the Mayor – who knew? Who was commoner, who was lord – who knew? Who was woman, who was man – who knew?

Regardless, they kept scrubbing, scrubbing and scrubbing and scrubbing. They used every rag and cloth, used them until they were worn completely away. When the rags ran out, they tore up their clothes, their fine hats and gloves, skirts and undergarments; shamelessly they scrubbed, becoming ever dirtier, dirtier and dirtier all the time. Their fingernails, and then their fingers wore away too, ravaged and raw, they scrubbed, endlessly, they scrubbed and scrubbed and scrubbed......

Finally one wall of one building became so thin and weakened from all the scrubbing, it collapsed; it was followed by another, and then another. Eventually whole buildings crumbled, and yet, the letters 'G', 'U', 'I', 'L', 'T' and 'Y' remained etched deep in the broken rubble. There was nothing else for it: the rubble was crushed by huge mallets, until the pieces were ground down to sand, and then taken away and cast into the sea.

It was not long before just about every building had disappeared. Random meetings were held, in amongst the ruins, futile suggestions raised, as to how the city might yet be saved, but there seemed to be no solution: wherever a single stone stood, the word 'GUILTY' would appear, and it was unthinkable to leave such a blemish visible.

Eventually, however, there was nothing left of the city. Not one single stone was left standing......

The people, all of whom had been forced to live in makeshift shelters, packed up their meagre belongings and moved away, disappearing into the forest, and the city became just a memory, a memory of a city that had once been so perfect, so pure, so white, so...clean. All that remained were the six letters, gleaming bright, bright red, scratched into six tiny pieces of stone left piled up and cautionary where the City Chambers once stood; all that was left of the guilty city......guilty ever more.

Post-Script:

Rumour has it, that the forest into which the inhabitants vanished, over time slowly...changed, and became infused with a delightful laughter, sweet and harmonious. If you visit the place where the city is deemed to have been, now overgrown, abandoned and turning to seed, you might hear this magical laughter, like pipes blowing softly, echoing from the forest, whispering to you and inviting you to follow. You might also see the forest glow, with colours, rich and vibrant, dancing from deep within the forest gloom; in the forest canopy you might see glimpses of the fanciful turrets of palaces and castles, pink, blue and gold, and you might see other structures too, hewn from rough timber or vehicles, stalled and painted, rainbow patterned as if dappled by a new born sun; and if you look, carefully, you might on occasion catch sight of people, strange, beautiful people, happily dancing, and oddly glowing, bright despite the darkness. You'll have to look really hard, though – for though there are many, so many as might fill a city, they are almost indistinguishable from the forest, from the heavenly trees, leaves, and flowers that surround them.

And yet, once upon a time, there was an invisible king......

THE INVISIBLE KING

Once upon a time there was a king. This king was the greatest king who had ever lived, truly, the greatest, for he was possessed of attributes that were equal to, if not abundantly in excess of, any preceding king.

For he was more ambitious than Macbeth; more brave than Henry V; more conned than Kong and as creepy as Burger; he was more deluded than Canute and as determined as Bruce; as eloquent as George VI and as exact as David; he was more foolish than James I and as fickle as Henry VIII; as great as Alfred and as good as Wensleslas; he was as hearty as Richard I and as handy as Midas; as intact as Tut, as jealous as Louie and as knotted as Gordias; he was as legless as Elvis, as merry as Cole and more mad than George III; he was more needy than Lear and more naïve than Arthur; more obsequious than Herod and as omnipotent as Zeus; he was as pardonable as Hearts and more pompous than Charles I; as qualified as Lion; as rotten as Claudius and as redy as Ethelred II; he was as satisfied as Richard III and as skilled as Lizard; as tanned as Louis XIV and as terrible as Ivan IV; he was as unique as Dravot, as visionary as Martin Luther and as wise as Solomon; he was as witty as Pupkin; he was as xenophobic as Edward I, as yellow as William I, and he was more zealous than Jesus.

He was all these things and more. There was, however, a problem, a rather significant problem: unfortunately, this king was invisible.

No-one would ever know of his greatness, therefore, for no matter how hard he might try, his tremendous acts, whether of gallantry or futility, of valour or foolhardiness, of cowardice, or of sadism, of heroism, of deviousness or of generosity; none would ever be witnessed. Nor would his worthy attributes of amenability, grace, care or diplomacy, nor attributes of dubious worth: of conceit, obsession and gullibility; whether vice or virtue, none would ever be recognised or acknowledged.

There would be no coronation for this king, no great celebration in respect of his ascendancy, and when he died, no great service of remembrance would be held in his honour.

Neither his acts nor his visage would be entombed for posterity: no statues would be raised in formal square, no portraits hung in sterile gallery; no tales would be told nor fables handed down, his great deeds and achievements would never be inscribed in voluminous tome.

No-one would mourn and no peoples would be made incumbent to treasure his memory, for no-one would know that he had ever existed, so invisible was the invisible king.

And yet, once upon a time, there *was* an invisible king......

But as darkness fully fell, the tree discovered what it was to be bathed, unmitigated, in the stars unworldly light...

THE SOLITARY SILVER BIRCHTREE

Once upon a time, there was a forest of silver birch trees. In tune with the seasons, every spring the forest would blossom, bright, bright green as the new leaf buds burst open and grew, abundantly in verdant rapture. Then, as the summer ended and autumn took hold, the forest would change, becoming red and orange, before the tiny leaves withered, and fell, brown and brittle to the ground.

So it was, year upon year: trees grew, leaves blossomed and died, others took their place, they too blossomed and died - and so the forest persisted.

However, somewhere in the middle of the forest, there grew one silver birch tree whose leaves never blossomed, they never turned red or orange, but remained brown and never fell. The tree stood as tall and straight as all the other birches, and in every other respect was the same as its neighbours, but for this unusual condition.

The other birches did not notice; if one of their kind was not quite right, well, it made little difference to them. They remained discreetly non-committal and preferred to ignore the fact that, at the height of every summer, when the forest was as green as it could possibly be, the silver birch stood, by contrast, its leaves laden brown; and in winter too, when all the other birches were bare, the silver birch tree would stand, oblivious to the change, completely covered in its withered little brown leaves.

Over time, however, the difference became increasingly obvious. Season after season, not a single leaf fell from the branches of the silver birch tree, and as more and more grew, each one already and forever autumnal, their ever increasing weight slowly began to pull the tree down – its branches hung lower and lower, and lower still, until they almost touched the ground. Unnaturally encumbered, it soon cast a sad and forlorn profile: where all the other trees stood straight and tall, this silver birch strained painfully even to stay upright.

Eventually the other silver birches had to acknowledge that they did indeed feel rather sorry for this particular tree. They were, however, confused and did not know what to do. They asked, but could not understand the reply: for the leaves tried to explain that they could not allow themselves to fall from the tree, for the tree would be left, abandoned and bare; bereft, its branches would be unprotected: how would the tree then survive the harsh, harsh winter? And the tree in turn tried to explain: how could it abandon its leaves? How could it allow them to fall, to be left to lie and rot upon the ground: such a terrible fate it could never condone!

This reasoning meant nothing to the other trees, they could only offer solace by sharing knowledge of their own experience: the joy they felt when the new buds bloomed, sadness, certainly, when their leaves fell, but the comfort they took in the unquestionable certainty that, come the spring, new buds would bloom, the tree would be full, and that birds would duly nest in their corpulent branches. The silver birch, though it listened attentively, knew itself to be different, and could not therefore take consolation in their solicitude. It bore no malice towards its compatriots, and could only wonder sadly at what they said: for no birds ever nested in its branches.

Perhaps, the other trees thought, the terrible affliction that beset the silver birch was because it did not get enough light (or so they told themselves, perhaps, conveniently, for there were plenty of other trees who did not get light) – regardless, in an attempt to do something, they gradually began to move away from the birch tree, ostensibly to help, but in truth because they were deeply embarrassed by their inability to do so.

Slowly, the forest thinned out, until eventually it disappeared altogether. Every tree was gone, except for a few loyal friends who remained, albeit at a distance, and the silver birch was left to stand, pretty much all alone in an empty field.

It was a lonely place where the silver birch stood, barren and now all the more exposed to the weather that blew remorselessly in from the sea, weather which assaulted the tree, unhindered and unrelenting. But no matter how much the wind might blow, nor how hard the rain might fall, still no leaf fell from the silver birch: it became almost unrecognisable as a tree at all, so low did it sit upon the ground. Its weight became intolerable, finally it lay down, flat, and so unbearably did it bore down upon the ground that the world itself seemed to slow, and to stop, its orbit around the sun appearing to halt prematurely, stalled and without any capacity to motivate itself to movement ever again.

And in that silent and deathly winter, a tremendous freeze fell across the land: it would have been difficult to predict a winter more bleak or severe - and it never seemed to end. Snow fell, slow and continuously, and so cold was it that the snow failed to thaw. Rarely did the sun shine upon the place where the tree lay - and yet the tree never yielded from its frozen embrace. It lay, prostrate in the snow and would have remained so throughout this winter and the next, and those ever after, were it not for the star, that careered suddenly and without warning into the tree one bright October morning.

The tree did not notice the star, it did not even see it coming – few would, so brightly did the sun shine that day (and of course stars don't exactly make much impression on the eye in the daytime!) It first appeared low on the horizon, whirling and tumbling, laughing and chortling across the ground, spinning and reeling and farting too! Its trajectory was uneven and yet not without direction: it would have careered right across the field and slithered right over the edge of the field and into the sea had it not been for the tree.

Without warning it clattered into the thick branches, and came to an abrupt stop.

The tree was stunned. It took a minute to realise what had happened. A star?! A star of all things had fallen from the sky and crashed right in to it! It was difficult, in fact, impossible, to believe - and almost as impossible to discern. But for its twinkling, the star was virtually invisible – it was difficult to locate exactly where the star lay until the daylight began to fade. Only then could the tree really see the star, and properly appreciate and acknowledge its radiant beauty. Although small, the star was perfectly formed - its long tender limbs flickered in time with its glowing centre; some were damaged and bent, but this did not detract from the sheer elegance of line. And the star was light too, as light as air. 'Are stars not meant to be heavy?' the tree wondered, and yet the star was anything but. 'And would their brightness not blind you?', the tree also wondered, but the star did not – it was in fact, pale rather than bright, and yet it exuded a light that was startling none the less, a light sweeter than any light the tree had ever known, an iridescent glow which seemed encompass the tree, imbuing it with joy, with frivolity and silly thoughts of such daft uncommon humour; it was all so unexpected, yet welcomed none the less!

And then, as darkness fully fell, the tree discovered what it was to be bathed, unmitigated, in the stars unworldly light. Strangely, being so close, the star's twinkling did not blind, rather the tree was caressed, sublimely, as the star, in the background, hummed, and snored – yes, snored! – and occasionally called out, soft guttural claims and careless demands. The tree could not understand the language used, none the less it was of such an elegant timbre that the tree could not help but be hopelessly enamoured by the stars odd yet endearing habits.

The star itself never seemed to mind that it no longer hung in the sky: when the tree asked, it would just laugh, and flicker, and laugh some more. In fact it didn't seem to mind about anything. If the tree asked, anything, anything at all, of where it had been, of what it had seen, what it wanted, the star just laughed, laughed, and flickered, and laughed even more! Only when the tree commented, how unusual it was that the star was so small – weren't stars suns? 'No, no, no,' explained the star – 'every sun was a star!' Otherwise, the response to the trees every question was the same: just laughter and flickering, flickering and laugher – and as time passed, the star's constant humour, its light heartiness and gentle glow infected the tree with an uninhibited warmth – it did not yield its prone position, but instead was content to simply lie, delighted and perfectly satisfied in the stars blissful presence. Occasionally the star's flickering would lessen, but its laughter, never, and the tree learnt to embrace its new found contentment, to accept, gratefully, its tremendous good fortune; it learnt to take pleasure, unashamedly and without any compromising condition, in the stars impartial company and unconditional friendship.

That is, until one day, the tree awoke to find that the star was no longer flickering, and that its laughter, too, had stopped.

The tree called to the star, and shook it, almost violently, to provoke it, and bring it back to its flickering ways – but the star just lay there, its limbs limp, its light, extinguished. No matter how hard the tree tried, it could not entice any reaction whatsoever from the star, nothing, not even the slightest movement - nothing.

For a long, long time the tree, numb, lay even more prostrate than before, so deeply distressed and saddened was it; its leaves, which had been forever brown, turned black. Once they had blossomed, soft before they became brittle and cracked; now they blossomed already dead. When the wind blew they crackled, some shrieked, frail but intensely and uncontrollably, they all twisted; frantically they hung onto the branches – and yet more still blossomed......

It was impossible for the tree to describe how wretched it felt - shivering, and shaking bitterly in the cold, it called to its few remaining friends, desperately searching for some sort of comfort - but they did not understand, and could only shake their branches in ineffective and impotent commiseration.

Gradually the tree began to wither. Hopelessly inert, it clung, habitually to the ground - but its rigid grip upon the surface of the earth began to slip. The world began to spin and turn again, but its orbit was unrecognisable, as if in revolt – it was exactly that...a revolt, in revolt, nauseating and inescapable. The world turned over, and over, and over, and the tree began to lose its capacity to endure, to endure the unendurable...

But then, slowly, the star began to rust.

At the sight of this something in the tree stirred, and broke –

something deep in its trunk, deep within the rings of its age, its heritage, deep in its lineage. It was wrong, so fundamentally wrong, to let this happen, to let the star lie like that: its place was not to be left tangled, low down upon the ground. Its place was up; up in the air, up in the heavens! Suddenly the tree no longer felt its weight, the weight of its trunk, its branches and leaves; what weight was there that could compare to the weight of the fallen star, a weight that bore down even more heavily than the trees own, a weight more heavy than any tree, unbelievably heavily, a weight, of unknowable and immeasurable proportions? Why, why had the tree allowed itself to be borne down under its own weight for so long?

As if in mutual unspoken accord, the tree, its branches and all its leaves elected then to lift the star from where it lay.

Painfully, but persistently, with a stubborn tenacity that the tree hardly knew it possessed, every leaf was shed, each and every one, like a ripped tear, fell from its limbs. For the first time, they were let to drift freely to the ground - and slowly, laboriously, the tree rose, aching as it inched ever, ever upwards.

Finally the tree stood erect. Some, indeed, many of its branches were broken, and some were rotted and some, gone altogether; some, inevitably still hung low to the ground, and yet the majority had risen, trembling and brave. Overall the tree was terribly misshapen – it had grown all the time it had lain on the ground, but unnaturally so: it was hardly straight: its trunk was twisted and gnarled, deformations and unsightly protrusions abounded, but nevertheless it now stood proudly, crippled, but upright.

Suddenly a breeze blew through its empty branches, a breeze unlike any the tree had ever known; it lit up the tree, as if the breeze itself shone, as if the air glowed. This luminous breeze, it ruffled the leaves that lay about the tree's trunk, scattering them, this way and that – and for a second the tree regretted what it had done, fearing for its fallen leaves, for it sounded as if they were hurt, for they were...crying. And then the tree realised that though they were crying, they were crying not with pain...but with joy...each one, crying, exclamations of wonder as they began to dissolve, wonder and delight in the discovery: that there had been no sacrifice in letting go, none whatsoever; only purpose realised, and in the same instant, fulfilment...

The solitary silver birch tree waited, in quiet yet patient anticipation for the spring to come. Never again would it lay down low upon the ground - it would stand forever upright; despite the vagaries of the passing seasons, it could carry any burden placed dispassionately upon it – because it would be protected, and perpetually bathed in the light from the silent star that spun gently sparkling from its tender branch: an eternal sunshine, burning both day and night, and throughout the years.

Birds, robin red breasts and magpies, would one day nest in its branches, branches that when the next spring came, the silver birch tree knew, would blossom full of buds, and though some may yet be brown, indeed, though there may be many, others would be green; green......bright, bright, green.

And as he drew, something incredible happened!

THE BOY WHO CHANGED THE WORLD

Once upon a time there was a little boy who loved to draw. He would draw all the time - he drew with a pencil; it was, in fact, a magic pencil, though the boy did not know it, not until one day, one remarkable day, when he drew something that he had never drawn before......

The boy lived in a fine villa, which sat facing the main street of a small, pretty town. To the rear of the villa was a gently flowing river, and all around was a large garden, abundant with all manner of bushes, shrubs and plants - and trees; trees, and lots of them!

Mostly they were large mature trees, oaks, maples and fir trees. There was however, one tree which by comparison, was rather unique: it was a red acer - an extraordinarily beautiful red acer.

Though young, the branches of this tree had grown both wide and high, and had spread with an uncommon and yet consummate grace: it was without question, elegant in form – but what really astounded was its colouring. Every spring the leaves of the acer blossomed the most delightful burnt orange colour, before turning bright green in the summer; but then, come the autumn, the leaves would reveal their odd, and yet astonishing splendour: they would turn again, to a deep, deep red, a red of almost unnatural origin. Set against its more prosaic neighbours, the tree would stand out truly as one of a kind: a magnificent and glorious vision in scarlet!

The little boy would often sit under the tree, especially in the autumn. He felt blessed to witness its incredible transformation, even when the leaves allowed their wondrous red to fade to orange as autumn too faded; blessed, to watch the leaves fall so softly, scattering themselves charitably and without reservation all over the grass beneath

- some even fell upon his head! Sometimes he would lay back, the leaves as soft a mattress as he had ever known and he would stare up into the branches, picking out patterns and allowing his imagination to discover all manner of creatures and scenes from within the entangled silhouette of the trees corpulent branches. The leaves would continue to fall, and on occasion the boy would gather some, throw them into the river and watch them slip away on the gently tumbling current - he would picture them washing up on strange exotic shores, picture a boy perhaps like himself, finding one and carrying it back to present it to his people, as the most wondrous offering, a gift bestowed from the most charitable of gods.

It would not be an exaggeration to say that the little boy loved the tree. Every day as soon as he awoke, he would rush out to see it, and the last thing he would do at night would be to say goodnight to it. His last thought before he fell to sleep would be the tree, his first thought on waking. He simply loved it – he loved looking at it, and of course, he loved to draw it!

There was however, one thing that troubled the little boy. His bedroom, being located to the side of the villa, had no window from which he could see the tree.

So one day, one magical day, when the red tree's red was as red as its red could be, the little boy sat with his pencil - it was a perfectly normal pencil, made of wood, with lead of course - and on a scrap of paper, drew his bedroom, but with a window in the wall which faced the tree.

And as he drew, something incredible happened! A part of the wall of his bedroom dissolved! The paint, the plaster, the stones themselves, just floated away and disappeared, and in their place, just as the boy had drawn it, appeared a window!

The boy could hardly believe it – he rushed to his new window, and looked out. It was just as he'd imagined – below him sat the tree, red, still, and redolent! Mesmerised, he sat at his window for the rest of the day, gazing at the tree glowing crimson in the autumn sun. He was very,

very happy – happier, in fact, than he had ever been.

His father, however, was not so happy...!

That evening, when he returned from work, as soon as his carriage pulled up at the villa gates, he couldn't help but notice the new window. His son's face was staring down at him.

"What have you done?!" he shouted, red faced with rage.

The little boy was upset that he had upset his father.

"But father – I can fix it," he pleaded. "Just tell me what you want, and I can fix it."

"I want the front of my house to be as it was!" his father roared. This was not, of course, what the boy wanted to hear, as he had already become rather accustomed to having his new window.

"If I put a window here...," he suggested, and quickly the boy sketched what he meant on another scrap of paper. As he did so, again, it happened – part of the wall in the front of the villa dissolved, and another window appeared, exactly as the boy had drawn it!

Well, his father was obviously, amazed – amazed, and appeased, for the symmetry that he so desired was once again restored. He happily said so.

However, now the little boy's sister was not so happy...!

The new window that the little boy had created opened directly into the bathroom, and his sister, who happened to be bathing at the time, was therefore very embarrassed.

"What have you done?!" she shouted, flushed and red faced, her towel pulled tightly around her.

The little boy was upset that he had upset his sister (even though she could be a bit of a pain at times!)

"But sister - I can fix it," he insisted, and with his magic pencil, he re-drew the villa, swapping around the bathroom, which was at the front of the villa, with his parents' bedroom, which was at the rear of the villa. As he did so, walls slid away, skirting boards and facias followed, and all the fixtures and fittings, the bath, toilet, bidet and wash-hand basin, lifted themselves up and out of their position. Pipes disconnected, taps too, and they all re-positioned themselves exactly as the boy had drawn them!

Well, his sister was, likewise amazed – amazed, and likewise, appeased, for the privacy that she so desired was once again restored. She happily said so.

However, now the little boy's mother was not so happy...!

The two rooms, now re-positioned, meant that the sun would no longer shine in the parents' bedroom in the morning, a fact which the little boy's mother only discovered when she awoke the following day.

"What have you done?!" she shouted, as she yawned, red-eyed and stretching in the unlit room.

The little boy was upset that he had upset his mother.

"But mother - I can fix it," he promised, and yet again, with his magic pencil, he re-drew the villa; it rose from the ground as he did so, the whole building, and turned itself, according to the little boy's drawing, through 180 degrees to face completely the other way! Concrete foundations scurried into their proposed location, cables and pipes snaked into position, and the building then settled itself comfortably back into place, its walls carefully aligned, its windows re-positioned mindful of both the father's concern for symmetry and the sister's concern for privacy, and not least the mother's concern for morning light: the window to the parents' bedroom was again facing east, exactly as the boy had drawn it!

Well, his mother too, was likewise amazed – amazed, and likewise, appeased, for the light she so desired was once again, restored. She happily said so.

So now everyone in the villa was happy; they were, in fact, happier than they had been *prior* to the little boy's adjustments: the father, content that his house was again, symmetrical, delighted that, if anything, his villa was now even more refined in its symmetrical composition than before; the sister, content that her privacy was assured, delighted that, if anything, her bathroom was now even more discreetly located than before; and the mother, content that the sun shone onto her bed in the morning, delighted that, if anything, it shone even more brightly than before! Of course, the little boy himself was also happy, happy that he could look down on the tree in the garden, through his new perfectly located bedroom window. But he was also happy that his father and sister and mother were happy, if not, in fact, happier than they had ever been!

However, unfortunately, now all the other people who lived in the street were not so happy...! In fact, they were exceedingly unhappy!

"What have you done to your villa?!" they all complained, as mystified as they were angry. "It is facing the wrong way!"

"That's no problem," declared the little boy. "I can fix it", and with that, he re-drew the villas in the street so that they all faced the same way as his villa! Lo and behold, as he did so, the villas lifted up from the ground, foundations again re-positioned themselves, as did various cables, drainage pipes, and gas and other power mains, and then settled themselves comfortably in their proposed locations!

Everyone who lived in the street was amazed, utterly amazed...and duly appeased, that all the villas now faced the same way! They were in fact delighted with their revised prospect, which was so much better than it had been - which was fine, except that, having now seen the wonderful changes the boy had made to his own villa, they all came to him and asked if he could change theirs, to better suit *their* specific needs, for symmetry or privacy or light or for any number of other reasons, whether personal or practical or purely aesthetic!

The boy was actually delighted. He loved to draw, and he drew and drew, and as he drew, windows, doors, and roofs, roof tiles and floor tiles, bathrooms and bedrooms and living rooms, all moved. Walls slid this way and that, up and down, and around and around. Bricks and stones floated up into the air, tumbling over each other. Globules of paint and clouds of plaster dust drifted casually past each other, and nails and screws and dowels flew here and there...it was truly a sight to see! And each and every item, from chimney-pot to chamber-pot, was re-configured exactly according the boy's drawings!

Finally everything was re-arranged to everyone's satisfaction, and everyone in the street was happy, happier in fact than they had ever been – everyone, that is, except the postman, the milkman and the newspaper boy: now they were not so happy...!

"What have you done?!" they complained. "We cannot deliver the post, the milk, the newspapers!" The bin men were not happy either: "We cannot collect the refuse!" they complained.

"That's no problem," assured the little boy. "I can fix it", and with that, he re-drew the location of the street: kerbstones, cobbles, pavement slabs and tarmac flew into the air, and all re-located themselves to lie once again in front of the villas.

The postman, the milkman, the newspaper boy, and the binmen were duly appeased, for the road was smoother, the pavements wider, and as such their jobs had been made so much easier. They were happy, happier in fact than they'd ever been and they duly said so.

However, now the mayor, his appointed associates, other governing bodies and elected representatives were not so happy...!

"What have you done!" they formally objected. "You cannot move villas and streets without permission!"

They had perhaps, reasonable grounds for their objection – because the street had connected the main square, with its town hall and marketplace, to the castle on the hill, and now...well, now it didn't!

"I can fix your street," the little boy proclaimed. He re-drew the street, in fact he re-drew all the streets, *and* the square *and* the castle; he re-connected them whilst at the same time re-arranging all the buildings: the town hall, the church, the library, the school, the hospital, the hotel, and every house and villa: they all floated into the air, every one re-positioned according to his drawings, until finally the town was completely and entirely re-configured!

Everyone agreed that the new town was infinitely better than it had been, though they would have been hard pressed to explain exactly why? Perhaps it was because all the streets were broader, the spaces between the buildings more harmoniously proportioned, the town square more spacious, the buildings themselves, more refined in their structure and composition, their fenestration more elegantly arranged...perhaps? It was hard to say, nevertheless, they were all exceedingly happy, happier in fact than they had ever been, and they duly said so.

However, now all the neighbouring towns were not so happy...!

"Look what you've done with your town," they enviously declared. "Why can't we have a town as fine as yours?"

Word had inevitably spread to the neighbouring towns of the little boy and his magic pencil; their complaint was incentive enough for the little boy.

"I can fix your town," he pledged, to each and every one. And so he drew, and he drew and he drew; he drew everything, from furniture to factories, from town squares to toilet roll holders, from halls to heating ducts, from warehouses to wine glasses, from greenhouses to garages, from patios to plugs, from living rooms to light fittings, from doorknobs to dormers; he drew and he drew, and as he drew - everything moved!

Soon, every town was re-configured according to the boy's drawings, and all their people, appeased, in fact, delighted, and happier than they had ever been, because their streets, their squares and their buildings were so much better than before. How was it so? Well it was as hard for them to say as it had been for the people of the boy's town – perhaps it was because now their town was so much better organised, and so much better arranged, and all its spaces and buildings, more elegant and more refined in their proportion and composition, and all of it so perfectly crafted in its construction...perhaps?

Well, whatever the reason, they were all exceedingly happy, and duly said so.

However, as for the people that lived in the city....? Now they were not so happy...!

"Look, what you've done to the towns," the City Fathers observed, in solemn admiration. They presented their city to the boy: "Our city...requires your help," they admitted, with statesmen like authority, for word had indeed spread, of the little boy and his magic pencil – and clearly, the city had need of his gift.

The streets were narrow, the buildings pressed close one upon another – there was no light, no air, and the city stank, for there was no sanitation! If the City Fathers were unhappy, the citizens were even more so, as they were the ones who had to endure such grim and wretched surroundings.

"I can fix your city," the little boy swore. He set about drawing the city, drawing everything, once again, but not before he had talked to the people of the city, the citizens, and listened to what they told him. He heard them tell of what they wanted - and then he gave them, in return, exactly what they needed. Neither the citizens nor the City Fathers could have predicted nor envisioned the city that the little boy then drew – and as he drew, the city dissolved, each piece of timber and stone and concrete and glass, re-configured, re-organised, re-made according to his drawings. Everything swirled through the air, vast slabs of wall, floor and roof, twisting and turning, and a new city, so unlike the old, slowly arose. It was white and it was beautiful; there were no ugly buildings any longer, there were no foul smells or dingy streets. In fact, there were no streets at all, but parks, endless parks full of trees and greenery, and all the buildings stood majestically tall on the parks edges, air and light pouring through them!

The City Fathers were duly appeased – in fact, they were delighted. They had a city the likes of which had never been seen! No longer had their citizens to live in the cavernous maze of dark and miserable streets - now they could wander uninhibited through green fields and fertile gardens to their homes, which seemed to watch almost paternally over them. They were truly happy, happier than they had ever been, and they duly said so.

However, as for the citizens in every other city...? Now they were not so happy...!

"Look, what you've done with your city," the other City Fathers observed with admiration, equally as solemn. "Our cities, too, need your help."

It was true, for each one had cause for complaint, whether too dense or too sprawling, too dirty or too sterile, too ugly or too remote, too noisy or too smelly, too poor or too insignificant, too bland or too ornate, too mean or too difficult to navigate; whatever the cause, each one hosted some aspect that was simply untenable!

"I can fix your cities," the little boy vowed. Again, he drew. He drew and drew, and drew and drew, and once again, everything dissolved and floated into the air - whole cities rose up, and moved, every part of every one according to the boy's drawings. And they were re-created in the image of the first one, cities that were white, and beautiful, full of trees and greenery.

The citizens of every city, and the City Fathers too, were duly appeased – in fact they were delighted, for they too now lived in a city that was devoid of all that they had previously found so abhorrent. They were happy, happier than they had ever been, and they duly said so.

However, now the governments of neighbouring countries were not so happy...!

"Look, what you have achieved with your cities, your towns, your houses," they appreciatively exclaimed, clamouring in languages both common and foreign. "Our cities, our towns, our villages, our houses, too, need your help."

It was true, for there was not one city, nor one town, nor one house that did not require some form of adjustment, some sort of improvement to better suit the need of the person who dwelt there.

"I can fix it," the little boy said, though he was hardly a little boy any more. He had grown into an old man, his eyes were weary and his pencil nearly completely worn away - but still he drew, he drew every city, every town, every house, he drew each one, and all the spaces within and between them, every piece and every part, down to the tiniest detail, and it was all created exactly according to the little boys drawings!

When it was complete, when every material had finally settled into its due position, everyone was duly appeased – in fact they were delighted. Every single person in the world was happy, happier than they had ever been, for each and everyone now had everything they needed: they had enough light, they had enough air...and everyone, like the little boy, had perhaps what they needed most of all: everyone, no matter where they were, or what they were doing, had a room with a view, a view of a tree, as beautiful as the view of the red acer that sat in the garden of the villa where the little boy once lived, and finally, as an old, old man, passed serenely away...

Side 2

'Everything you can imagine, is real.'

Pablo Picasso

"Have you ever wondered, about corners?"

THE GIRL WHO DREAMT ROUND CORNERS

"I think...this is a song of hope."

> Robert Plant, introduction to 'Stairway to Heaven',
> Madison Square Gardens, 1973 (from 'The Song Remains the Same.')

Preface:

Once upon a time there lived a princess, a pure and beautiful princess, who dwelt in a tower, a tower so high that it stood higher than the highest cloud! All around stood other towers, each as high, and each host to a princess, as pure and beautiful as the first.

The towers were so tightly packed together, it was difficult to tell where one ended and another began. Every morning, when the princesses bathed in their exquisite pink and perfumed boudoirs they could murmur sweet greetings to each other, their windows being so close that their shadowy shapes appeared like sisters in an adjacent room. Washed and dressed, they would breakfast on terraces, terraces so close they could pass favoured foods to each other: toast that lingered still warm and buttered, perfectly; grapefruits covered in soft crusted sugars still not yet melted into insidious syrup; divorced cereals still crunchy despite being drowned in chocolate milk or honey; or eggs, scrambled in oils and herbs, served still hot on plates of the finest steely china.

Breakfast concluded, their days were then consumed with all the dutiful requirements of their station – they studied, they exercised, they prayed, and at night, their kingly fathers would tuck them into their silken sheeted beds, whisper goodnights to their precious daughters - their beautiful princesses - after filling their heads full of tales of the towers within which they all dwelt, content and secure. Their doors closed, in the darkness the princesses would feign to sleep, but instead, would chatter through the walls, walls that were so, so close they could share, intimately, their hopes, schemes and petty conspiracies.

So their days and nights revolved, and not once would they ever look down, for why would they? There was nothing to see, only shades of shadowy greys, slowly shifting beneath – if there was an earth below it was unknown to them, for all their lives they had lived in their shiny towers, and their earth, the surface of the planet which they inhabited was therefore the parquet flooring beneath their manicured feet, permanently smooth, lacquered and varnished to a finish so soft it felt like a carpet between their tiny toes.

The princess had no cause to object to her life – her every need was catered for, her every desire – she lived, and to all intent, lived happily. And yet......she harboured within her an unease that she found difficult to discern. Why that should be, she did not know. She was no different to the other princesses – or so it seemed, for they were all, in turn, no different from any other collection of princesses. Typically, each one had her own thing, her own look: one was frumpy, one was diva, one was glum, and one was fun; one could fake, one could bake, one could dance, one could sing; one could mock, one could talk, one could act, and one could walk; one could skip, one could parry, one could cry and one could hurry...and one could worry. Each one was special therefore, but then so was she; she was the same: she could do something that none of the others could: she was the one who could dream.

It was this skill that differentiated her from the rest – and it was such an implicit skill, difficult to ascribe any outward signs of mitigating evidence. It was simply something she could do, just as the others could bake and sew and sing and dance...... but by comparison it was an elusive ability – and pervasive: she could dream where and whenever she liked, and she did it all the time: every second of every day, and every day of every month.

It made no difference whether she was asleep or not, in fact she slept the appropriate hours expected of her, but still she dreamt, day or night. "Wake up, wake up!" her perfect friends would shout, her royal parents too, her wisely teachers. "You were dreaming again. What on earth were you dreaming about?" they would kindly inquire, but she could never explain, for how do you explain, the dreams you have? How do you...?

It was simply impossible, to tell anyone of the things she saw, especially those revelations, disclosed so vaguely when she stole time into her bedroom – where, alone, she fretted, she agonised, where she negotiated with herself and never won, where she discovered how to make-up and where she travelled millions and millions of miles inside her head, this way and that, and in every direction at once, over landscapes of people and places, making incredible discoveries exclusively only to her. Great truths abounded in her mind, observations and constellations of emotions that collided and exploded behind her eyes. Truly she was a princess, though she did not know it, for her capacity to embrace the world was entirely different to that of everyone else: she could see things the others couldn't – she was unique, because she, and only she, did look down: from her balcony, she secretly stared into the shadowy clouds below - and staring, saw things she could never imagine...worlds worthy of inhabiting, worlds, though hard to believe, that were worthier than the one in which she lived.

For years and years she gathered imaginings of these wondrous worlds; together with her thoughts, she stored them tight inside her bedroom, piled higher and higher, vision upon vision, until it seemed that the walls of her bedroom would burst! She could hardly breathe, and became frightened, fearful that the visions would finally crush her – until, by chance, she discovered a simple and easy way to unburden herself.

She wrote them down.

Like a dam bursting, she poured her visions into innumerable stories, stories set in these unseen worlds, the stories that only she could tell, stories, not unlike the story of the girl who wept round corners......

Prologue

Once upon time, there was a king, an old, old king, who lived in a city, gleaming, pure and white.

The king was no fool, he was not one to entertain falsehoods or be subject to self-delusion: on account of his great age, he knew that his life was nearing its end; he was soon proven to be undeniably correct - his health began to fail, suddenly and with serious consequence: he was diagnosed to be beyond hope of any possible remission, and was confined, subsequently, to see out the rest of his days recumbent in his bedchamber, atop the tallest tower of the royal palace that sat high in the mountains overlooking the great white city below.

Select physicians, nurses, and trusted courtiers willingly attended to the king, but their presence was more for comfort than for healing – a conspiratorial silence prevailed, for all knew that the king's life was irrevocably fading, and no words could counter the inevitable. Discretion was maintained and no visitors were allowed, in respect of the king's unspoken wish, to reign undisturbed until the end.

However, as the king had no children, the Royal Court, knowing the kingdom would be left without an appointed heir to the throne, requested reverentially an audience with the king. They hated to do so, as they loved their king, a king who had ruled over them with such consummate grace and kindly authority; therefore they respected their king's wish for solitude - nevertheless they felt that their concern was justified. They genuinely wished to know his expectations for the succession over their great land, presuming that the king would be as assuredly concerned for the future of the kingdom as were they. Moreover, they wanted to record for posterity, his life, so that tales of the king's great achievements might be handed down from one generation to the next. The king was a singularly humble man, therefore no account of his reign had ever been instructed – an oversight that the Royal Court considered within their remit, indeed, their duty, to rectify.

An audience was finally granted, but the king expressed little or no interest in the concerns of his Royal Court, appearing distracted and withdrawn; the Royal Court, courtiers, nurses and attendant physicians all worried that he was of an unreasonably melancholic disposition, attributable presumably to an inconsolable grief at the thought of his impending demise. Though they tried, the Royal Court could do nothing to lure the king away from his apparent absence of spirit. So worried were they, they chose to ignore his wish for solitude; acting in good faith, they invited all manner of consultations on his behalf: they tried to elicit confidence from familial friends and respected peers - but nothing worked: every consultation was to no avail. Frustrated, they elected to try to reach the king by other means: musicians were brought, to play for the king, soft sweet harmonies composed in string and voice, accompanied by jesters in the hope they might elevate the king's mood, raise a laugh or even a smile - but this too, was to no avail. An artist was commissioned, ostensibly to prepare a portrait of the king, but more so in hope that the artist's benign presence might encourage the king to a confessional state of mind; again, this was to no avail. Respected authors and playwrights, masters of letters and intrigue, were invited to orate dramatisations of their fantasies, stimuli that might inspire some response or comment from the king - but this too, was also to no avail. Monks and priests, ministers and seers, all of great repute and known for their singular capacity to empathise with their respective congregations, came to offer consolation or private counsel in expectation of the king's need to unburden himself: again, to no avail.

Throughout, scribes were permanently on hand, should suddenly the king make utterance of any kind - but he never did. Finally, in desperation, a pronouncement was made to the people of the city: was there *anyone* who could be of beneficial assistance to their sovereign?

Many, many people came forward, willingly and well-meaning in their intentions, whether comedic or serious contenders as confidant, but not one could establish any rapport with the ailing king.

The Royal Court eventually abandoned its efforts, and resigned themselves to the inevitable: all hope of a secure and determined future would die with the king. All the efforts that they had made, including the commissioning of the king's portrait, became forgotten in their inflicted woe.

However, the artist selected to produce the king's portrait was born of a persistent nature, and she continued regardless, the task asked of her. Every day she sat sketching the king as he lay, prone and silent in his bed, and every day she reported obediently and in accordance with instruction to the Royal Court of her progress. With diligence rather than in expectation, she would be asked if any conversation had transpired - but despite sitting together daily, for weeks on end, the king said nothing, the artist simply noticing the fine lines in the king's face as he slumbered, recording each in sketch after sketch, in preparation for the portrait that she had been prevailed upon to create.

A considerable number of sketches slowly accumulated, the bedchamber became adrift with them, all manner of drawings in charcoals, pencils, crayon and ink – and then eventually, deeming her studies complete, an easel was set up and the artist set about the production of the portrait. She began in confidence, but almost immediately her confidence evaporated - she felt a tremendous pressure upon her to complete the portrait as properly representative of the king: he was obviously old, but he had become enfeebled, and made so transparently frail by his illness – and yet, she wanted to try and capture that great wisdom and authority for which he was known, for which he symbolised to his people, to his kingdom, and indeed, to her. She worked and worked, tirelessly - but it was without question, a struggle. Often she became frustrated, that she could not capture in the image, the proper recognition she desired. She could accurately represent his physical condition, his fine features regardless of his ill health: the sharply defined line of his jaw, his high cheek bones, and long thin nose, his fine, though thinning, grey, indeed almost white hair, pulled back straight from his high forehead, hardly creased despite his age. But his eyes were sunken, his cheeks too, and his lips, thin and almost colourless. These debilitating facets confounded her, she tried but could not disregard them, and they hindered her capacity to compose an image properly imbued with that regal aspect prevalent: all her attempts conveyed rather the impression of a sick old man, albeit one with attendant, some subtle yet considerable quality of refinement.

But the artist was tenacious: she was determined to complete, successfully, the task. She asked, and was granted with the barest acknowledgement, the permission to stay, so she might work on the portrait, day and night. She worked almost in isolation, as the bedchamber had become effectively abandoned, the physicians having left, the nurses and courtiers too; they returned, but only occasionally, to effect the merest of examinations – there was little else they could do. Even the Royal Court withdrew; it had become nothing more than a perfunctory conglomerate of despairing individuals, so distressed were they by their beloved king's deterioration. They were resigned, and rendered ineffective as a collective; their behaviour reflective of that of the populace at large - for there had settled upon the land a sense of quiet foreboding, as everyone in the great city - and even the city itself - waited, idle and numb, as if prematurely incapacitated, for the kings final breath.

Silence reigned, and sometimes it seemed as if the artists brush was the only thing that moved, that and her long red hair, fluttering in the gentle breeze that blew in through the great undraped terraced openings overlooking the city.

Rarely did the artist pause, but when she did, it was to the terrace that she would go, to gaze out and marvel from such an inimitable perspective, at the city laid out below. She would stare, enraptured, her artist's eye tracing the wonderful lines made by the buildings that stretched out across a landscape more verdant green than anything else. It was a city unlike any other, and she marvelled at the incredible inventiveness of it, at its sheer conception. The pattern of buildings formed such an exquisite grid of walls and forms, all set together in faultless harmony; she could not help but wonder: had there ever been a finer place, a more perfect place, built, than this? It was paradise...

It was on one such occasion, late one glorious evening, when the fading sunset seemed to cast its light even upon the delicate sounds of the city sleeping, echoing distantly from below, that the artist, weary after another frustrating day's work, was moved to utter, quietly...: "Beautiful."

"Beautiful?"

The artist turned, startled. The king had not moved, and his eyes remained closed. For a second the artist thought she had imagined it, but then the king, in the same shallow voice, said again: "Beautiful?"

She felt obliged to respond, indeed to explain: "Yes.....yes. The city. It is beautiful, quite beautiful."

"So you know, then, what beauty is?"

"Oh...," the artist was taken aback slightly. She had averted, respectfully, her gaze, but the king, *her* king, was initiating conversation with her. It was disconcerting, despite the unequivocal invitation so willingly offered. Still, she hesitated before answering, she hoped, with the appropriate deference: "Doesn't everyone? To me, yes, yes I think I know."

"And can beauty be true for one, and yet false, for another?"

"Why, most certainly......the eye of the beholder....." The king opened his eyes, eyes that were surprisingly bright. They glistened as he regarded the artist.

"Yes......the eye of the beholder...," he conceded, with a soft laugh and subtle lifting of his thin hand. He smiled. "Many who come here, they tell me what you have told me, that the city is beautiful."

"Well, then perhaps it must be true...?"

"Indeed, perhaps, perhaps it would be so if everyone agreed?"

"Do they not?" The artist was incredulous – for it was difficult to imagine a scene more magnificent than the one that she looked down upon. "But they must agree......?"

"I could imagine one, who would not......," the king said, quietly, his eyes cast downwards, as a sadness seemed, suddenly, to consume him. The artist was left not knowing what to say, or indeed whether she had the right to do so. She was grateful that he broke the silence, even if it was only to comment: "You are an artist......"

He indicated her easel, its back to him. She did not understand, exactly, if he were asking it of her, or simply stating a fact – or for that matter, imbuing her with an authority or respect that might be expected of such a title. It was however, not a title with which she had ever felt entirely comfortable, despite her successes and dedication to her craft.

"As are you," she countered, again, she hoped, deferentially. She indicated towards the city. "The city...?"

"Ah, the city. You flatter me," he said. "But I fear that I am not the creator – I did not make the city, I had assistance, and what parts I did make, I had considerable material to work with. You have neither, neither assistance nor material."

The artist couldn't help herself. "Oh, but I do...," she protested instinctively.

"Indeed...you do flatter me."

The artist was very embarrassed. She hung her head, and made to kneel. "I'm sorry...my king – I –"

The king halted her admissions of regret with, again, a gentle wave of his hand.

"You paint...?"

"I try, my king..."

"I don't doubt it...and do you succeed?"

"I...think so, my king. My work is liked......"

"Does it matter to you, what others think, then, of your work?"

The artist's first thought was to present a denial to the king's query. His manner, though, was so charmingly indulgent and sedate that it eased her capacity to simply tell the truth: "Yes," she replied, "yes, it does. I do not like it when my work is not liked."

"And you like it when it is?"

"Well...yes." She hesitated a little – the king prompted her: "Even if *you* don't like it?"

She hesitated again, unsure as she answered: "No, no..." and then added assuredly: "No."

"No." The king acknowledged her confirmation. He regarded her, steadily with his sharp clear eyes.

"Do *you* like it? Your work," he asked.

"Sometimes..."

"Sometimes?"

"Sometimes, yes, sometimes......sometimes, I do something, yes, which I think is...ok."

"How do you decide?"

"Oh, I don't know...many reasons, I suppose."

"Perhaps...if it is beautiful?"

"Well, yes, I suppose so...yes."

"So...beauty..." The king's voice faded as he said it, adding, as if to himself: "Is beauty enough?" quietly, and without rhetoric. Again, the artist didn't know what to say – she pretended not to have heard the king, pretended, indeed, to have misheard him, and repeated unnecessarily: "I believe yes, I know beauty when I see it."

"And what if you can't...?"

Before the artist could reply, the king, his tone suddenly light and inquisitive, said:

"Have you ever wondered, about corners?"

"Corners?"

"Yes, corners."

The artist hesitated. "What about corners?" she asked.

"Well, have you ever wondered: corners, what are corners for?"

The artist felt that she was being mocked, and said so: "You mock me, my king...I think...?"

He smiled again. "Indeed......well let's see......let me put it another way: have you ever wondered, what might be around a corner?"

"Which corner?"

"Any corner."

"Do you mean, as in, you never know, what is around a

corner?"

"In a way, yes – but, more explicitly, and less metaphorically – what is around *any* corner?"

"I suppose so, yes...doesn't everyone?"

The king paused before answering. "No, I think not. I might agree, that everyone 'wonders', 'wonders' implicitly perhaps, but I know that few realise what they 'wonder'."

"I'm not sure I understand...."

"Ok, I shall put it another way: have you ever hoped around a corner?"

"Hoped?"

"Hoped, yes."

"Hoped for what?"

The elderly king paused, again, before whispering: "Perfection."

The artist could only look back, blankly.

"There could be perfection around a corner," the king intoned. "Any corner, or indeed... every corner." He looked with kindness but keenly at the artist. "Wouldn't you wish it so?"

"I've never really thought about it.....but now you mention it, yes, I suppose so. It depends on what you mean, by 'perfection'."

"Yes, yes it does."

The king fell silent once more, and closed his eyes. The artist could tell though that the old king did not sleep, but rather appeared to be waiting. Waiting, waiting ...for what? For her? To ask him......what? The king said nothing, and waited.....

Finally, it dawned on the artist, perhaps what the king was getting at. She hesitated a little before asking: ".....have you ever found, perfection around a corner?"

The old king smiled.

"I thought you'd never ask," he said, and, lying back into the soft comfort of his great bed, he proceeded to tell the tale of an astounding life......

ACT I

"Leave? Who would be so foolish?!"

ACT I

Scene i: The Creatures in the Saucer

'Once upon a time, there lived a young prince. He was all the things one might expect of a prince: handsome, brave, charming, to those who longed to be charmed, unknowingly vain and therefore forgiven for it, impulsive and impetuous.

Less a product of his upbringing, some aspect of the prince's character demanded that he prove his worth, and, hardly a man, he elected to seek his destiny, to travel and to conquer, lands and peoples unknown.

However, his father, the king, and at the invocation too, of the late queen, lamented his son's decision: "Why?" he pleaded, "why would you wish to leave, your people, your land, your kingdom, your city?"

It was incomprehensible, and in particular to this king, because his son had grown up at his side, as he, the king, had built around them a city the likes of which had never been seen. It was a splendorous place, delightful beyond words: a glorious construction, every building raised in golden stones and unblemished marbles, hewn from local quarries burrowed deep down into the earth, and shaped into forms and details impossibly refined, honed by master craftsmen, stonemasons skilled beyond comprehension; craftsmen, carpenters as gifted as the stonemasons, carved the hard timber of the mighty trees felled like giants from the local forest: they jointed the pieces together without a sign, filling the spaces between the golden stones and perfect marbles: every door, door frame and window frame, every floor and every piece of furniture too, was made by those gifted hands – and slate, quarried hard from local mines, stored and piled high as mountains in upturned strata, was laid upon every single roof; and massive cobbles, shaped smooth like pillows made the surface underfoot, as secure as the slate overhead.

All these materials united to form a composition of streets and squares unquestionably absolute: a cityscape, exquisitely arranged, with every part set in wondrous harmony. If a more perfect city existed, none could tell, for none had ever elected to leave, not one. Every citizen instinctively knew that their city was, indeed, perfect – and every visitor would be so overwhelmed by its beauty, they would never elect to return to their place of origin, so paltry was it by comparison!

Leave? Who would be so foolish!?

For the king then, it was unimaginable: how could his son, his joy, his heir, how could he of all people, wish to leave? But the prince's steely resolve thawed the parental will; and the king, reluctantly, relented.

On the day of the prince's departure, the whole city turned out, as much to wish kind farewell to the frustrated heir as to witness the great gates in the city walls being opened outwards for the first time. Trumpets blared, drums thundered and banners waved feverishly as the prince rode proudly through the streets, carrying lance and sword, glistening fresh from the furnace. Bedecked in roguish masks, voluminous capes and with feathers fluttering in their caps, a small army of willing and excited compatriots followed. Enraptured by the prince, their natural trepidation was overcome by his charisma and enthusiasm. They should have feared properly the unknown, but they could talk only of the great adventure upon which they were about to embark, the valorous conquests they would doubtless make, and the great riches and treasures they would surely accumulate.

Through the city gates they passed, and into the distance the small cohort disappeared, the music gradually receding until the city vanished entirely from view.

They proceeded with confidence, but it was not long before the prince's campaign turned to ignoble failure. He was not a fighter, and certainly not a navigator, and least of all, a leader of men. Ignoring advice from his advisers, unrepentantly he drove his small army into uncharted lands, lands which were perpetually hostile and forbidding, despite expectation. Slowly but steadily both the will and character of his troops was eroded. Illness and plague beset them, and defeat and resentment bested them, led as they were into landscapes that became ever more desolate, landscapes that were dispassionately unforgiving, without sustenance or shelter whatsoever. Without respite, they travelled, through these landscapes, made of materials both unfamiliar and cruel: some were so sharp and hard, that flesh was cut mercilessly from bones, others, by comparison, were so soft, limbs were wearied by the very act of walking – and some were shrouded in venomous fogs, vicious vapours which drew breath from lungs, abrasively stung bleary eyes, and left mouths parched, and throats, bitter and raw.

For many, many months they struggled forwards, and the memory of the great city they had so willingly left behind, haunted the prince's followers persistently and with increasing anger. "We were fools to follow such a foolish prince," they declared, they whispered and muttered it, until finally, what remained of the prince's glorious little army rebelled.

They had forced their way through a forest of brittle glass, set in a marsh made also of glass; the shards had torn to rags what was left of their fine robes, shredded their feet and their legs, and any that stumbled and fell were cut, literally, to pieces. When they finally reached the outskirts of the forest, they found themselves confronted by a bleak and uncompromisingly vast lake of frozen salt. They halted, exhausted, and refused to accompany the prince any further.

Mutinously they stated their case: they would rather return back through the forest of appalling glass than take one single step further away from the city, from their home. In ragged robes, the prince raged at them, but it was useless – he was in truth, not a man, but a boy, and in the face of their justifiable resistance, he stormed off alone, disappearing into the frozen wilderness as his army turned around and abandoned him to his fate.

Only pride drove the young prince onwards, onwards into what could only be described as a wasteland, a wasteland of nothing: nothing, but emptiness. There was no rock, no tree, no mountain in the distance, there was no distinguishing feature whatsoever – just a blank, frozen landscape stretching endlessly in every direction – even the horizon disappeared: the prince could hardly distinguish the land from the sky, nor could he determine distance or direction. He walked and walked in the empty silence; his steps made no sound and left no prints, the pain in his limbs being the only indication that he was moving at all. Finally he could walk no further: overwhelmed by the great labours of his failed campaign, he fell to his knees, defeated.

Had it not been for the weeping, he would have perished, right there. But as he lay crumpled and broken, the sound of weeping, softly echoing, came to him from out of the dim misty air – distant, and quiet, but disturbing none the less, for it was distinctly, the weeping of a girl.

Pulling himself up, the prince drew his sword and struggled in *the direction of the sound. (He may not have been all the things expected of a prince, but in one capacity he excelled: he was, truly, a prince valiant!)*

He tried to call out, but his voice was gone. He tried to run, but his exhaustion precluded it. Doggedly, he stumbled forward - but the source of the pitiful sobs eluded him. Where did it come from? It seemed to come from everywhere and yet nowhere. He persisted, stumbling on and on, until, from out of the mist, a figure emerged! The prince pushed towards it, his eyes blurred and burning. Again, he tried to call out; the shadowy figure loomed larger and larger in front of him.

And then suddenly - it disappeared!

The prince stopped, stunned - but he hardly had time to wonder what had happened, when the figure, suddenly, re-appeared! For a second the figure was in front of him, it disappeared, then for a second it was to one side of him, then to the other – the prince spun round. What was going on? He became dizzy – and then, without warning, something black rose up from the ground: the prince tripped right over it, heard the thing, whatever it was, grunt, before he fell again, and then he was tumbling, down, and down and down...the world reeled, meaningless, he fell, out of his senses, senseless –'

The king paused in the telling.

"I have interrupted your work," he said to the artist. Was the king chastising her? If so, it had been done amenably, in kindness even. He was right, though; she had willingly sacrificed her efforts, abandoning herself to listen to the king's account, and she felt slightly guilty, despite the king's most gentle admonishment.

She cast a glance at her sketches, at her easel, and at the attempt of a portrait she had hardly begun: the rough outline presented itself accusingly. It drew from her the admission: "Sometimes the choices are just ...impenetrable..."

"Perhaps it is the tools you use?"

"Perhaps..."

"Or perhaps it is the subject...?" The king smiled.

"Yes...my subject...is difficult to capture."

"Perhaps... your subject is too beautiful......"

Again, the king smiled, as he indicated his own face.

"Perhaps......" She smiled in return.

"Too much beauty can be ugly, no?" the king added, still indicating his own face, but somehow his tone did not mirror the lightness of the gesture. It pre-disposed the artist again to honesty, as she instinctively replied: "I have never seen enough beauty, my king, truthfully, I would not know. I have not lived long enough-"

She regretted immediately what she'd said, thinking it rude of her - but the king did not seem to mind.

"Age...makes no difference," was all he said, and though he might have said it in riposte, there was, again, no admonishment, only that same lingering sadness that had penetrated his manner before. He sighed. "Neither age, nor time...opportunity perhaps, chance, maybe...though maybe not. Maybe it is just the way we are?"

The artist did not know what to say, as again, the king did not appear to be inviting a response. But suddenly he sat up clumsily, his voice loud, demanding: "Is it? Is it, the way *we* are?" He stared furiously at her, before slumping slowly, quietly, back into his pillows.

The artist was shocked, and hardly heard the king whispering: "And even if it is...is beauty enough?", again, as if to himself. He fell silent, and remained so, until the artist, still taken aback by the outburst, eventually felt confident enough to encourage him to continue. As deferentially as she could, she asked: "The prince...? What happened to the prince?"

"The prince? The prince was bewitched...," and with that the king, seemingly once again composed, closed his eyes and resumed the account.

'How long the prince was unconscious he did not know. When he awoke he thought for a second that he must be drowning: eyes, like pools of warm sea water, deep but crystal clear, enveloped him. They stared without blinking back into his - eyes, which seemed to see right into his very soul: they penetrated with a surgical ease, piercing painlessly, but

with such transparent honesty and innocence - eyes, that had no centre and no reflection. They were truly the most beautiful eyes – but they were set, however, into a face of dark rims: it was a gorgeous face, the face of a girl, but ringed in a melancholy impossible to condone, the face of a ghost, and a haunted ghost at that; it had to be, for how could a face be so insipid, and so devoid of any colour, or aspect of expression, and still be alive? And yet, somehow, a vibrancy emanated from it, and from too, the cascade of shocking red curls that tumbled as lightly as feathers over the girl's shoulders, shoulders as pale as the face, and so, so pale, that by comparison, those beautiful eyes appeared dark and ominous, foretelling of something forbidden and incomprehensible, like blackened rocks protruding but a little from the snow.

The prince tried to stand, but he could hardly move – though by his stirring, he apparently frightened the girl, for she scurried away. He couldn't see too well, he was still was dizzy and it took him a few minutes to sit up. He tried to clear his head.

Suddenly, something fluttered over him, past him and settled clumsily onto the ground. It clattered as it did so: what was it? Despite his blurred vision, the prince could contend, that he had never seen such a creature. Slowly his eyes cleared, enough to make out that it looked, mostly, like a bird, like a magpie in fact, although also, a little like a butterfly? Curiously, it had a wing of a butterfly, and two of a bird, which was very odd. In fact, the whole creature was odd: it had a beak, and part of a nose, it had legs of a donkey, but arms of an insect. Mostly its hide was of feathers, the colouring of a magpie for certain, but in part it was covered in what appeared to be cow-skin, coarse hair in places, scales in others, and even skin. It had talons at the end of one limb, webbed feet at the end of another, hooves too. Its back was humped, its head, strangely misshapen – and set into deep, deep sockets were two mean beady eyes, eyes that evidentially sought to filch, and a third that protruded swollen, veined, and weeping, and constantly twitched, staring scattily about.

Whatever it was, the whole thing looked like it had just been thrown together from bits and pieces of various animals, and though in parts it was quite impressive, the overall impression was one of: ugliness. Truly it was the most ungainly and hideous looking creature the prince had ever seen! It was disgusting, and the prince could not help but stare, open mouthed and aghast.

"I used to get that a lot," the strange creature sneered, but with *an indication, albeit slight, that it was at the same time, flattered. That it spoke seemed, somehow, fitting from such an unusual creature.*

"I heard weeping," the prince said, still trying to clear his head.

"Yeh......I heard it too. She does that, from time to time. Don't mean much. Forget it, that's what I say." The creature looked over at the girl, and growled at her: "And what use is it.....you can weep, you can cry, you can howl all day, if you like. Ain't no-one gonna hear......" - it looked back at the prince - "'cept, well, 'cept you......"

"Who is she......?" the prince asked, rubbing his eyes.

'Who is she.e.e.e...,' mimicked a thin and rasping metallic voice, suddenly, from out of nowhere. It echoed loudly. The girl did not move, but the prince noticed that she shuddered slightly as the voice erupted again:'Who is she, who is she, who is she.e.e........,' it repeated.

"Exactly!" the creature shouted. "Who is she!!!" It flew up into the air, buzzing and hissing, before settling back down onto the ground.

The prince sat back, bewildered – where had the metallic voice come from, and what was this creature, this 'thing', which sat before him, and which, without provocation, behaved so oddly? And where was he? He looked around – he was in what could only be described as, simply, a vast saucer, a vast white saucer, that appeared to have been carved out of the ground as if by a single stroke – there were no markings at all on the surface; it was so smooth that, had the slope not been as shallow, the prince felt he might have slithered right to the bottom. The circumference of the saucer was wide, very wide, and overhead, a gridded canopy, made of some sort of opaque fabric, stretched across the whole vast space with no visible means of support. It cast a dull flat light, which settled over everything, what little there was: at the bottom of the saucer there appeared to be the remains of a fire, and some rugs made of animal skins – otherwise the space was empty, except for the creature and the girl.

She cowered some distance away. Even from where he sat, the prince could still make out those incredible eyes – they stared at him, unflinching and unafraid.

"Who is she?" the prince asked again.

"Who is she!?" the creature screamed back at him. "Who is she?! Who are you, more like?! Who are you, comin' here with all yer questions, 'n all yer demands! Who is she? Who are YOU?!!!!"

The prince bristled, and in his defence snapped back, coldly:

"I did not ask to be brought here."

"Nah...your kind, you ain't got no need to ask fer nuthin'... shoulda', shoulda' just left ya' out there..." Huffily, the creature turned away.

The prince thought it pointless to contradict - if the creature wished to pretend that it had in some way been responsible for the saving of the prince, then so be it. The prince knew better, and had little time for useless appeasement. He did however, wish to know where he was, what had made that sound, and above all: who was the girl. She still sat, huddled, and unmoving, but she was looking intently elsewhere, apparently at something which the prince could not see.

He was about to ask again, the identity of the girl – when suddenly, she disappeared!

Involuntarily he exclaimed: "Wha-." Despite still being groggy, he jumped up and staggered over towards where the girl had been sitting. But all of a sudden she re-appeared, then disappeared, then re-appeared again!

The creature gibbered, and sniggered. "Relax......it does that..."

"It?"

"Yeh...IT!" The creature fluttered up, and began kicking what appeared to be fresh air – but clearly its hooves were hitting something. It settled back down again.

"What is ...it?" asked the prince.

'......l.l.l.ttttt.' *the metallic voice repeated.* 'iiiiiii....t.t.t'

"It? Oh...the Mirror Machine? It, is a Mirror Machine."

"A Mirror Machine?"

"Yeh ... it don't work though."

"It doesn't work?"

"Yeh...it's broken."

"A broken...Mirror Machine?" The prince looked sceptically at the creature, who in turn sneered. "Gee...you gonna repeat everythin' I say? Bad enough one'a ya...It's a Mirror Machine, right? An' it's broken. Enough!"

"Why-?"

The magpie like creature leered at the prince. "Idiot." It spat out the word. "Idiot!! Idiot!!!" It squawked and drooled, and again, the prince couldn't help but recoil. His hand went instinctively to his sword.

"Idiot, idiot, idiot!!!!!" the creature howled, and furiously pecked

and grasped at his own hairy hide. But as suddenly as it had started, it stopped. It smiled benignly at the prince.

"Anything else ya' wanna' know?"

The prince was almost afraid to ask. He took a moment. "It ...stutters...?" he said, his hand still grasping his sword.

"Yeh...wouldn't you? It's bloody cold...for a mirror."

Nonsense, thought the prince. A mirror that was cold? Ridiculous! Who ever heard of such a thing? There must be some other reason that this curious machine was here, here, there - or wherever it was.

"It's her protector, apparently," *the creature clarified, and not without some measure of sarcasm.* "Not that she needs one - YOU'VE GOT ME!!!" *The girl recoiled from the creature as it swooped down on her – but it banged suddenly into a reflection of itself and fell to the floor! Grumbling it crawled away. The girl had disappeared again.*

The prince had no time to react, however, as the metallic voice announced: 'S u p p e r.s.s.s.''''''.s re.a.d.y.'

The girl re-appeared, and immediately jumped up. It was the first chance the prince had really had to look at her; she was thin more than splendour, lithe certainly, but there was not a pick on her. She indicated insistently to the creature, and the prince, to come closer. The creature muttered obscene objections, but lumbered down towards the centre of the saucer nonetheless.

"Yah betta' come...," *it recommended.*

The prince struggled to stand up. He still had no idea where the strange metallic voice came from. It repeated its deliberate message: S u p p e r s.''''.s.s r.r..e.e.a.a.d.d.y.y.'

Following the creature down to the bottom of the saucer, there appeared in front of him another creature, then another, then another, and then an infinite number stretching apparently into infinity. It took a minute for the prince to realise what he was seeing: reflections, reflections, no doubt, from this 'Mirror Machine'. They shifted around and disappeared. Then, from nowhere a fire appeared, a pot boiling upon it. It was accompanied by a foul smell.

"You get used to it," *the creature said.*

The prince wasn't sure to what the creature referred: the strange visual tricks that the Mirror Machine created or the smell: he doubted he would ever get used to the latter!

After their meagre and frankly disgusting meal, both the creature and the girl curled up next to each other on the rugs, and fell, almost instantly asleep. The prince sat for a while, waiting expectantly for the night to come - but it didn't. The pale light faded, but only a little.

He had hoped to learn more from the creature, but he would clearly have to wait – the creature snored brutally, and the prince was not inclined to try to wake it. How the girl could sleep next to such a horrendous beast the prince could not understand. He was still none the wiser as to who she was, and was even more confused, as to her relationship with this 'creature', and this 'Mirror Machine', of which there was absolutely no sign - he looked around: no, nothing.

Perhaps in the morning he might learn some more. Wearily he lay down, pulled his cape over himself and fell asleep.'

The king paused again, but for a moment, allowing the artist to ask: "What was this 'creature'?"

"A mistake, I think," hinted the king.

"A mistake?"

"Indeed...don't you think?"

"I don't know..." The artist was confused. "A mistake...what kind of mistake?"

"Well, I'd say, there is only ever one kind of mistake."

The artist was still confused, and though she might not wish to admit it, a little irritated by the king's cryptic manner. Only one kind of mistake? What did that mean? Before she could ask though, the king continued: "I knew a man once, who had never made a mistake. He was very irritating – he was very stupid too."

"He was?"

"He was, yes – because he made mistakes all the time, and he never knew it. How stupid is that."

"Yes..." It dawned on the artist what the king meant, as she said it, instinctively: "One learns from ones mistakes..."

"Indeed...otherwise, it is not a mistake..."

Any irritation the artist had felt evaporated, under the king's kindly gaze - and in simple acknowledgement of the king's subtle wisdom. It encouraged her, and provoked her to ask: "Have you ever-"

"Made a mistake?" the king interrupted. "I am a king – I never make mistakes. I'm not allowed......" Again the king seemed to be overcome, suddenly, by a profound sadness. He added: "Actually, I did make a mistake, once..." before turning to the artist: "And you, have you made any....?"

"Oh yes......many," she admitted.

"But of course you have... of course you've made many, haven't you? In fact, all you do is make mistakes."

The artist was taken aback at the harshness of the king's words. She flushed red, and turned away.

"It's alright," the king said, his voice appealing and conciliatory. "You're meant to - you're an artist." He smiled at her. She smiled back warily.

"You make it sound like a curse," she said.

"Well, it's curious you should say that...," and on that cryptic note, the king continued.

'What is this thing, this Mirror Machine?' the prince said to himself. 'It is everywhere and nowhere…'

Scene ii: The Curse of Corners

'The prince was awakened by a tugging of his belt. He jumped up, pulling out his sword. The creature drew back sheepishly, its taloned fingers held out in guilty submission.

"Nice," it said. The sword glinted, despite the absence of any bright light. "Very nice," the creature repeated, unable to take its eyes off the sword.

The prince turned the sword slowly, before sheathing it again.

"You like?" he said.

"Oh yeh, yeh..."

"I have other things you might like," said the prince, taking some silver coins from his pocket. He waved them slowly, hypnotically, in front of the creature. It reached out one of its talons towards them – but the prince pulled his hand away. The creature scowled, but the prince just shook his head. He nodded towards the girl, wrapped up in the rugs.

"Who is she?" the prince asked.

The creature said nothing as its eyes followed the coin without blinking.

"Who is she?" the prince asked again. Mumbling, the creature answered, its eyes still focussed on the coins dangling in front of it.

"Some say, she is a princess, of the treeless forest, orphaned here......her mother entrusted me with her safety...for she was a great queen, despite her failings. Some say she is an alien, abandoned here by her race for some heinous crime she committed, and some say she is the daughter of a cruel and vicious ogre...some even say she is my daughter!" The creature suddenly became agitated, and its voice rose to a grating squawk: "Some say that, yes, and some say...whatever they want to say! Ah, say what you like!" it snapped. Once again it flew, literally, into a rage, flapping its wings as if they were broken. It screamed. "Some say yes, some say no, some say know......I don't know!!!" Its words became meaningless, and soon turned to incomprehensible gibbering. The prince, feeling that it would be best to calm the creature down, handed it one of his silver coins once it stopped fluttering madly about – but it just continued to gibber, as it turned the coin feverishly between its taloned toes.

The prince tried again. "You don't know?" he said, softly, hoping to prompt a more lucid answer. The creature looked at the prince, apologetically: "No...well, yes, well, no, not really," it said, and shrugged, and started gibbering again, and then began to drool. The prince gave up – all this creature does is talk rubbish, he thought.

Just then, the girl woke, sat up and stretched. Overcome by her beauty, the prince couldn't help but stare – she was simply adorable, and such a stark contrast to the creature, which continued to slaver over its silver coin. The prince threw it some more, and then crawled over to the girl. He was about to speak, when suddenly his reflection surrounded him! The girl had disappeared.

'What is this thing, this Mirror Machine?' the prince said to himself. 'It is everywhere and nowhere...'

Without warning, his reflections came closer and closer, until they were pressed in all about him on every side! A mirror surface, colder than anything the prince had ever felt, touched his skin. Instinctively he pulled back – behind him though a similar surface pressed against him, just as cold. He could feel himself begin to freeze.

The creature's voice echoed from somewhere, near, far – it was hard to tell.

"You just take it easy fella' – it'll let ya go...I think. Just take it easy."

The prince tried to do as the creature suggested – he tried to stay calm, but the Mirror Machine closed in tighter and tighter! Everywhere it touched him, he froze instantly! His breath too, froze on the mirrored surface, and he found it harder and harder to breathe as the mirrors continued to press slowly in on him. He became colder and colder, and began to lose feeling in his limbs, and then in his whole body! His image, all around him, became a hazy blur as his consciousness began to slip away – and then, just as he was about to expire, the mirrors disappeared!

He collapsed, gasping for air. The creature was sitting where the prince had left him, the girl too. Neither seemed troubled by what had just happened. The Mirror Machine had vanished.

"You best not talk to her," the creature advised, nonchalantly as it groomed its feathers with its long talons. It was hardly something that the prince could not have gleaned for himself. He nodded, still not able to talk.

"Told ya...it's her protector."

"Protector from what..?" the prince eventually managed to ask, through chattering teeth.

"Well, from you by the looks of things!" The creature chortled, and began talking to itself, though not in any language the prince could understand.

The prince sat up, and wrapped his arms about himself – he was freezing. But then he felt the girl's hands on him, as she wrapped some of the rugs around his shoulders. She began to rub him, to warm him up. He could only stare, dumbfounded as she did so, her concerned face so close to his – her beautiful face, so, so close...

He was about to thank her... "Best not," the creature cautioned. It mouthed the words, and for a second the prince thought he saw the slightest glimmer of a smile pass fleetingly across the girl's pale lips. She turned, though, abruptly, and scurried away again. The creature smiled crookedly at the prince. "Don't know what you see in her," it said, sniggering. The prince blushed.

Just then, the metallic voice announced: 'B.b.b.aaa.ttth...ti...mmm.e.'

The prince looked up, puzzled: "Bath-time?"

"Yeh, y'know...bath time..." The creature made motions as if it was washing itself - which was not a pretty sight! Then it clambered up to the canopy, the girl followed, it pushed the canopy open, obligingly, and the girl crawled out. Once she'd gone, the creature looked down at the prince, and indicated for him to come up. It was a tougher climb than it looked. He was breathless by the time he reached the creature; it winked salaciously at him. "Don't go too far," it warned, and with another nod, let the prince crawl out under the canopy.

Immediately the prince found himself back on the frozen salt surface. A brutal wind blew about him, and salt pelted harshly into his eyes, momentarily blinding him. He covered his face with his hands, trying to let his sight clear.

The creature's voice sounded, again, distant in his ear, sniggering: "Don't go too far." Its deformed eye stared up at him from the under the lip of the canopy." Don't go too far..."

Don't go too far? Dropping his hands, the prince looked around: where would one go? All around was simply emptiness!

He covered his face again, to protect his eyes from the blinding salt. Squinting through his fingers, he could just make out the girl, standing on the far side of the canopy (or, rather, a roof, a roof to the saucer like space below, as the prince now realised, that that's what it was.) The girl was doing something, he couldn't make out what. She appeared to be – undressing? As soon as he realised, he looked away, embarrassed. She had little enough in the way of clothes as it was, hardly more than rags - she must be freezing, he thought.

He was about to head over to her, his princely chivalry overcoming any discomfiture, but the creature stopped him. "Come on," it whispered insistently from under the lip of the canopy, "mirror boy'll be getting nervous".

"You mean, it's not here?" The prince looked keenly about, but discreetly, trying to avoid looking in the girl's direction. He couldn't see anything.

"Naw, don't think so...nevah seen it outside, not much anyway - not when a storm's comin',..."

The wind was indeed blowing harder. It was becoming almost impossible to see anything.

"The girl-?"

"She'll be fine," the creature said adamantly. "Come on!"

Reluctantly, with a brief backward glance, the prince slipped back in under the canopy. A short time later, the girl too, reappeared, and joined them. The prince tried not to look directly at her; his cheeks still burned – but the girl hardly seemed to notice him. She sat, distracted, and then began to whimper. Tears ran slowly down her cheeks. The prince made a move to console her, but again the creature mouthed the warning: 'Better not'. So they sat, in silence: the girl gently weeping, the prince, frustrated, that he could not help, and the creature, muttering, and ignoring them both.

Later, how much later the prince could not tell, the metallic voice announced that supper was again, ready. They were treated to another disgusting meal, after which the prince tried to sleep. But sleep eluded him - the permanent pale white gloom was deceptive, it was far too bright. He sat up, and watched the hideous creature preen itself; the girl, who had stopped weeping, just sat, either doing nothing at all, or furiously moving her hands, as if cleaning something.

Finally, the girl and the creature settled down to sleep, as did the prince - there seemed to be nothing else to do. He thought it fruit-

less, but this time he did fall almost immediately into a deep and dreamless sleep.

And so the days, if they could be described as such, passed. Of the three wayfarers, marooned effectively in the vast white saucer, their routine revolved around eating, sleeping, and bath-time, and though rarely in the same order, tedious nonetheless. On the whole, the prince rested and tried to recover his strength. He had misjudged how weak he was – the place he found himself in was, without question, unusual, and hardly hospitable; had he the strength, likely he would have left without compunction. But he did not want to leave: the girl had captivated him.

He struggled to take his eyes off her. She was so beautiful, despite her rags, her dishevelled hair, her rough hands and broken fingernails, and despite her all too apparent misery. She never smiled - in fact she rarely countenanced any expression at all, other than on occasion to adopt an attitude of such infinite and incomprehensible sadness, accompanied by her awful weeping. Such a face, consumed as it was with such distracted longing, could not fail to stir the prince's heart: a face, so still, so smooth, so perfectly formed, and yet, so lowly hung as if weighed down by an intangible load of the most desperate woe.

He simply adored her, whilst she sat, oblivious and crying.

He needed to know more, who she was, what had happened to her. His only resource however, was the ridiculous creature – but it was of such an unpredictable nature, unpredictable and untrustworthy: it was impossible to know what, if anything that the creature said was true.

Alternatively, he had the option of trying to engage in dialogue with the Mirror Machine - but it could hardly even be seen! Only by moving around very slowly could the prince make out where it was. Ever so subtle changes in the surface of the saucer were all that indicated the machines location: it appeared to be a box, a big, big box, as best as he could discern, sitting precariously and rather ungainly on the curved surface of the saucer. If it was, indeed, made of mirrors, they were certainly curious mirrors – they did not always reflect! Was this what the creature meant, by 'not working'? The prince had no idea. How do mirrors 'not work'? Certainly though, it was true that his reflection, or that of the girl or the creature, they were never present continuously on the machine's ever changing surface.

Only the girl seemed to have an accurate inkling of where the machine actually was. It became clear, that the motion she made with her hands was exactly what it seemed: she was cleaning: she was cleaning the machine, forever polishing it, or so it appeared. It was bizarre: she would sit, for hours, moving her hand around, a dirty rag in her grip. She would carefully examine what she had done, and then begin again, furiously polishing – polishing nothing!

The prince longed to talk to the girl, if only to interrupt the sight of her so disturbingly employed, polishing the empty air – but he couldn't risk trying that again.

Unfortunately, the creature appeared to be his only option.

Occasionally, in comparison to its usual erratic behaviour, the creature could appear almost rational – at such times, the prince could be slightly more convinced of the creatures credibility. It was on one such occasion, as they sat, picking at the foul stew prepared for them, the creature told the prince of the curse.

The prince had not expected to hear tell of it – their conversation had begun much more casually. They were sitting near the fire, which, curiously, had no warmth whatsoever, when the creature, without any prompting, offered the admission: "You think I like being here? I come from a place much better than this..."

For a second the prince felt a little bit sorry for the creature. "Why-?"

"Why? Why? Why did I leave...? That what you wanna know? Wish 'ah knew..." The creature hung its misshapen head, then lifted it abruptly: "For her of course!" it shouted. "Fat lot of good it did me..."

Before the prince could ask, the creature explained: "See ...where I come from, ain't two things the same, see? We ain't got, what you might say, is a system – for anything. Ain't that anyone minds – ain't no-one gonna complain! Ain't no-one to complain to! You takes what you want...and I ain't done badly, as you can see." Vaguely, the creature waved a dripping bone around, as if it were a trophy.

"So, how did you end up here?" the prince asked.

"Well ...let's just say...ah kinda' fell in with a bad crowd. Wasn't ma fault...y'know, they just kinda , well they kinda had a plan ...for somethin' better, y'know?"

"Better?"

"Yeh – like, they'd heard of this princess, from the treeless forest, that had been orphaned-"

The prince interrupted: "You mean to tell me that this is true?"

"Yeh – well, they had it all written down...the curse...naw, wait, we kinda' worked that out later....nah, see we wanted the no colour y'see? That's it, that's it... They'd heard about it....we kinda' figured it out, said she lived in a land of no colour, well, all we knew was colour, ah tell ya'. Colour ....so much colour. Colours you never even hearda! Colours, colours, so many....Ah don't think they were that bothered about this princess stuff...just a bit of relief ...thought we could make a buck or two, bring something back maybe, somethin' special...? Treasure, y'know? Treasure...somethin' dull! Dull'd be special, no? You betcha!"

The prince began to lose faith in what the creature was saying - it wittered on and on, before pausing, eventually to rake some grains of the saucer's surface into one of its deformed hands. It sighed. "Special?" it mused. Then it spat on its hand! "Special? Yuck –!" Angrily, it threw the grains of impacted salt away. "You betta' watch what you wish fer..." it muttered. "Never thought we'd find something like her though...," it added, without looking up.

Encouraged by the mention of the girl, the prince asked: "But...how did she come to be here...?"

"Ah, well...I'm glad you asked me that...see, that's where me and smiler mirror boy come in, see – things it could tell ya...anyway, when we found her-"

"Found her? Was she lost...?"

"Well...funny you should say that, as it turns out...seems not......seems we are..."

"Yes." The prince duly acknowledged the accuracy of the creature's observation. He cast his eyes around. "Yes – seems we're the ones that are lost - in the middle of nowhere."

"Yeh, yeh...middle of nowhere! Ah like that! We ain't lost no more ...hear that? We're in the middle of nowhere!" The creature began shouting, as if to others, of whom the prince had no idea. He looked around, half expecting other creatures to appear.

"You said 'we'?" he asked.

"Yeh – me mates...we found her, we found her..."

"So what happened to your 'mates'?"

The creature sniggered. "What you think you've been eatin' all this time...?"

Stunned, the prince dropped the bone he held in his hand.

Surely not, he thought, in horror!? The creature just stared at him. It sniggered again.

"*Good, ain't it?*" It crunched a bone into its beaked mouth - the prince turned away in revulsion. Deliberately, he changed the subject.

"*She never speaks...?*" he asked, indicating the girl.

He wasn't expecting to receive the reply that came, so immediately, and with such candour: "*Nah, and she never will, not until the curse is lifted.....*" The creature dropped the bone from its dripping jaws, and began to pick at its own hide, grooming itself in a way that was almost like self-flagellation. The prince could hardly watch. "*The curse?*" he said.

"*Yeh......the curse.*" The creature continued to groom itself, without offering any further explanation. The prince couldn't help himself: "*What curse?*" he demanded, in irritation. The creature could be so infuriating: one minute, it would talk, openly, and the next, it would become sullen and angry - or say nothing at all! The prince didn't care if he caused offence: "*What curse?!*" he demanded, yet again.

The creature sighed. "*The curse......the curse!*" It sniggered, and leered, and the prince's patience finally broke - he jumped up and grabbed the creature, drawing his sword. The creature tried to pull back – its two mean eyes squeezed shut, its big bloated one literally scurrying around in its own socket, in a feverish panic – but the prince held tight to the creature's neck.

"*What curse?*" the prince whispered sharply into the creature's frightened face.

"*I ain't gonna tell....if you ain't gonna listen...*" The creature grimaced. "*Ask the machine if ya don't believe me.*" The creature did its best to nod towards the girl, who was kneeling, and making her pantomime gesture of cleaning and polishing. "*Ask it anything, anything a't'all. Needs to be in rhyme though.*"

"*What do you mean?*"

"*Rhyme...y'know...*"

"*Are you serious?*"

"*Yeh...of course. 'Mirror, mirror', you know.*" The prince relaxed his grip, and the creature smiled smugly.

"*You're telling me, I can ask this Mirror Machine, anything, as long as it's in rhyme?*"

"*Sure.*"

The prince looked sceptically at the creature.

"What ya got to lose blondie?" the creature added, rubbing its throat. Stubbornly, it sneered: "I tell ya...I ain't gonna tell..."

The prince knew there was no point in arguing further. He re-sheathed his sword. Feeling slightly foolish, he walked over to the Mirror Machine. As he approached, the girl stopped her polishing, and looked up at him, a worried look on her face. The prince put his finger to his lips.

Turning to the Mirror Machine, his reflection for once perfectly reflected upon it, he cleared his throat, and said:

" *'Mirror mirror, tell me true,*
Who is this girl, who, who, who?' "

The creature sniggered. "Gullible ain't in the dictionary..." But before the prince could respond, from the Mirror Machine there came a slight click, and a voice of peculiar but gentle timbre, intoned sweetly:

Listen well, ye who seek tell of this wonderful yet terrible tale of tangible woe.
For you ask to know, but once you do know you'll ne'er not be able to not know:
Of what it is, the duty that lies full square in the heart of this world
For you'n me, and all that be – t is most truly reflected in the dreams of this poor girl.

Mark, in fact does this tale extend; hostility in truth make imposition of impossibility
That doubt must desert you, all loyalty too, for you to embrace it, nay readily.
But if ye are prepared to take on this call, to hear and see and burdened be,
Then to this cause, state yer name, yer faith and yer commitment, for posterity.

There was another clicking sound, a beep, and then nothing.

The prince looked back at the creature: "Go on then!" it said, impatiently. Irritated, but determined, the prince turned back to face the machine, and recited: "I am the prince of the Eternal City, my faith is in my God, and I vow to commit myself, my sword, my valour, and my honour, to this cause".

The creature sniggered. "Idiot...," it said.

There was a slight whirring, the clicking sound again, and then the sweet voice continued:

Our tale must begin then by setting the scene, but patient though kindly ye be,
For this girl she did hail from once an elsewhere, that none could not see. T''is
Not your eyes to burden the blame, fear not, but your mind that renders such blindness.
But sight be damned! – come, let us lead, post-haste, no time to waste, to her lightness!

She was known to have dwelt in the strangest of lands
Where all colour it seemed, appeared to be banned.
Mind it was a curious land, of which there was no kind, nor alike,
A land that was toned only, both in Black and in White.

Where lay this land, well no-one doth know, nor where even to look,
Most likely it lay where the river never bends, or in an unwritten book.
All that is known, this world is in words as they have been told,
From one child to the next, once the child, is grown old.

So doubt, no doubt does easy arise at such facts so handed down,
Like lineage challenged in dubious claim for an aged heirless encrusted crown.
For fables abound, sprouting full in such fertile ground of sceptical mystery,
And reasonable questions most reasoned raised, consequence of what is hear'say

For can one imagine, such a land might exist without hue?
'A lie' one may say, but t'was most certainly true:
Neither was there grey, for nought could e'er be merged,
Black and White, was that all, and nothing was diverged.

One was both up and down, and inside and was out,
One could both speak softly as one rallied for to shout,
One was both near and far, and far, far away, yet ne'er in-between,
And no conception of it either; for all were kings being fit to be queen.

For men were both as females, and the females both were males,
Both loved as much as they hated, and neither could tell tales,
In measure for measure they lived, ever equal in unspoken equality
Can you imagine, what it means, to both be, and not to be?

For neither was there commoner, without veins of royal blood,
Neither was there rich who lived in robes but rags and mud,
Neither was there wise man who could stupid often make,
Neither was there taken from whom one could never take.

In this place there was some gravity, and at times there was none.
And nought really mattered, no, nothing, for no consequence could come.
There was no 2 nor 3d nor other unproven 'd', for how could there possibly be?
For black and white, side by side? – can't be, you see? All's cancelled, free, is free of free.

So there could be only straight, and not straight: for front was behind,
And behind was in front or nothing, no, nothing was lost yet to find.
Without lost there was no cause for a loss, and so there could be no mourners.
And so it was, in this world of white and black: a world: without any corners.

And yet, born into this land, came a child of curiouser mind –
Though no-one could know it, for none could wonder at the time.
She looked so much the same as a sweet child of mine
Though if one cared to look, one could have spotted the sign.

If she had a dear mother, or a father, or anyone to care
Perhaps they could say, but ne'er two had e'er been a pair, (unfair!),
For father and dear mother, daughter and or son,
Were terms undecided – so nought detection could be done!

For she had all her fingers, her hands and her toes,
She had her two eyes, her ears, her nose, like any child born that normally grows,
But her eyes, prey, were grey, which was surely not quite right,
For everyone else's were – you guessed it – one black, and one white!

In a world without order, there were none worthy, nor known to be asked
For order means there's rulers, and rulers mean ruled, and taking things to task;
Patient then, by nature, the people they relied on their lacking of employ
To secure by osmosis, an understanding, of this girl, who clearly was no boy!

As a baby she cried or laughed very loud, she smiled or frowned
Or ransacked the feelings, of those found all around, in stereo sound!
But never it seemed, did she settle quite right in
To the land of black, and white, she lay somewhere, in betw'en.

At first it was strange and exciting, nae feart to discover
A child, being of one and not one or the other.
The people they stared, affected, they loved her though dumb,
For they had no idea of the horror yet to come.

151

It was much more explicit, however, as she got so much older,
How different that she was, as her acts became much bolder:
Everyone accepted the world simply said as they found it –
And saying as simply as it can be said: she simply didn't.

She changed this and that, left things rearranged
One could only be staggered that something was changed!
And this then sent ripples, not yet of fear, but in consternation
Invitation, inflicting the minds of the people with hints of imagination.

But time did proceed, unnoticed, and senses did slowly thin, in
Acceptance the girl who was with such strangeness, did acknowledgement dim.
When initially, she was anomaly, but one amazing black or a white,
Surely would be realised, unobserved, another, to make right this oversight.

But one day it did pass though many would wish
That such a day would memory, perchance to dismiss.
For the girl, she took a handful of rock, and rolled together
And lo and behold – a corner was made and so ended peace, and contentment forever.

Let us pause a while to ponder on the state of begat:
Where things that we see are nought more than that?
When one is but naked, there is no naked eye state duplicity,
When one is but used, there is no use needed for clarity.

But what would you say to the blind in the night?
That they were blessed, or better to have sight?
Doubtless you'd wonder and wait on advising,
Until you had reached the end of surmising?

And what would you say to the dead, left to rot,
That life now goes on, but how much worse it has got?
You could make best proposal as best you compare,
But how would you know, when you've never been there?

But how do you wonder when night and day are but one?
How do you wonder, when wondering's not done?
How do you know what is wrong and is right?
So was it: impossible in the land of Black and White.

But now – where nothing was secret, now all could be hid.
Such were the ramifications of what the little girl did.
Where once all the lines had been straight as a die –
Now they all realised, that anyone could lie.

Such was the shock that a crime could exist
Was only exceeded seeing innocence desist.
But worse, so much worse, than truth being descripted
Was that a crime had already been, so foully committed!

So a trial was announced, to consider the case
Counsel invented, that could stand face to face.
Argument was born, was raised and purpose was lost
As each of the counsels would count, to their cost.

The opposing counsel, they learnt first: attack!
"You have unjustly brought, white to colour our world pure of black."
The opposing counsel, they learnt how to fight, back:
"You have unjustly brought, black, to colour our world pure of white."

So the argument floundered, and right judgement was made
Caused divisions to be formed, and, of course, carnage:
'And' was now guilty, nought now knew what 'and' meant,
And 'Or' became reason, reasonably cause for dissent.

Now and no longer could one be one and the other,
One had to be now, not one, but one or another,
And if one promoted it so, well, one just could not:
One had to be punished, for one was now crime, and every one fought.

For eons and eons the troubles they raged
What landscape there was, was destroyed, nay, erased!
What structures that stood, such shapes that could be raised,
Were rendered surrendered and simply, were unrecognisably razed.

At last, nought was left of the land the grey eyed girl had been born into:
All shapes and each space was destroyed, all forms of life, all cells dissolved too,
All was distilled, and returned, to whence or beyond it was first made,
And nothing remained, save same shadows of black or whitened shades.

Shades, only shades, conflicted, they blurred and shrouded over all,
Shades, only shades, cast halos non-anointing in clammy and cold pall.
As unfathomable as non-entities, they were formless without mass,
Swirling into and between themselves, endless, indeterminately: gas.

At once there were dark evil shades, meagrely mean, diseased and self help-less,
And then, put sure into their place: the sweetest of shades, un-naturally generous.
They writhed and they twisted, together, enraged they fought all as one,
Their individual strands, pleated to go on, and wage war, on and on and on.

Held in the centre of this squall, was the girl – she had grown,
And the conflict, strife around her, was all that she had known.
She'd cowered in the fallout of the shady milieu; she grew,
Until at last from conflict, the shades, they finally withdrew.

Then down then upon her, fell their anger, and their love, now as one
Eyelessly, they glared, and adoringly demanded that something be done.
Swithering and dithering, the shades, now sounded without sight,
And spoke in a tongue both measured and full too of spite.

"There she is," they both muttered, in a voice that did sizzle
In goodness and evil entwined, nay in honey and poison drizzled.
"There she is, aye, she is......the wonderful and dangerous one,
There she is, aye, there...where all our sweet troubles begun."

The girl could but watch, in fear as the shades swirled around her,
Furious and soft, they caressed o'er her skin like tickled barbed wire.
She pleaded and pleaded, that her voice might be heard, but was ignored.
The shades set to whisper, repeating like echoes their word each for word:

"She is the one – who could not resist, from playing with Promethean fire.
She is the one – who could not resist, from taking it, higher and higher.
She is the one – who could not resist, to make not like this, but like this.
She is the one – who could not resist, to dare to forgive – and suggest..."

And so they went on, and on and on stating their complex tirade in exchange.
Twinned it droned on, but the more the voice whispered, the more it did change:
The kindness retreated, defeated, ruled by dominion reigning in ruined remains.
Inward it delved: muttering, stuttering, cackling and hissing, in swirling insane.

Then the swirling it stopped, and the fury it froze,
And in troubling silence, alone, a great echo arose.
White, without power, evil quenched full its first thirst:
Black, hissed like a viper as it laid its most terrible curse:

A curse upon ye,
For ye 'are destined
Tae dream around corners,
Til perfection ye find.

A curse upon ye,
For seek though you may,
Perfection round corners?
Exists? or disnae '?

A curse upon ye then,
For ye 'to create,
Around every corner
A dream, incarnate.

A curse upon ye, mind,
For ye shall not speak
Of yer dream around corners
The perfection ye 'seek

A curse upon ye,
Mute, ye 'will weep
Every corner around which
Yer dream, does not keep.

A curse upon ye,
Fer a haven to find
Around any corner.
Ye'll need to be blind!

A curse upon ye,
Or pluck out yer eyes
For around every corner,
Yer hope, never dies!

A curse upon ye then,
A curse ye 'deserve
For dreaming round corners
Wha...? The nerve!

A curse upon ye,
Yer fate t'is decidet!
A curse, a curse,
An' ne'er tae be lift-it!

With a flurry and rage, the black uttered its whining in sane!
But white interjected, as black cackled o'er its mean stanza-d refrain.
In a gasp it proclaimed, 'No, this is wrong' and spelled soft dissention,
A chance, albeit slim, a chance for redemption:

A curse is upon ye,
Yer dream may come true
If around any corner
Come, a reflection of you.

Black cursed, it repeat'it its crippling curse: to dream around corners, each corner turned;
White held out in hope its hope for to find, perfection, a prince – perhaps, a one charmed.
Black scorned: in silence you'll waste, away your days for your dream don't come true!
White wished: unless you do meet your perfect prince who dreams around corners too;

Black then expelled, and uttered: shoo!...

A curse upon ye,
For now ye are cast 'oot!
To a world without corners?
Aye, ye 'wish... ...but nae luck!

Outraged, black had grabbed the thin upper hand - in vengeance famished,
With a vicious swirl of its visible vile the girl was forever banished.
But white in keen haste, made a last gasp and took chance to protect her
And built this machine, this defender, this mirror reflector.

They both of them vanished in an instant, a flash,
Black howling profanely, but words of the white lingered last
Take care, only child and know, where you go,
That love will be with you – stay safe, and close, to the straight and narrow!'

And so it was ended, this tale of some woe.
What became of the girl no-one does know,
For the land does not lie that could console her so,
To carry the cruellest of curses wherever she go.

But if you should find her, wandering long,
Doubtless she'll be weeping her curse's sweet song.
Prey don't desert this girl and her wishes,
For her dream must come true, for her curse to be lifted.

And if you should seek, to seek and to win her fair hand,
Be sure that you can withstand – understand: for you too will be banned
From living together, such life as you now know it,
To life in sweet bondage, all profit forgotten and defencelessly forfeit.

The machine clicked, there was a slight whirring sound, and then nothing.
The crippled, magpie-like creature guzzled on a bone, and smiled crookedly at the prince.
"Pretty grim, ain't it?"
The prince could only nod, dumbly.
"Yeh...pretty grim. Oh well..."
The creature casually threw the bone into the bubbling pot, and began to chew on another. Its complete lack of empathy infuriated the prince; he was tempted to rip its head off! But he still needed to know more – trying to remain calm, he asked: "The curse said something about her being blind? But she's not blind...?"
'She has e.e.eyes...but she cannot see.e.e.' the Mirror Machine stated, mechanically. The creature threw the bone at it. It missed. "That was what I was going to say!" it snarled.
"I don't understand," said the prince.
'No.o.o.' said the Mirror Machine.
"NO!" shouted the creature. It threw another bone, which bounced off the Mirror Machine and fell to the ground; it threw another which seemed to disappear into the machine altogether.
"No," the creature repeated, turning to the prince. It screamed at him: "No, no, NO! She can see! Didn't you listen? You nevah listen! You...idiot! You, idiot, idiot, idiot!!!" A tirade of expletives followed; the creature then hung its head, and squatted, miserable and silent.

The Mirror Machine once again announced that supper was ready, and in truth, the prince was grateful for the distraction: he could have killed the creature right there and then - but there had been enough grief, more than enough, hearing the tale of the girl's apparent origin.

He looked at her as they ate, trying to evaluate the legitimacy of it – it eluded him; after supper he hardly slept, so troubled was he by the account, and by the curse, that echoed repeatedly in dreams, which were full of dark and troubling images, indistinct and yet of malevolent derivation.

When he awoke, he found it difficult to shake off a lingering sense of dread. It persisted, from that day to the next, that some evil waited, unseen, and harbouring malicious intent against the girl. It was impossible for the prince to ratify why, or how this evil might manifest itself, but he became increasingly convinced that the Mirror Machine was anything but a protector for the girl.

It never harmed her, that was clear – but it enslaved her, of that the prince was certain.

Inwardly, he was incensed.

Somehow, the machine demanded that she clean it, over and over and over again! Would it matter, that a blemish be evident on its frigid surface? Apparently – and here she was, this girl, this beautiful girl – to him, a blessed princess – condemned to perform this utterly pointless task, clothed in nothing but rags! She should be clothed in the most valued finery of the land!

His love for the girl caused his rage to blossom, unfettered, to see her demeaned and so devalued. Whatever hold the Mirror Machine had over her, it was a hold he would have to break - or at the very least, disable - in order to take her away from this barren place. (For of course, he knew it was his duty to do so – to take her away: she could not possibly wish nor voluntarily care to remain in such an ill-befitting environment.)

If only he could speak to her. Perhaps at 'bath-time', but that hardly seemed appropriate. Even if he did, would she be inclined to listen to him? Why should she? She clearly dreaded any attempt he had made so far, for fear of reprisal by the machine, he assumed, on behalf of his well-being.

So the prince decided to wait, and in the meantime, to try and win her trust, if not her heart, whilst at the same time, gain some further *knowledge, and to better understand the intentions of this elusive 'Mirror Machine'.'*

'*She will w.e.e.e.e.p to death*' blared the machine
stuttering. '*W.e.e.e.e.p to deat...t…th…th.th.!!!.!*'

Scene iii: The Escape Plain

'The very next day, before either the creature or the girl had wakened, the prince searched the saucer, crawling across it, until finally he found the machine. His head actually banged off it - though to his relief, without provoking the machine to then encase him in its frozen embrace! The memory still unnerved the prince, as he tentatively held out his hand – but the mirrored surface was cool rather than freezing; slowly and carefully the prince ran his fingers across its whole surface. It was a box, unquestionably. Occasionally it flickered, the prince's reflection leaping out at him, making him jump, but, gradually, he got used to it. Taking a rag in his hand he began to clean – not that the Mirror Machine needed cleaning, his intention though, was that the girl should see him doing this from the moment she woke up, and take due notice of his honourable action on her account.

So intent was he on the task, he was unaware that the girl had wakened: she sat up, stunned. She stared for some time in grateful awe at the prince, kneeling in front of the Mirror Machine. When eventually the prince did look round, he smiled – and to his utter joy, the girl, hesitantly, smiled back. She came over to him, rag in hand, and together they knelt, cleaning and polishing. They sat like that all day, stopping only for 'supper'; and again the following day, and the next. The creature occasionally fluttered past them, muttering sourly, but the prince threw coins at it, and it crawled away gibbering and drooling; left alone, the prince and the girl cleaned and cleaned, as the Mirror Machine sat impassively, tendered and accepting without malice their ministrations.

Despite the meagreness of the surroundings, the prince had never known such contentment. His knees hurt, his arms ached constantly, but he barely noticed: sitting next to the girl filled him with feelings of such incomprehensible happiness. Occasionally she looked at him, and once their hands touched, accidently: their eyes locked, and the prince was overcome yet again by the beauty and depth of intense longing expressed in hers. On another occasion, they were both reflected, together, looking at each other's reflection: for an instant the prince felt as if he had disappeared - and yet his reflection remained! Shocked, he gasped – fearfully he looked over, but the girl was there, right beside him.

She smiled then, too, and just for a second he thought he saw her eyes change, the longing: vanish. Then the moment was gone. 'Normality', such as it was, re-asserted itself, and they resumed in tandem their quiet and silent communion of cleaning. But the prince could not forget that terrifying yet wonderful moment. He thought on it often as they sat cleaning – distracted, he did not notice that not once, since they had sat down together, had the girl wept.

Of his ulterior objective, the prince learnt nothing further about the Mirror Machine. The creature appeared to be correct: if it was intended to 'reflect', in order to protect, then they were strange mirrors indeed: they rarely reflected anything, and when they did, the reflections lasted only for seconds, and were of a rather unusual quality, difficult to discern: some aspect of the prince's features seemed not quite accurate, some embellishment or aberration seemed apparent, though it was impossible to know exactly what. That, and the occasional clanking and whirring noises, fuelled the prince's belief that the machine held a malevolence within it. He felt more than ever that he had to get the girl away.

But the opportunity to talk to the girl did not present itself, and the prince reluctantly decided that he would have to do so at 'bath-time'. It would be the only chance he would have.

The very next time the machine made the announcement, the prince, as discreetly as he could, slipped out under the canopy. The girl appeared shortly afterwards; before she even realised he was there, he called to her. Her face, turned, startled and afraid, as the prince whispered intently: "Come with me – I know a safe place for you. Much safer than this." *He cast his hand around the desolate landscape that surrounded them.* "You can't live like this..." *Gently he took her hand.* "You can't live like this..." *he repeated, insistently. Fearfully, she pulled away, but the prince persisted.* "Come, come away..."

Suddenly, their reflections burst upon them, the Mirror Machine was all around, the prince was thrown backwards by his own reflection, and the girl was gone.

'She will w.e.e.e.e.e.p to death,' *blared the machine stuttering.* 'W.e.e.e.e.p to deat...t...th...th.th.!!!.!'

"That's ridiculous!" *the prince shouted back.*

'She w..i..ll weep to death.........if y.y.y.ooou take her from h.e.r.e.'

The Mirror Machine, with this threatening statement, abruptly fell silent and sat, immobile; the prince could sense that same malevolence that he had felt before emanating from the blank façade. His own reflection stared, flickering back at him, and for a second he thought that the machine was actually reading his mind.

Then, as suddenly, his reflection vanished, and the prince was left, alone, staring at the empty white landscape, that disappeared into nothingness.

Instantly, his mind was made up: 'I will take her from here, for anywhere is better than this' – and if the machine decided to stand in his way, he would destroy it. His hand clenched around the butt of his sword, for reassurance. 'The next chance I get,' he decided.

That night, such as it was, the prince took the creature to one side.

"I can get us out of here," he said.

The creature was unashamedly suspicious. "You can...? I doubt it..."

"I can...but I need your help."

"Hmmm, my help...?" *The creature began to giggle.* "My help..." *It giggled some more, and then stopped. It grinned maliciously.* "And if we get out of here, where will we go...?"

"To my city..."

"Yeh...ya don't say. And how do we get there...?"

The prince, without blinking, lied: "I know the way."

"Really?" *the creature said, scornfully but its eyes narrowed, intrigued.*

"I can see things you can't," *the prince said, turning a coin between his fingers. The creature stared at it.* "And there are many, many more of these where I come from." *He handed the coin to the creature, who grabbed it with his taloned foot. It squinted at the prince.*

"I only need you to ...distract...: it..." *He indicated vaguely towards the Mirror Machine.*

"Oh yeh...and so you make your escape, and you leave me stuck here?"

"No, no...all we need is something to leave a trail...and you follow us."

"And you'll leave me a trail, will you?"

"Yes – yes, of course..."

163

"Yeh ...right, sure you will. You think ah'm stupid!" The creature flapped its wings angrily, as it pushed its beak hard up into the prince's face. Its breath stank. "You think ah'm stupid?" it repeated, quietly. Its three eyes glowed, angry and mean.

The prince didn't flinch. "No..." he said, softly. "No...if we had a rope..."

"So...where do we get a rope from? Where do we get a rope from, where do we get a rope from....ha! ha! Ha! You're an idiot!" The creature flew around, its reflection repeating, here and there and everywhere. It howled, and sang: "Oh where will we get a rope from, my dear, where, oh where, oh where!"

Erratically, it flapped and flapped its wings, as it flew around madly, and then it disappeared! Suddenly a rope dropped at the prince's feet.

The creature's voice whispered, close, from behind: "This betta work, blondie...this betta work. You cross me, you don't cross me...you'll be a dead idiot."

The prince feigned acknowledgment, but ignored the creature's threat – he had his plan, and now all he needed to do was wait.

His opportunity came the very next day. Even from beneath the canopy, the storm could be heard, whistling overhead. It had happened before, but never so violently. 'Perfect' thought the prince. He'd primed the creature – it was a simple plan: he would grab the girl, and they would simply hide from the machine in the storm. To get her out of the saucer, the creature would distract the machine, and then follow them. They'd talked it through during the night, and the creature had tied the rope itself, around its own leg and that of the prince: the knot bit into the prince's skin, so tightly was it tied. The prince had acquiesced - one thing at a time, he thought.

He waited – and then, when the storm seemed to be at its height, lowly he instructed: "Now!"

He grabbed the girl, but the creature just sat, staring at him.

"Now!" the prince repeated.

The creature did nothing. It was too late – the Mirror Machine flicked over the creature, it disappeared, as did the girl, and the prince's reflection was everywhere.

The prince swore. He pulled his sword and began to swing at his own image. It danced crazily in front of him and then – SMASH!

164

Glass shattered all over him. He swung again, and again! SMASH!! More glass. The girl reappeared.

"Run!!!" the prince shouted, "RUN!"

He swung madly at the machine – it shattered, and shattered again. More and more glass showered over him.

"RUN!!!" the prince shouted at the girl. She just stood, like the creature, paralysed, and stared, in shock. Glass showered over her, and soon she and the prince were covered in tiny cuts. The machine whirred and clanked.

'Where...where is the creature?' the prince raged – he pulled on the rope, whilst swinging his sword with his other hand. 'Where?' Glass fell all around, but still his image pressed closer and closer upon him. He felt the first tinges of frost prickle his fingers.

Suddenly the creature appeared above them – it swooped down upon the Mirror Machine. "Go!" it shouted. "GO!!"

The prince grabbed the girl, and dragged her behind him. "Run!!!" he shouted.

They scrambled up the slope, and threw themselves under the canopy. The wind hit them, hard. All around was white, blustering white.

"Run!" the prince kept shouting. He had no idea if they were going in the right direction – he never had! He just pulled and pulled on the girl. Behind, they could hear the creature, shrieking, glass, shattering. The girl was crying.

They ran and ran, and ran until the sounds dwindled, and could hardly be heard. On they ran, blindly – and then, from the distance, suddenly they heard the sound of flapping! It got louder, and with it, screeching. The creature was chasing them.

"Run!" the prince shouted.

"No, no, no!!!" the creature shrieked. "Wait...!"

The girl pulled on the prince's cape, trying to make him stop, but he kept going. "Don't!" he shouted, urging her on. She grabbed the rope, sharply, and the prince staggered and fell clumsily to the ground.

He looked up, his cheek stinging and badly grazed. The girl was standing over him – she indicated behind them, and then back at the prince – her eyes pleaded into his, 'please, please', they seemed to say. Please...what? The prince gaped. "What?" he mouthed. She pointed behind again – for what? For the creature? To wait – for the creature!?

"No...," defied the prince. "No." He got up and, lifting his sword,

sliced through the rope. The girl stared at him – in horror? The prince had no time to wonder. He grabbed her and began pulling her away again.

But it was too late - the shape of the creature loomed suddenly up from out of the white shadowy mist. It swooped screeching down upon them, drooling and sweating, its talons flashing. The prince flayed wildly, but it was no use. The creature knocked the sword from his hand, and pushed him to the ground. It raised its talon, and was about to strike – when the girl threw herself over the prince.

The creature hesitated – it stared, but for a second, at the girl, her eyes shut tight as she clung to the prince; in that second the creature's rage evaporated, its jealousy too, turning from realisation to acceptance and forgiveness, all in an instant. The merest flicker of a sad smile crossed its twisted features; it was about to turn away – but the prince had not seen the creatures intention. He had rolled out from under the girl, and grabbing his sword, leapt up and with one swing, lopped the creatures head from its body! It flew off, and tumbled across the ground. The creature's body stood for a second before crumbling under its own weight.

The head came to rest a few feet away; balefully its eyes looked at the prince. "You're an idiot..." the creature said, and then its misshapen head tipped onto its side, and in a ridiculous parody of death, the creature's tongue lolled out and slapped pathetically onto the ground.

The girl opened her mouth, as if to scream – but no sound came out. The prince grabbed her, roughly, and dragged her away. She cried and cried, until finally she fell into a faint. The prince pulled her over his shoulder and staggered on, until, finally they reached the edge of the great plain and collapsed into the glass forest.'

The king stopped, and sighed, and as he lay, his eyes closed, his mouth, slightly parted as if in an aspect of death, the artist could not fail to notice how ill the king was: his pallor was extremely faded, his skin, nearly grey. Though he rested, the effort of telling the tale had clearly caused him to be affected by an extraordinary weariness. His breathing came in uneven and shallow breaths, his chest hardly moved.

"Do you wish to rest?" she asked.

The king did not seem to hear the question.

Instead, he said, quietly: "It's a curse, no? To be cursed?"

"I...wouldn't know."

At this response, the king shook his head and smiled, but so weakly that the artist asked him, again, if he would care to rest. The king could only nod in consent, and slipped almost immediately into a delicate slumber.

Darkness had fallen. The braziers that lit the room cast, sharply, shadows that flickered and jumped across the walls, and fell across the kings frozen face, making it appear strangely animated, albeit mute, receptive, and vulnerable to suggestion; as if flighty ghosts had been freed, and authorised to disclose temporary truths the day kept hidden.

The artist felt inclined to smother the braziers, to banish their freakish light, and would have done so had she not a greater fear that the darkness would give free reign to encourage ghosts of genuine malevolence to work their evil magic. It was illogical, she knew, but she was weary, and her mind was inordinately susceptible to such fancies.

Her work beckoned...she tried to paint, but the shadows distracted her. She sat down again, and she slept, her head resting upon the edge of the king's bed.

She was awakened, not by the light of the morning sun, but by something softly stroking her head. She sat up, embarrassed.

"I should work," she said, straightening her hair.

"Indeed."

The king pulled back his hand. An awkwardness hung between them, which the artist hastened to break.

"You never married?" she asked, continuing to straighten her hair and her dress as she rose and stood beside her easel.

"No."

"Was there none suitable?"

"None."

He answered abruptly and it was clear that the king did not wish to discuss the matter further.

"The prince...?"

"Yes...?"

"Did he marry...his ...princess?"

The king's voice lifted. "Well, let us see, shall we?"

ACT II

His steps, though aching with pain, were light, and by the time the city came into view, he felt as if he had been granted wings.

ACT II

Scene i: The Longing Return

'The prince, in search of some unsung glory, had set out from the city proud and certain that glory would automatically be deposed upon him.

He had envisioned all manner of riches – but none could compare to the treasure he now escorted homewards. She was treasure indeed, treasure, not of accountable worth, not diamonds nor rubies nor golden doubloons, but treasure in human form, and priceless in his eyes.

When she had awoken from her faint, it was as if their flight from the white wilderness had been completely forgotten. She held no anger or resentment towards the prince. Her manner was sublime, she looked at him with wonder in her eyes, and the prince imagined that it was love: she loved him, for his integrity, his honour, his charm notwithstanding: for all he had done, he had done for her: his selfless and explicit acts of kindness, his fearless acts of bravery. She loved him - and the prince, in turn, had no doubt of his love for her – he had loved her from the moment he had set eyes upon her, and nothing since had given him cause to question his love; indeed it had grown deeper, and deeper still, every time he looked at her. She was a treasure, in both mind and body, and he could not wait to display this treasure to his people, and especially to his father: his princess to his king.

Their journey however, was not short of incident, for they were far from the haven of the prince's kingdom, and the consequence of extreme endurance was inevitable: they had little to eat, little to make shelter with, and little really, in the way of suitable or appropriate clothing – the girl was covered only in rags that barely hid her honour, and the prince too, had lost most of his princely attire – his cape alone catered for them both, to protect them from the winds that blew, bitterly and without remorse, from the rains that fell, in torrents, almost drowning them, and from the suns that beat down mercilessly upon them.

Gratefully, and without compunction, they curled under the prince's cape at night and held onto each other for warmth and

protection, sleeping wherever they lay, exhausted from each days
walking.

  Their limbs ached, inevitably, from the hours and hours that
they walked, and their cuts still bled from the fight with the Mirror
Machine, but such minor wounds paled in comparison to those sustained
consequently: their feet in particular became torn and bloody, for they
hardly had the necessary protection of sturdy footwear: they were
virtually barefooted, and tramping across surfaces that racked and
gouged without respite at their skin. The prince did his best to remember
the way back, but it was difficult to recall; there were no clear routes, no
pathways to follow, and no-one to ask. He was unsure therefore whether
they passed through those same exact landscapes that he and his small
army had passed through before; regardless, they were equally as
desolate and forbidding, and as hostile to his and the girls well-being -
landscapes again formed entirely from singularly uncompromising
materials: of smooth and green slimy rocks; of twisted strands of tortured
steel; of thin sharp slivers of blackened stones; of soft and undulating
sodden fabrics, like porous carpets, that caused them to continually
stumble and fall. Their lungs too strained at times from such a lack of
oxygen, as they climbed high into mountains of ice, curiously and
ironically red like a blazing fire; and they froze or burned accordingly to
the vicious climates within which they were enveloped.

  Both the prince and the girl shouldered each other's distress
with equanimity - but unquestionably, the most distressing aspect of the
journey was the girl, forever weeping. It broke the prince's heart: for she
could hardly see, so blurred was her vision by the constant stream of
tears. The prince had thought that the landscapes he had traversed to
find the white plain would be devoid of implication of the curse (the truth
of which the prince still doubted: he honestly did not believe it, and held
true to the idea that what ailed the girl was nothing more than an
unusual fancy that had inflicted an infection in her mind. His physicians
would be able to cure her of these ridiculous and unfounded notions.
Regardless, if indeed true at all, his father's city would, without question,
be the tonic she required to dispel both curse and ailment alike.)

  But in the meantime, the girl's dismay was considerable: she
kept her head down, most of the time, her tears dripping to the ground
as if to steer her way, as a torch might (though the prince fancied that
they in fact stained the ground where they fell, leaving a trace of their

journey, a trail few would care to follow.) If she looked up, she would be so overcome with grief the prince would have to steady her, and increasingly she held onto him, weakening it seemed with every step. He wrapped his arm around her, and did his best to protect her from whatever was causing her such distress. The Mirror Machine's warning that she would die if taken from the plain echoed in his head, but the more the prince thought on it, the more determined he became. Not once did he think to return, and not once did he doubt what he had done. They would go on, they must go on. The curse, if cursed she be, would not defeat him. And anyway - how could she be cursed? It wasn't possible: what corners there were, were hardly corners at all: there were no buildings or structures of any kind; this curse was a fantasy – but he desperately needed to find means to help the girl, because his efforts, though well intentioned, were futile: the girl continued to weep - he needed somehow to shield her from her perceived source of complaint.

Slicing a sliver from his velvet cape, he tied it as a bandage across her eyes, and led her, forward then, step by step. She trembled, and clung to him, each step infused with a dread borne of uncertainty that any who are sightless could attend. But the prince held her tightly, and spoke to her constantly as he guided her forward. If the way became too difficult, he would kneel before her, in some bizarre parody of betrothal, and he would lift her worn and bloody foot with his hand and place it steadily on the ground, and then he would repeat it again with her other foot; patiently and with infinite care they would inch their way forward: she, blindfolded, on occasion weeping still, and he, kneeling ahead of her, holding her befittingly and allowing her hand to rest on his shoulder, or his head, clumsily and without ceremony.

Only at night, when the light had finally faded, and the darkness descended fully upon them, would the prince dare to remove the blindfold; oftentimes the girl would be asleep as he did so. He longed to look into those wondrous eyes, but he daren't invite the grief that waking her would doubtless entail. On those nights when the moon was full, he would hesitate to remove the blindfold at all; but once removed, the sallow light would reveal her lids, sunken and even more darkly rimmed, and the prince would be overcome yet again by her pale beauty, irritated when cloud stole the light away, and spurred guiltily to replace the blindfold the instant the cloud passed should she stir.

Step by painful step they made their way ever closer to the prince's kingdom. The prince learnt to accept the girl's enforced silence, the permanent muteness of her demeanour. However, he felt the need to fill the void, and so he talked to her incessantly; in the first instance he did so to offer reassurance, and to comfort her.

But as the days passed into weeks, he talked also of his life, as a prince, and his obligation as heir, and of his father, and of his father's city: he conjured it into his mind, and walked her through its wonderful streets in his imagination. He knew every part of the city, so intimately had his father described to him his intentions as it had been constructed; he had watched it rise from the ground as he too had grown; it had been his childhood playground, his athletic field in his youth. Though elusive, he could recall exactly how it smelled, the way hot air carries a scent; how it felt, whether rough or smooth; he could describe his fondest impressions: of the perpetual colonnades and cornices and capitals, carefully crafted but carousing none the less in comparison to the sombre rustication and perfect mass of the city's vast stone walls.

It hummed in the prince's mind, the city, and he searched vainly to find the words to properly describe the wonder of it. The distraction was invaluable, as he was reticent to talk to the girl of his love for her – he refrained to do so for some time, but his resistance eventually collapsed: with passion and with increasing ease, he talked of the happiness they would share, and of their future together. She would on occasion squeeze his hand; emboldened he would describe to her his dreams, and too, his fears. He revealed his deepest thoughts, his harshest memories, his guiltiest and most awful secrets – until eventually he had told her everything he could possibly tell. He sought out words to do so, as accurately as he could; he struggled often to find the right words, but he persisted none the less. Shame abandoned him; he entrusted without reservation his innermost cares and concerns, and not once did he doubt that his words would fall on deaf ears, but rather that they were heard with perfect forgiveness and understanding. Her eyes, though blindfolded, still bored into the prince, as if freeing him from all the constraints of a life he had once led, unknown constraints revealed in an instant, and unchained at the very same moment.

Though their journey was long, and of almost unimaginable hardship, the prince embraced an undiscovered enlightenment in its progress. His steps, though aching with pain, were light, and by the time the city came into view, he felt as if he had been granted wings.

The girl, by comparison, sagged in his arms. Limp, and agonizingly thin, the prince lifted her up, easily and carried her forward.

From the distance, shouts and cries of wonder drifted from the walls of the city, from those who witnessed the terrible tableau of the prince's return: like a husband whose wife had died on the very day of marriage, over the threshold the prince regally carried the lifeless girl, through the gates of the city, her tattered rags blowing in the breeze like a helpless and haunted wedding veil; weeping, he fell helplessly into the collective arms of his beloved people.'

The artist couldn't help herself: she smiled. The tale the king told, and the manner in which he told it, though much of it full of hardship and pain, was laced enough of love and affection to charm her. It stimulated her natural capacity towards the goodness in life - though she rarely found much opportunity to embrace it: she was an artist, and forever conflicted, particularly whenever she went to work.

She was grateful therefore, for the time the king was spending with her. Listening to his account allowed her room to breathe, and to forget for a while her own concerns. Though somewhat confused at the king's frankness, she was nevertheless honoured that he was confiding so openly in her.

Food was brought to them, but the king ate little. Afterwards, as the king appeared tired and disinclined to talk, the artist left him and went to sit on the lip of the balcony at the terrace. Dark clouds had gathered in the distance, hanging over the mountains as if taunting them; a smattering of rain fell. She turned her face upwards: if she had to choose she would rather have the rain than the sun - she loved the sound of it, the patterns that it made, she loved that it touched you, as it did now, droplets freshening her as they landed in a mist on her forehead – she'd sooner drown than suffer drought, though she had to admit, the sight of the midday sun punching through the clouds and scattering its rays across the city below was utterly captivating.

The day wore on; the king slept, and eventually the artist felt obliged to work on the portrait – it remained a struggle however: whether to balance lines of varying weights, soft lines, harsh lines, and the colours, whether to adopt hues of serious connotation or to mix complimentarys – she could not decide. Her temptation had been to present a king sharply defined, keen, strong – but her initial attempts had revealed themselves almost immediately to be insufficient, as they were inaccurate.

She gave up, and turned to her various studies, pouring over them and looking for clues – but it was as if her eyes could not see what she had drawn. Images of the prince, and the girl, clouded her mind, as did the tone of the king's voice, his soft yet firm intonation. Distracted she returned to the terrace, and allowed herself to drift into a kind of dream…

The king roused, though the artist did not notice; he coughed.

"Would you object, if what you made, was destroyed?" he asked.

The artist turned – and some sketches that dangled loosely from her fingers, slipped from her hand and fluttered out and away over the terrace. In a panic, she tried to catch them – but they tumbled away on the breeze.

The king smiled.

"Would you?"

The artist was confused – she stared at her sketches as they floated away into the distance. "Would I what?" she said, preoccupied and annoyed.

"Would you object?"

"Yes," she said, finally turning away from the terrace. She said it sharply.

"But nothing lasts…"

The artist frowned at the king.

"Yes, yes, I know…" she said, "but you said destroyed? I wouldn't want my work destroyed…" Momentarily she glanced back at the terrace.

"Does it matter, the circumstances of ruination?"

"Well…yes? Surely…"

"Perhaps..."

Again, he smiled, and again, the artist had the impression that the king was toying with her. She was already upset at losing her sketches – she didn't need the king's cryptic interrogation. Deference forgotten, she snapped back: "What purpose does it serve, to destroy...?"

The king did not flinch.

"Yes indeed, what purpose..." he agreed, and still smiling, began again, his account.

Once again, the city resounded with the cacophony of destruction, and once again, a cloud of dust rose up, billowing high into the sky and blocking out the sun;

Scene ii: The Edicts 3

'Inevitably, for many, many days the prince and the girl were confined to rest, attended by physicians and nurses, who carefully dressed and bound their wounds, and stayed by their side throughout the night as both the prince and the girl were plagued by appalling fevers.

For the prince, his fever was manifested in terrible rages, and outbursts of unfathomable anger. He would scream profanities at unseen monsters, trying to fight them with clenched fists, balled so tight and flung with such abandon the nurses feared he would injure himself even further. He had to be restrained for his own safety, and prescribed medicines in considerable dose to calm him, and protect him from visions that seemed to be luring him towards madness.

The girl on the other hand, her fever presented in a manner that neither the physicians nor the nurses could comprehend: she did nothing, and lay as rigid as a board, her eyes staring and blank, and never blinking. It shocked the physician who first removed the dirty blindfold, to witness such an expression and though he had no knowledge of the exact hardships that the prince and the girl had encountered on their long journey, he was left with the impression that no matter where they had been, the blindfold, presumably applied to protect the girl, had caused some unforeseen consequence of a magnitude that could be construed as having been worse than anything the girl might have seen had it not been applied. The physician had no reason to credit it, and it seemed such an unlikely a thing to believe, but he was convinced that the girl had not closed her eyes behind the blindfold; he could only wonder at what it was that the girl had seen, or rather, imagined, to cause her to become so transfixed and left in such a paralysed and comatose condition.

Compresses, warm scented baths and painstaking massages were prescribed, and slowly, as each and every individual muscle was teased, reluctantly, back to life, the girl's body relaxed its tense and prone position. Her eyes finally flickered, and her eye lids finally blinked, spasmodically, together. She slept then, to the physician's relief, her eyes closed; the tears that slipped from them the instant before she fell into unconsciousness, assumed to be tears of relief.

The king fretted constantly over his son's condition, and the girl's too; initially, when word had arrived of the prince's return, he could hardly contain his joy – not one member of the prince's small army had ever returned to the city; the king had long since given up hope of ever seeing his son alive again – it was as if the dead had been brought back to life.

His joy however, turned to worried concern when he saw how ill his son was, how deathly pale he looked, and also how ill his companion appeared. He had no way of knowing who she was, nor why she was with him; for an instant he feared that they both carried some contractible disease, and certainly the girl in particular seemed to be suffering from some sort of ailment that defied any other conclusion.

But as time passed, and as the health of both gradually improved, he allowed himself to take absolute delight, again, in his son's unexpected deliverance; he ordered that the soft coverings, worn over every shoe and hoof in the kingdom, be removed; that the church bells be rung, albeit only on the hour; and that music could once again be heard; trumpets, strings and bows were duly brought out, and blown and plucked with celebratory enthusiasm. Only the drummers were cautioned to temper their performances, so that the prince, and the prince's princess, as the girl had soon become known, could be allowed to recover in respectful peace, and relative quiet.

Perhaps on account of his lingering youth, the prince recovered first. As soon as he could walk, he hastened to the chamber of his beloved; unaided he stood over her as she slept, and remained there, until the king, informed by his aides of his son's sudden improvement, joined him. He could not fail to notice the affection with which his son stood sentinel by the girl's bedside – he was reminded of a time when he too had stood by the bed of his then ailing wife, the queen. He had loved her, as much as his son clearly loved this strange wraith of a girl. She was not of a type that the king would have normally approved: he had no idea of her lineage, or of her status - his son was heir to his throne after all. Such things were of considerable import, but he was a good father, and in witnessing his son's entranced demeanour, he bent his dutiful inclination for disapproval to one of paternal acceptance. She would be his son's betrothed, of that the king had no doubt.

If the king retained some reservation of the girl's worth, he had to admit that he had none regarding his son. Rather, the prince, on account of his travels, appeared to have a gained a maturity that the king had long thought lacking in his heir. The attentive care that he showed over the succeeding days and weeks towards the girl, as she gradually, and on occasion, painfully, (for she wept, for apparently no reason that any physician could ascribe), regained her strength, was admirable. It confounded the king - if he had not been still somewhat blighted by the joy of having his son, once again by his side, he may have noticed that in fact the prince was not properly shouldering his princely duties, nor carrying himself properly as befitting his position. But the king did not: all he saw was his son, the prince, responsible without limitation for someone other than himself. If he issued commands somewhat abruptly to the nurses and physicians, so be it, and even if some of these demands seemed questionable, if not in fact ludicrous – why was it so necessary to keep the drapes and blinds so permanently closed throughout the day? Why did it matter what the girl did or did not see? Why did it matter if he was to be informed the instant she awoke? - it was of little concern, compared to the authority the prince displayed by his intensity of his directives.

"Forgive him," the king advised his aides, courtesans, his Royal Court - and to dispel the chagrin of the attendant physician and nurses: "The prince is in the throes of his first love," he said, "let us indulge him – and help him shoulder this burden!"

They laughed, in turn to appease the king, but the beginnings of resentment settled within them, and some who had lost sons of their own in the prince's foolish campaign, secretly harboured treasonous thoughts against the prince, who remained in their eyes, a fool - their opinion of him only embellished by his pathetically entranced behaviour; their animosity festered.

Unbeknownst to the prince, and to the king, of the bitterness seeded within the royal household, they were immune to its potential implications; they were content, therefore, and found themselves, for the first time, as father and son, completely comfortable in the company of the other. The king joined his son on many occasions as he watched over the girl, but of her the prince said little. He recounted to the king, the mutinous behaviour of his army, and of the hardships of the journey, to and from the white plain, but of the creature, the Mirror Machine, the 'curse', the prince said nothing; only that he had found the girl abandoned, in the forest of glass trees, apparently left to die - and had

181

elected to save her from her tragic fate. He said nothing of his love for her – and the king did not ask. He only smiled, and patted his son warmly on the hand.

"You are my heir, my son – you are my blood, and I am proud of you for what you did," he said.

The prince smiled in return, and would remember that moment as one of his happiest memories: sitting, in the warm stillness of the girl's grand bedchamber, she wrapped up in silken sheets, safe at last, tended gently by obedient and caring physicians and nurses, and he, basking in his father's unprompted approval.

When finally the girl awoke, the prince hastened to bring her out from her bedchamber. He had no wish for her to be subjected to unnecessary interrogation, nor had he any desire to explain, or make reference to her 'affliction', certainly not on account of some arbitrary and fictitious 'curse'. Rather, he wanted desperately to display her to his people, so that they too might rejoice in the presence of her incredible beauty. His father acquiesced immediately to his son's request: that an event of almost coronationary proportions be hosted to present the girl to the populace - for the king too had been entranced by the hesitant wonder of the girls perceptive gaze. That she said very little seemed, consequently, to be of no account – her incredible eyes said enough!

Pronouncements were made, and shortly thereafter, the great day arrived: trumpets blared fanfares loudly across the city, a cacophony of church bells rang, banners were unfurled, once again, and streamers and confetti fell from every building. The king, his Royal Court and whole household, all his courtesans, his aides, advisors, his governors, his lords, ladies, and his every subject were in attendance; the main square was packed, and the cheer that arose when the prince stepped onto the royal dais, erected especially for the event, was so loud that the tiles on the roofs of the square's glittering palaces rattled alarmingly, as did every little pane of glass held by slender mullion in the palace's numerous windows.

The prince waved, and then, having thanked the assembled throng for their adulation at his return and for the warmth of their affection, invited them to be witness to his engagement to, as he described her, simply the most beautiful princess in the world.

The girl, finally dressed in clothes fit for a princess, a gown of red as crimson as her hair, cowered behind the prince, but trusting to the reassuring grip of his hand, she stepped forward, and cheers turned to gasps as her beauty radiated out across the assembled crowd. The people parted like curtains as the prince, and his princess, stepped hand in hand from the dais.

With immeasurable pride, the prince then escorted the girl around his father's great grid of a city. He was certain that the splendour of it could not fail to impress the girl, and that any fears she may have had would dissolve confronted by the sight of such a wondrous place. The city, was, truly, perfect, in every way, of that the prince was certain, and as such he had no worry whatsoever that the perceived 'curse' would prevail. "You will weep no more," he had promised, again and again, on their perilous journey, and his vow was as sure and confident as was his stride.

That day, and daily for weeks afterwards, he escorted her, as proud of the city as he was of the love the people clearly felt for both him, and the beautiful girl that he held by his side. Everywhere, the streets were lined with the people of the kingdom; they cheered and cheered as they passed, and the girl, though she did not smile, did not weep. Each corner they turned, more cheering would erupt, and the prince waved, appreciatively, forever glancing at his beloved escort, and feeling his heart warm at the steady expression on her face: 'She does not weep', he told himself with satisfaction, 'she does not weep'.

If he were honest, however, he felt, deep down, that something was not quite right, a seed of doubt born perhaps from the fact that still the girl did not speak – but he ignored it, preferring to celebrate in tandem with his people, the great rejoicing of his return, the unfettered adulation for him, and his soon to be bride.

Their days were spent endlessly tracing routes through the great city, the boulevards, the streets, the squares, the lanes, the alleyways: every inch of the city had been carved with loving care, and the prince relished the opportunity to present this endless finery of construction to the girl. But as time passed her expression, which had remained stoically calm and composed for so long, began to slump - and then, one day, as they turned a corner, a corner like any other, from one street to another, the prince heard the girl sigh, and saw, with unmitigated distress, a tiny tear slip from her eye......

Another tear followed, that were soon followed by more – accompanied by a gentle weeping.

The prince was aghast. How could this be? He tried to explain to her that it was impossible, but it was no use – for a number of days he continued to lead the girl around the city in the desperate hope that the weeping would stop, that some corner they had not yet turned would resurrect her composure, and that she would recover – but it was not to be. With each corner they turned the weeping increased.

The people, at first they tried to offer condolence and sympathy, offering advice, and endless handkerchiefs; but slowly they turned away, and then hid. Doors, windows and shutters closed surreptitiously as the prince and the girl approached, opening only slightly as they passed, to peer out at the retreating backs of the distressed pair. Gossiping ensued: that this strange girl, who never spoke, though beautiful, was clearly afflicted with a terrible disease, a disease that affected her sense as it did her senses. It was not long before some concluded that she was a witch, come to cast her evil spell upon the city, for soon her weeping became the only sound that could be heard, and it caused the people of the city to cover their ears for fear that the sound would harm them, that it would infect them and cause them to become as distressed. Others, of a more rational mind, could not harness enough of their better nature to contradict such ridiculous notions, for the inexplicable truth of it confounded them: she wept at what she saw, and how could that be so, for everyone considered their city to be beautiful, and what right, or evil capacity did this girl have, to cast such a slight upon their kingdom? It was not uncommon, to hear others talk, sympathetically, not on the prince's part, but on the kings: they put themselves in his shoes, and lamented on his behalf, that his son had brought this burden down upon him, and of course, on his loyal people. In many ways they were correct: the king was also deeply distressed to see the girl weep so, but his heart ached to see how it affected his son, to see him almost drag the poor girl around his city day after day, to no avail whatsoever.

It was with such relief, to king and populace alike, that the prince eventually realised he had no choice but to return with the girl to the palace, where, though her weeping did not cease, it was at least intermittent and, if the term be appropriate, manageable.

He called for the best physicians, doctors and finally psychologists to come to his, and the girl's aid: but there was nothing they could do. They examined her, they analysed her, they asked endless questions of her, they stared into her eyes and made prognosis after prognosis, and tested all manner of cures upon her, but nothing they did served any purpose: she wept, and their every attempt to stem her tears was proven futile.

The girl, they all concluded, wept, for no reason that they could ascertain, and she must therefore be afflicted with some unseen and mystical ailment, of other worldly origin – or else she must be faking her condition.

At this, the prince, in a rage, threw the physicians out of the palace; but subsequently he was left distraught and bereft of hope. He'd clung desperately to his denial, but now he had nowhere else to turn: he confided in his father, late one night, as he sat by the girl's bed, she sleeping her familiar sleep, unmoving apart from the tears that continued to leak from under her eyelids and run perpetually down her cheeks. He recounted the tale he had been told, and the 'curse' that had apparently been placed so unjustly upon her. His father though was not one to indulge in such fantasies. He was a practical man, and his instinct was to respond to such notions as nonsense. However, he wished to be supportive on behalf of his son, who clearly had come to the end of his tether. There seemed no other option: if the corners were the cause of the girl's grief, then, for the sake of his son and in turn, his beloved, the offending corners would need to be removed.

It would not be true to say that the king embraced the decision without reservation. His son was delighted - but it was not his city, it was the king's, and he alone had striven to create it, and held the same view of it as did his people: it was indeed perfect. To change it would come at considerable cost to the king, to both his person and his pocket: nevertheless, an edict was passed, and soon the day to day business of the city ceased as the alterations were initiated.

All the builders, tradesmen, contractors and craftsmen were gathered, and the works duly began. Every building was painstakingly altered: where they all once had corners of 90 degrees, now each and every one was modified to be of 45 degrees. And where the city had once been rich in the variety of spaces that existed between the buildings, now it was made uniform throughout: each street was made the same, and each city block was made the same: the prince did not dare risk that any one should be less perfect than any other; he hoped upon hope that the perfection of the one deemed most perfect would prove itself to be the solution, the obvious solution – obviously - to the problem.

Day and night the sounds of construction echoed throughout the city. The king, if distraught at the changes, outwardly appeared to accept them, and with regal composure oversaw the progress of the works. Privately though, he longed for his city of old, and could not help but harbour some resentment towards the girl, who had been the cause of such upheaval but lay sheltered so comfortably in his own palace, saying nothing and continually weeping. Many of the king's people had had to vacate their homes, and some had even elected to leave the city altogether! This fact, almost more than any other, upset the king. And to what purpose? - the king, who was not blinded by a blinkered optimism like his son, shouldered an unspoken yet uneasy conviction that the changes being effected would not produce the result that his son so hoped for.

Finally the works were completed, the offending corners, removed. The prince, once again, prepared to lead the girl proudly through the streets (though this time devoid of cheering onlookers).

His pride turned to utter despair however, as the girl, immediately upon removal of her blindfold, wept.

Almost pathetically, the prince re-tied the blindfold, and led her to another street, and then another – and each time he withdrew the blindfold, the girl wept, and wept it seemed even harsher than before. He could barely look at her, so painfully did it appear to hurt her, and yet he rushed her from one street to the next – but every street was the same, as was the girl's tragic reaction.

Eventually, at his father's sad behest, the prince allowed himself and the girl to be led back to the palace, where he hid for many days in his bedchamber, refusing the company of anyone, his father included.

The prince could hardly sleep, so troubled was he that he could not resolve this terrible, terrible problem. And then it dawned on him: if the corners at 45 degrees did not work, then there should be no corners at all!

He rushed to his father's chamber, and burst in upon him as he rested, exhausted from long sessions trying to placate his Royal Court and their many complaints as a consequence of the edict. The people were not happy, his Royal Court had told him, and neither were they. They refrained from making explicit complaint against the king's son; but their comments were less discreet when it came to the girl. The king had dismissed them, and retired, without resolution. His eyes, like his head, ached, and he was not in the best mood to receive this excitable visitation from the prince.

But the prince took no heed.

"We must remove ALL the corners!" he exclaimed, breathlessly.

"All the corners?" the king replied, mystified. He rubbed his temples. "But how-"

"Yes – all the corners!" and he went on, enthusiastically, to suggest that as the affliction which beset the girl was caused by what she saw, she should see nothing at all: she should see no corners!

"We need to lift every building up!" he said. "Lift them up – so that she sees nothing at all?!"

"Sees nothing...?"

"Yes! If we lift them all up, then she will not see any corners – you see?"

Hesitantly the king replied, not wishing to point out the obvious. "I...see," he said "But-..."

It was no use – the prince seemed touched by a madness that was almost of unholy origin, and the king feared for his sanity, should he fail to support his son's proposition. But he retired to his bed that night, deeply troubled, knowing the probable consequence this second edict might bring – he made no concession in his mind to the potential complaints of his Royal Court, nor his people. He was king, and his son's concerns outweighed any other: the edict would be issued. But he remained deeply troubled none the less.

It turned out he had good reason to be - the edict was met with considerable criticism and barely disguised disdain; some expressed outright anger. The king had to invoke his regal authority to enforce it. He overruled every objection, outlawed every act of dissention. Guards were instructed to remove everyone who lived in the ground floors, by force if necessary, and those same builders, tradesmen, contractors and craftsmen were once again gathered together, and instructed as to the sacrifice that must now be made: that all the ground floors of every building were to be removed.

Once again, all the normal day to day business of the city ceased as the work began. All those who had lived or worked on the ground floor were forced to work on the city re-building, though many chose instead to leave. Disgruntled, they headed out from the city to join those displaced by the first edict, settling into the mountains that surrounded the plateau upon which the city sat. It made no difference - others were conscripted to contribute their labour, and soon the whole populace was involved. Day and night, the works continued, unabated.

It was of course impossible to raise the buildings from the ground – without support, they would simply collapse. Columns, therefore, thousands upon thousands of them, were required to be inserted, between the first floors and the ground, many piled deep below the surface in order to be robust enough to carry the weight of the buildings towering above. For months all that could be heard was the remorseless hammering of steel and concrete, as each column was pummelled down, like a stake, being driven mercilessly into a dumb beast, defeated but refusing to succumb.

Once in place, the columns, like a forest straining suddenly under the weight of the sky, were confirmed sufficiently numerous and properly located, to allow every wall on the ground floor to be removed. For months and months more, all that could then be heard was the sound of demolition, as walls were battered down, with mallet, hammer and saw.

But progress was slow - so great wrecking machines were commissioned, which crawled slowly through the streets like insatiable insects, ripping out doors and windows of houses and shop-fronts alike – until eventually, not one was left standing. In the process, a great cloud of dust rose up, it hovered constantly above the city, every building, and every person was covered in it; grey, they worked like ghostly shadows in the artificial fog, the sounds of demolition accompanied by the constant coughing of the people. They could not open their mouths to talk – only at night, as they washed off as best they could the grime that now settled permanently over everything did they secretly mutter oaths and share their treasonous thoughts.

The king, for a while, looked on. He took no part in actually overseeing his second edict, leaving his son to do it – he seemed to relish the prospect; the king on the other hand did not, and eventually he retreated into his palace, and refused to entertain any counsel whatsoever. He could not watch as the city- his life's work and that of his forefathers before him – was destroyed. He confined himself to his bed, overcome by the dust that seeped poisonously into his lungs, and lay, listening to the sounds of wreckage; horrendous sounds that filtered into his bedchamber despite his windows being shuttered securely and *covered in drape upon drape. Silence occasionally reigned, as the works ceased to allow some rest for the workers, a reluctant accede on the prince's part – and yet even in the silence, the king could hear a more horrendous sound: the soft yet insistent and increasingly irritating weeping that echoed through the apartments of the palace. Again he felt the same foreboding: that the edict was folly, and that his son's enthusiasm for the success of this ridiculous undertaking would only result in disaster.*

True to the king's assessment, on the day the works were completed the prince led the girl out into the city – to have his hopes instantly dashed once again, the very moment he removed the girl's blindfold.

He had been so sure that this would have been the solution – as far as the eye could see, there was nothing other than columns to block the view. From any point in the city one could see any other, and indeed, beyond, to the distant mountains that lay far from the city boundaries – for even the city walls had been removed! The prince was certain therefore that this second edict would result in healing his beloved's condition – but it did not. The girl wept, uncontrollably, her tears pouring down her dust covered cheeks.

The prince spun her slowly around, but in a hope forlorn. He replaced the blindfold and led her back to the palace – overhead, the people stared down in silent condemnation, and not once did the prince look upwards.

That night, the prince sought out his father. Though the king had not witnessed his son's sad denouement, word of it had been brought to him by the Royal Court, insistent on an audience that they might state their 'most rigorous concerns'. Again, the king had dismissed them, without resolution, and again, his head, his eyes, and now his heart, ached.

"The edict did not succeed," the prince said, shamefully, his head hung low, unable to meet the frank look in his father's eyes.

"So I have been told," the king replied.

The prince looked up, surprised – but then of course the king would know, of course he would have been told, doubtless by a delighted Royal Court, of his son's failure.

"They failed me..." the prince said, defensively.

He waved his hand loosely in front of him. "They failed me.

They didn't build it properly!"

The king thought for a moment that the prince might stamp his foot.

"They built it as you instructed," he said.

The prince shook his head, but then frowned and admitted: "I know, I know......it just wasn't right...It wasn't-"

"Perfect?" the king interrupted.

"Yes, yes – exactly!" the prince agreed.

"My city...my city, was perfect...," the king stated, quietly, with significant authority and barely concealed resentment.

"No - it wasn't ! It wasn't!" the prince retorted, angrily. "How could it have been...! She wept......"

"She still weeps!" the king retorted in return. "And why should we worry about her? She weeps? I should weep, for the damage she has done." He glared at his son.

The prince felt tears well up in his own eyes.

"I have to keep her locked in a tower...blindfolded. I don't understand, I don't understand...this pain. And this weeping, the weeping... it never stops...," and then he held his head in his hands and he too wept.

The king longed to put an arm around his son's shoulders, but he could not - he sat, watching dispassionately until his son regained his composure, then said gently: "I love you my son...but you are the one who is blind, not her. Nothing will ever be good enough for her...do you understand?" He paused, to cough, before continuing. "You cannot eradicate all the corners of the world...and even if you could, why would you? Why?"

But the king knew his words were falling on deaf ears. He coughed again, and waited as the prince wept, once more, dribbling disappointment like venom on the king.

"Maybe ...maybe if I change the walls, to glass maybe?" the prince said, finally, drying his eyes. He looked at the king, expectantly. "Walls of glass...yes..."

The king sighed: "No, my son, no, no more......"

"Father, please," the prince pleaded. "I love her father, I love her. I would do anything for her. Please father, please... wouldn't you, do anything for the one you love?"

The king, despite himself, could not counter the prince's

argument. He was reluctantly convinced to pass a third edict: that the city should be destroyed, and replaced with a city made entirely of glass!

The edict was met with outrage, and outright revolt: but the king, now confined to his bed, presented grounds for its justification that were impossible to contradict. Wracked by bouts of coughs, gasping painfully for breath, he explained to his Royal Court, and in turn to his people, that their city could and would be beautiful again; as it stood, it was already ruined – why not remove it, and replace it with a vision of beauty, a place of wonder made of glass, and filled with light? The king still had the regal authority enough to convince those that mattered; outspoken detractors were silenced with extreme prejudice, whilst many others, who might otherwise have objected, were too worn out; they held their tongues, but remained sceptical nonetheless.

Furious in his zeal to create a place that his princess could finally live, the prince threw himself into the realisation of the edict. He did not notice the rapidly failing health of his father, neither did he notice the barely hidden resentment of the people, conscripted once again to the task – he did not notice how depleted were their numbers, nor the numbers of those same builders, tradesmen, contractors and craftsmen. Instead, he rallied his father's guards, and issued demand upon demand, though the work was in and of itself, simple: demolition.

Once again, the city resounded with the cacophony of destruction, and once again, a cloud of dust rose up, billowing high into the sky and blocking out the sun; the city was plunged into almost complete darkness. But the work went on regardless – as the plans were drawn for a city that would arise from the ashes: a transparent city! All that would be retained of the old city would be those buildings duly cherished by the population at large: the palace, the cathedrals and other buildings perceived to be of similar value and worth. Everything else would go.

But the people had had enough: like the buildings, the people too, disappeared: in droves they abandoned the crumbling city, and sought refuge in the mountains.

The prince did not seem to notice – "Tear it down, tear it all down!" he gleefully encouraged his sullen workforce; he was consumed with the task, and consumed too with telling the girl. Late every evening he would visit her; in the darkness he would enthuse of what had been achieved that day, what had been destroyed – he described it all joyfully, for he was of a mind that the destruction of the city was akin to the removal of a cancer, each corner like a tumour: he told her in considerable detail the circumstances of their removal, and he insisted that everything would be fine – there would be no more corners, and no cause therefore for grief. The old city would be gone - in its place there would be a wondrous 'invisible' city, and once it was complete, they would live there, happy and safe for the rest of their lives. He told her every night, and every night, the girl lay, silent, and softly weeping. He wiped her tears away, convinced his ambitions would cure her – he did not see the handkerchiefs that piled up through the day, nor the industry of the nurses that attended to the girl: they had to remove handkerchiefs by the bucket-load, incessantly rinsing them, and wringing them out with innumerate wrangles.

The demolition work went on, and on, and only when the city had been virtually destroyed did the prince suddenly discover that he had been left without adequate means to complete the edict.

He suddenly found himself, standing, virtually alone, in the middle of a wasteland.

Some few structures, erected in glass, stood; otherwise there was nothing other than remnants of the once great city, a wilderness of ruins, crisscrossed by lines where streets had once been, and here and there the odd building, either partially demolished, or left, isolated and sitting almost embarrassed to be abandoned in such a desolate landscape. Rubble lay everywhere, as did the various machines for construction – but they were useless, and redundant. The city, what was left of it, was virtually empty.

In frustration, the prince howled! He shook his fists at the sky – and in a rage, ran to the palace, demanding of his father, that he must do something! But his rage evaporated, almost, immediately, when he discovered his father to be comatose, wasted away and hardly breathing, unable to hear his sons ranting proclamations. Shocked and appalled, he stumbled from his father's bedchamber...... and then, drifting down from high above, he heard the sound of the girl, weeping.

He was overcome, incandescent, by fury – he took the stairs, three at a time, as he raced up the tower. The door to the girl's room was locked – it had been for some time, for the girl's protection, the windows barred, bolted and shuttered too.

The prince kicked the door in.

On seeing his face, twisted and ferocious, the girl scurried to the far side of the room, cowering. The prince grabbed her and pulled her to the window: he pushed the shutter open. Light flooded the room.

"See what you've done!" He breathed it at her, through clenched teeth, forcing her head towards the opening. She struggled, her weeping turning to cries of panic and fear. "See!"

Far below, the city lay like a torn and ragged patchwork quilt. Hardly any part of the city remained, and for a second the prince's hope flared: he dragged the girl out of the room, and stumbling, pulled her down the stairs and out the palace.

"Where are your corners now?" he cried, his hand gripping her wrist, his other hand pointing to the wasteland in front of them. "Where?" He demanded of her: "How can you weep – for there are no corners here!" But weep she did.

Disgusted, the prince dragged her back to the palace. She could only stare at him through her bleary eyes. He shook her. His rage outweighed his reason; he hurled the girl to the floor: "All you do is weep!" He screamed it at her: "Weep, and weep! I have done everything for you. My father's city, ruined, my father... my people......"

The prince felt a loathing rise within him. Her face, distorted in tears – he could hardly stand to look at her. He could not believe that he had ever deigned to think that he loved her! Not even her eyes, her beautiful, beautiful eyes, could resurrect any feelings of affection – he looked away in revulsion. "There is nothing more I can do. Nothing."

Without turning, he said: "If this city does not satisfy you, then no city can!" His anger subsided enough to recognise the truth of what he had said. Calling guards to his side, the loyal few that remained, he walked the girl, blindfolded, back through the barren grey and empty landscape, stumbling over its broken surface, crunching gravel and glass underfoot.

Still she wept, ever so slightly...and still she did not speak.

When they reached the edge of the city, where the city walls had once stood, they stopped. Evening had fallen - in the distance, millions of tiny lights flickered from the ramshackle slums that now covered the mountains.

The prince turned to the girl.

"All you do is weep......but who do you weep for? Who? Me? My people? Or do you just weep......for yourself?"

She said nothing. He pulled the blindfold from her face.
"Well, if weep you must, then weep you shall......forever!"
The prince gave instruction to his guards, and without another
word, banished her to the slums in the mountains - mountains which
were now, nothing but an eternal maze.'

The artist stared at the king, as aghast as the prince had once stared at the girl in the king's tale.

"You think the prince was wrong?" the king asked.

The artist wanted to shake her head, implicitly she loved her king - but she could not. "Yes," she replied, regretfully but with sombre conviction.

"Have you never been wrong?"

Hurt, she said defensively: "Yes...yes, of course I have," but the king barely acknowledged her; he carried on regardless: "I don't blame him, for doing what he did, you know......I don't blame him," he said.

"You don't blame him?" The artist was incredulous.

"No...I understand why he did what he did."

"You do?"

"He was angry......"

"That's no excuse......"

"No? Have you never been angry?" Before the artist could respond, the king added: "I know what you mean...but what I mean is: he had his reasons."

The artist said nothing for a minute. She could feel an anger mount in her. Struggling to control herself, she said: "But he was still wrong." She said it without fear of recrimination, adding: "Don't you think he was wrong?", when it appeared that the king had nothing further to say.

The king shook his head.

"Wrong – or right – everyone can have their reasons. Who can say, who is right or wrong?"

"But – you don't blame him?"

194

"No – how can any one person blame any other, for any act that every one of us is capable of? And how can one ascribe blame, when one understands?" The king looked at her coldly. "And anyway, is blame not pointless - for what good does it do? It does not turn back time."

"But what he did... was terrible!"

"You want justice?"

"Don't you?"

"I would prefer it if there were no injustices in the first place."

The artist shook her head – 'what nonsense', she thought. She could feel her respect for her king rapidly waning. "I'm sorry," she said, with a respectful finality, "but I think he was wrong."

"Yes," he said. "Yes – as well you might, and as, in fact, did I. Of course I could agree, that he was wrong, that he should have done better, that he should have tried harder......I could agree, couldn't I, that I could never forgive him, never forgive him for abandoning her like that?"

The king paused.

"But I have to forgive," he said, with the same intense sadness that the artist had witnessed before, a sadness that consumed the king, and rendered him almost unrecognisable to her.

Sunk low into his bed, his voice almost as quiet as his breath, he added: "I have to, we all have to, forgive – ourselves. We're only human after all."

He smiled then, ever so slightly, and at once the frustration the artist had felt was replaced by compassion of such intensity it confused her and left her speechless.

Still smiling, the king said: "He tried to say sorry,"......

*He vanished into this world, with no horizon, where there was
no steady or secure place to rest, where there was no comfort,
and no respite from pain or loss – he vanished, into a world
without hope.*

Scene iii: The Mountains of Regret

'One might have thought that the prince would have regretted his decision – but he did not. He was deeply hurt and angry, which blighted his compassion. If he were honest he would have acknowledged his shame, but he convinced himself otherwise: he had done the right thing, for all around was the destruction caused by his efforts to satisfy the girl, and he consoled himself by making attempt at reparation.

His efforts though were half hearted. He initiated meetings with what was left of his father's Royal Court, but it was with little enthusiasm that he presided over plans to re-build the city. He could not muster the energy to motivate either himself, or his depleted workforce – indeed, such resentment abounded that his plans provoked a sullen revolt in those of the populace that remained. If he had had his father's capacity for leadership, he might have been able to negotiate with them, to placate them – but he did not. He had not inherited such simple authority and their anger was both justified and entrenched: this prince had destroyed their city, and for what? For nothing - all of it, for nothing; a vain attempt to appease the peculiar whim of some strange girl from nowhere, a miserable girl who they had never, ever really liked.

Had the prince created plans comparable to those of his father's great city, even plans that mimicked its graceful splendour, he might have had some collateral to bargain with, but his capacity to create was unfounded. He could not ask his father, who remained comatose and sank further every day into ill health. He had to rely on his own capabilities - he was not entirely unable to apply self-critique, but where he had an aptitude for problem solving, he had none for invention. Consequently, the task of re-building was beyond him. In truth, he did not know even where to start, and his meagre efforts were further impaired because he was, to all intents, in mourning. Despite his anger, in truth he longed for the girl, for her company, her presence, her beautiful eyes. But she was gone, and cruel rumours exaggerated his grief, that she had been bruised and battered by the people of the slums, that she had in fact been killed, brutally in a grievous act of revenge for the ruination that she had effectively wrought upon them. Whether these rumours were true, the prince had no way of knowing.

He could not properly trust his advisors, for they did not trust him; they had not elected to coronate him as their rightful king, despite his direct lineage, and he too had fostered no impetus on his own part to promote the idea. He did not want to be king; so he became effectively besieged within the royal palace, by both the resentment of his own people and by his incapacity to motivate himself.

Isolated and alone, he was overwhelmed with guilt. At night he would be plagued by the most terrible dreams – it was the same dream, over and over – he re-lived the awful words he had uttered so dispassionately to the girl, but instead of abandoning her to the slums, he constructed a vast maze around her, a maze made entirely of mirrors. 'Weep,' he would shout, as he built, by his own hands, the incredible maze, a labyrinth of infinite dead-ends around an infinite number of identical corners. Her weeping would diminish as he distanced himself further and further from her, building as he went; his hands would bleed as he cut and cut, endlessly, glass and set the cut pieces in place. His blood smeared the maze – his blood, that he knew the girl would be obliged to wipe clean, with her own threadbare rags – she would lick it clean if she had to! The maze complete, the prince would rest against its outer wall, and all he would hear would be her weeping, from far, far away. She would never find her way out – but then he'd be overcome with remorse; he would search and search for her, but try as he might he could never find her. The creature would fly overhead, supposedly guiding him – 'This way, that way, you idiot!' it would shout – the mirrors would repeat the words, echoing stuttered and crazy in the mirrored halls – 't.t.t.this way, that w.w.w.ay...' He would run and run, the mirrors would become a blur, all around......and he would finally reach the centre, but nothing would be there, there would be no sign of the girl, only her weeping, weeping and darkness.

The prince would wake then, sweating, the sound of weeping still ringing in his mind. His dream haunted him, it haunted both his nights and his days, until finally he had had enough. Early one morning, he simply abandoned the palace, abandoned the ruined city, and went to the slums in search of the girl.

He had no idea what he would say to her, once found, but he went with an optimism imbued by his belief in her capacity to forgive. He did not think that he would struggle to find her – he knew that she would weep, *and weep perpetually by the very nature of the place to which he had banished her.*

He did not realise though, that in the slums, many wept.

If he had not seen it first hand, the prince could not have imagined that such an awful place could exist. The stench was the first thing that hit him – it was overpowering: the product of so much humanity crammed together into such unsanitary conditions. How could the slum even stand, being of such density, each building built so precariously on the next - it rose endlessly upwards, almost vertically; steep, and narrow uneven steps were the only means by which to traverse the slum, set in slivers of space between infinite numbers of random and ramshackle buildings, buildings that literally teetered overhead; a vast mountain of buildings piled high like some incomprehensible mound of rotting garbage.

The higher the prince climbed the worse it got. He had brought no provisions – he had not expected to be there for any great time, he had absolutely no comprehension of the slum's scale. The sun beat down upon him, and in his dehydration, he became faint, and even more disorientated. He became completely lost, and knew only that he should climb, higher and higher.

It was only when he finally reached the summit that he found some remission from the claustrophobic conditions and unbearable stench. He took a breath - and had it almost taken immediately from him: the view was stunning!

Behind him, the plateau where his father's city had once stood, lay stretched out, scared and pitted like some incomprehensible hieroglyphic, its meaning long forgotten; and in front, hung between clouds that clung resiliently to their surface, were mountains, innumerable and continuous: there was no horizon – just one mountain, one after another, each unnaturally shaped like a deformed cone, and each covered in the same dense pattern of discordant structures. Like a terrible disease that ravages the skin, leprous, and putrid, the mountains had been literally consumed by a fungal maze of irregular structures. It was distressing, and yet compelling, in its untrammelled beauty: a landscape, made awesome by its expanse and uniqueness of form – and distantly from each mountain, the prince could hear the steady hum of weeping, echoing through the clouds: a vocal outpouring indicative of depravity borne by such horrendous poverty.

It was desperate in the truest sense of the word, as desperate a sound as befitting the place, and somewhere, the prince was convinced, somewhere in this appalling place, was the girl.

If nothing else, the prince was stubborn in his chivalry, and inspired by his need to make amends – tirelessly, he searched. He searched, deeper and deeper down into the slums – and the deeper he searched, the quieter and sadder it got: the people he passed, squatting in open sewers or huddled in tiny doorways, they were beyond humanity – some watched him as he passed, staring, their eyes blank, their bodies emaciated and thin almost beyond human recognition: the prince could hardly recognise man from woman. They were grey, lifeless creatures, who lived in an almost impenetrable darkness, a perpetual gloom, airless and devoid of any kind of natural light whatsoever.

Nearer the surface, what light there was often blinding – the prince had elected to look deeper inside the mountains, partly to be protected from the light, but also because it was safer. His first attempts to find the girl had been met with ridicule; a girl, without a name, in rags, and deathly pale...that could be any girl belonging to the slums! People laughed at him, and worse, they beat him. He learnt quickly to deny who he was, after three times admitting, that yes, he was the unfortunate prince who has caused their suffering. His vain honesty provoked the people to rain blows upon him, and he had to run through gauntlets of abuse to escape. And his attire did him no favours either – his fine robes were so at odds with the clothing of everyone else, and he was often beaten for his garments, and for his ridiculous manner, as much as he was beaten for his lineage.

Undaunted he searched, into the slums which went on and on forever, and soon the prince lost sight, entirely, of the world he had once known. He vanished into this world, with no horizon, where there was no steady or secure place to rest, where there was no comfort, and no respite from pain or loss – he vanished, into a world without hope.'

"I don't think I like this story anymore."

The king, though interrupted rather abruptly by the artist, said simply, and indeed, kindly: "Do you want me to stop...?"

"I ...I need to get on with my work."

It was a feeble excuse, and the artist knew it.

"There is nothing to stop you working."

"No...no." She stared at her unfinished portrait. "I can't ...I can't. I just can't get it right..." Frustrated, she flung her brush at her easel; it tipped, but did not fall.

"It does not matter..."

"It does matter...how-"

"No, it does not....it does not matter, if you get it wrong."

"But-"

The king insisted: "No." She stood mute as he repeated it: "No – you will never get it right. There is no 'right' in what we do. Or rather, what you do. By default...you *will* get it wrong - only if you believe in right and wrong of course."

The king was provoking her, but she refrained from allowing herself to be drawn back into that conversation again. She stared at the unfinished portrait, frowning, until the king kindly asked her: "Is it worth the cost?"

The artist sighed. The portrait, half finished, stared back at her. She was tired, so terribly tired, and in her exhaustion she visualised the portrait melting – the lines she had worked so hard upon blurred, merged, and seemed to slip as if softened like pasta to the bottom of the canvas. She imagined all her sketches drying up, crinkling and spontaneously bursting into flames – for a second she wished they would. She picked up her brush, turned it in her hand as if seeing it for the very first time. 'Is it worth it?' she wondered. She couldn't answer the king, who watched her intently from his sick bed.   Eventually he said: "Everything we make, costs – and everything we make, fails to live up to its expectation, does it not?"

The artist sighed again. "You make it sound...pointless," she said.

"Yes, I can understand why you might think that..."

"Are you saying we should not try?"

"That," said the king, as he resumed his account, "is exactly the point..."

'How much time passed, days, months, years, the prince did not know. Slowly, he began to take on the same hue as those around him, a hue as grey as death. He had to scavenge for food, from leftovers thrown into the street or spilling from mounds of waste that accumulated everywhere. He had to shelter in shallow doorways or on crumbling roofs, and he could only wash, occasionally, in the rainy season, standing under whatever pathetic dribble might find its way into the depths of the slum, or in the putrid water that flowed down the streets.

It was not out of spite, nor malice that sustenance was kept from the prince. The people of the slums, they forgot who he was, they no longer cared, and he in turn became almost unrecognisable as the prince he had once been.

However, he never gave up on his quest. He searched every day for the girl. He never lost hope that he would find her. Indeed, with every corner that he turned, his hope would rise, and fill him with an almost delirious expectation that, around this corner, yes, around this corner, she would be there! His hope would be obliterated, immediately to be resurrected, for around the next corner, surely, around the next corner, she would be there? It was a cycle that repeated itself without relief - for that is all the slums were: corners: corners, one after another, each one barely distinguishable from the next.

Yet the prince never rested, never – his hair grew long, as did his beard, his fingernails and his toenails. His eyes became fixed, and focussed ever in front: he rarely glanced to one side or the other, in an effort to remember where he looked. He began to make notes of where he was and where he had been, but it became impossible; he could not find sufficient scraps of paper, and the slums were so vast and complex, no map could ever be made. So he took to drawing on the walls of the buildings he had surveyed, to mark them, to confirm his passing.

There may have been a shortage of paper, but there was no shortage of drawing tools: broken materials lay all about; bits and pieces of slate, and stone, and charcoal. His hand became deft and quick; where his first marks were random scratches, which became identifiable before long as a kind of signature, he soon turned his marks into definitive lines, and then shapes and forms. He drew on every structure he passed, every building, both inside and out; he invaded every house, and drew on the walls there too, politely asking the inhabitants their permission, to leave charcoal marks that might remind him of his presence.

*The children of the slums took delight in following the prince –
they called him names, the crazy man that shuffled manically through the
streets, glaring at every surface, and peering so close to the walls that his
nose was forever scraped and bleeding. 'Bloody nosey man's coming'
they'd cry, as they pretended to be him, mocking his efforts by scribbling
on the walls too – but the prince didn't mind; in fact he enjoyed their
noisy, nosy, presence.*

*His marks became in themselves a map – they helped the
prince to navigate the slums, and the people too began to follow his
signs, to recognise where they were, and where they might go, some
other way of making their way through the density of the slum that was
always, ever, ever so persuasive. Some tried to mimic the marks that the
prince made – but he had developed a skill, unbeknownst to himself, and
unable to be copied by others; for as he made his mark, his eye began to
reflect upon what he had drawn: the marks he made began to be more
than merely indications of his presence. They became decorative, stylised
renderings, refined, carefully executed, not rough scratches hastily racked
into the walls surface. He spent more time on them, his desire to record
his presence overtaken by a desire to place upon the wall, pictures,
visions, shapes, patterns, any manner of illustration that pleased him. He
studied his marks, his drawings, he looked hard at them, he drew them,
and then drew them again; he became obsessed, borrowing ladders,
climbing over roofs, crawling along the ground, to get his drawings just
right.*

*His inspiration came from, initially, his memory, the memory of
his father's great city, but this resource was soon exhausted, and he
turned his hand then to the transformation of what he saw, to what it
could be: this wall could have perhaps a window here, a doorway there,
this street could perhaps turn sweeter here, bend more naturally there.
His drawings were no longer marks on the wall – they were perspectives
of the place as he imagined it.*

*So consumed was he, that he began to forget about the girl,
though her presence, or lack of it, was the thing that fundamentally drove
him, every day; to get up, and draw, draw, draw, from morning until night
- and even then, he would beg for lights, miniscule bits of candle, that
burned over his hand as he scribbled, or a match even, or even just a
sliver of light from a window prised open enough in response to his
fevered request – anything, to allow him to draw.*

He retraced the places he had been, re-drew everything, again and again – for around every corner, suddenly the prince discovered......possibilities. There was no end to it – and no end to his capacity to visualise some other way for the slums to be. Though physically exhausted, he was not tired. His eyes burned bright, and his hand never stopped, drawing.

And then – something remarkable began to happen ... the walls as marked, became reality...

People began to re-build their homes as the prince had drawn on them, first one and then another made alterations: within their limited means, with the most meagre of materials, walls were reconstructed - and to immense joy, they discovered how wonderful it was, the improvement made.

Soon the reputation of this crazy man spread: this unkempt creature that could see possibilities in the walls, that he could by the mark of charcoal re-invent their world, that he could decorate their lives with his imagination. It became the desire of every person in the slums that the crazy man, the bloody nosey man, might visit them, that he might search their house, their home, and that he might then change their home and their lives forever.

Gradually then, the slums began to change: light began to enter, spaces began to flow, what had been thought to be mean and ugly became almost beautiful.

The prince though did not see the change: he could not. He became, by his work, delirious, and in his delirium, he saw visions, visions that were as real to him as reality. He saw the creature. It had lost what little charm it may have once had. Nothing remained – no sign of its unique form, its colouring – it was just an ugly shape, that curled around him, and tugged on his arms as he drew, pulled on his sleeve, caused him to shake and make marks that offended.

And then he saw the girl. She was there. He saw, her, standing right there. She smiled at him, beckoned to him, and then she disappeared around a corner. He chased after her, and there she was again, waiting for him, smiling, beckoning – he wanted to follow, but he couldn't. There was so much to be done, so much. He called to her, begged her to wait, as he drew and drew on the walls as quickly as he could. He wanted so much to follow her, to catch her, but he couldn't. She would disappear around every corner, and every time he followed, *he'd be so close, so, so close, but she would slip away. He could never get close enough to her. He would be stopped, stopped by all the possibilities that rushed out at him, which he scribbled furiously on every wall.*

The creature tormented him: 'Go to her' it would insist, 'go on. Go', it whispered, as it curled around him, its foul breath stinging his eyes, its shadowy tendrils pulling on his arms. 'You're an idiot', it would snigger, and it was everywhere, wafting and foaming and drooling all over him. 'You're an idiot...go to her.'

The girl beckoned, and the creature harried, 'Look, look,' it would insist, 'Look. The curse is lifted. Look – go to her,' and the prince tried to draw, draw, draw, draw, one hand on the wall, one hand waving......but it was impossible. Impossible.

If he rested he did not know it, but rest he did, and in his delirious sleep the creature would torment him still; from its indistinguishable shape, it would take on human form: a body would appear, with three heads: of a camel and a pig and a crow. The body was impossibly thin, as thin as sticks, and the heads wobbled unnaturally on top, as if supported on enfeebled stalks. It reeked, this creature, worse than the stench of the slum, a foul, foul, thing: shaped like a man, but in fact, it was a beast: a three headed beast. Each lambasted the prince, quoting facts and figures at him, meaningless nonsense but about which the prince worried nonetheless, and each plagued him banefully with its own particular rancour.

The pig was bald; it shouted louder than the others, its breath stank worse than the others, and its guttural nonsense was full of more obscenities than the others; it drew over the prince's drawings, discoloured them and flattened their perspective, reducing them to discordant and meaningless multi coloured graphics.

The camel was blind; it frowned more than the others, it moaned more than the others, and offered snide and pointless observations, berating the prince behind his back for his efforts, insinuating: why bother? Where it passed, what little colour there was drained from the surroundings, flowers drooped, and even the light itself seemed to dim.

The crow though, the crow was the worst: its feathery head was grey, it had eyes, but they were black, dead lifeless eyes - behind them there was nothing. It whispered to the pig and the camel, and laughed quietly to itself, walking aloof from the prince, speaking in slow incantations, observations that were as dumb as anything the prince had ever heard. The prince argued with the crow, trying to make sense out of its infuriating statements – but it was pointless: the crow could not tell the truth, and there was no argument that the prince could make that the crow could not answer.

Together, the three headed beast shook their gruesome heads. 'Rubbish,' they would write on the walls as the prince drew. 'Rubbish, rubbish, rubbish!', and they rubbed out his drawings, they erased them almost as fast as he could draw them. He drew faster still, as fast as he could - especially whilst the three headed beast slumbered. The girl still beckoned, and the prince pleaded: 'Please, please, wait – I'm nearly finished'. And she would disappear again, around another corner.

But he would keep drawing.

"Rubbish!" he would mutter, "Rubbish." Nothing made any difference to the prince – he drew, and drew. His delirium became worse, much worse. He could hardly see, his hands were bloody and numb, his fingers worn down to the bone.

Finally he collapsed.

He did not know it, but he had drawn over every inch of every single building, and as he drifted into nothingness, the slum around him slowly, transformed......'

Darkness had fallen once again, and with it, the expectation of confession. Though the king threw the question at the artist somewhat un-expectantly, his voice was soft, and turned in upon itself: "Would you ever ask it, of another – whether they wish they could dream around corners?"

"I suppose one should be careful what one wishes for...dreaming round corners might make you weep...," the artist replied, thinking her response humourous, and that it would lighten the king's mood. But he replied in earnest, and said, sadly: "Yes – indeed it might."

"It's good that someone does...," the artist added, respectfully.

"Perhaps..." His eyes turned downwards, and the artist couldn't help but ask: "Do you?"

"Do I what?"

"Do you...dream around corners...?"

The king didn't answer; for the first time, the artist sensed a hesitation in his demeanour, a reluctance to continue their conversation. When he next spoke, his voice had taken on a very different timbre: darkly he looked at her and said, in tones deep and withdrawn: "There may be danger, around a corner."

"Danger...?"

"Yes, danger. Don't you think there might be danger, around a corner, something there that will do you harm?"

"Well, yes of course, I suppose so...yes."

"Around every corner?"

'Yes, there might be, if you say so' she wanted to add, but said instead: "Personal harm? Harm to one's well-being? One's safety? Well, yes...perhaps, yes, I suppose there might be. Not always though..."

"Yes, yes indeed. I'd suggest that yes, there is danger – there is always danger, danger around every corner."

"Always?"

"Yes – always. There is always the danger..."

"Danger of what?"

"Danger - that what you find there does not live up to your expectations..."

Suddenly the artist felt herself lose interest in the king's pronouncements. 'So what?' she wondered. Did it really matter? Did it matter what the king thought, the prince, the girl...did it matter what she thought? She was tired.

Obligingly, she said: "Perhaps it *is* more terrible to hope?"

"Perhaps it is hope...," the king said, and added as if he were pronouncing a sentence on her: "You dream round corners...did you know that?"

The artist didn't know how to answer. The king himself had said already, that everyone did, or at least, had suggested as much – she couldn't understand why he was saying this so directly to her. She was grateful when he closed his eyes and resumed his account.

'Silence greeted the prince when he recovered his senses. Slowly he became aware of the world about him - he recognised it, not for what it was, but what it had once been: the slums – but hardly slums any more.

They were clean and fresh; where the stench had once permeated everything, now the streets were unsoiled, the walls, spotless and smooth, painted in warm comforting tones and colours that reminisced of fond and happy memory.

The sun cast sharply, dramatic shadows across every façade, from roofs, overhanging their curled burnt amber pantiles; from proud delicate awnings carefully cantilevered over doorways and windows; from window boxes blooming with flowers; and the warm light threw patterned lines across floors and walls, as it filtered through half closed shutters and lacy drapes, which fluttered in the occasional breeze.

In the warmth, gentle sounds slumbered – sounds of industry and conversation, of birds, calling and children contentedly playing. Delightful sounds all – and the only sound that could not be heard was the sound of weeping.

The prince, once fully recovered, basked for a time in the affection of the people, wondering through the narrow alleyways, up and down the steep steps that trickled through the slums like tributaries of some revered and enriching river. He was greeted kindly by every man, woman and child. They laboured, happily in open doorways, chatting to neighbours and passers-by alike. Consequently, an atmosphere of congeniality wafted through the air, rich like the odour of cooked meats and wholesome sauces that forever drifted alongside; bright conversations and laughter bounced off the walls; joyous banging and scrabbling merged with the sound of music played enthusiastically on strings and accompanied by hearty voices - and at night, those same voices would slur, but be no less joyful, as they echoed like prayers, finally answered. It was a mood relieved – even when a funeral cortege paraded through the slum, it would be attended by the tinkle of bells, and slow but comforting clapping, and even then, there would be no weeping.

It was wonderful to behold, the transformation – slums: that had been the sullied product of the princes own desperate folly, now made into the most wholesome of places.

For the prince it was redemptive – and yet, secretly, the prince, in his heart longed to hear weeping.

He longed to hear the weeping of the girl.

His longing distracted him from savouring any further delight from the refreshed slums, and presently his wanderings took on new purpose – or rather, a purpose of old: he began to search.

Steadily, and again as persistently engrossed in his singular purpose, he searched around every corner – hoping. And with each corner turned, his hope evaporated – though each was as joyous as the one preceding, none fulfilled. As he had wandered amongst the people when things had been bad, he did so again, but good times, bad times, it made no difference - she was still not there.

How much time passed, the prince could not tell – he wandered throughout the fullest extent of the slums, but ultimately and with a distressed reluctance, though none could nor would confirm it, the prince accepted that it must have been true: the girl had been killed in some furious, but forgivable rage.

Either that or she had abandoned the slums, though he doubted it - for even transformed, they were endless. How could she possibly have found her way out? And even if she had, where would she go? There was nowhere safe for her. Corners were everywhere.

Suddenly, it made sense, at last, why the girl had hidden in the vast saucer in the white plain. It had been a safe place for her, despite its meagreness: the Mirror Machine had been her protector, and it had been proven correct in its prediction: effectively, the girl had wept to death.

And it had all been the prince's fault.

Grief and guilt combined settled in the prince's heart – he struggled daily to engage at all with the people around him; still they sought convivially his assistance to advise them on their properties, their homes and places of work; they invited him to educate their children and show them the ways of his craft. He did as best he could, but his heart had lost its passion, indeed his heart felt as if it had lost even the capacity to beat at all, and yet was able still to pump the blood round his body- but for to what purpose? What purpose life, without her?

Wat purpose then: the world?

The faces of those around him, reflecting back at the prince their contentment, their joy, their vibrancy, they became intolerable reminders of what was lost - and the prince eventually realised that he could no longer live in the slums, for no matter how hard he might try, he would never be able to live in harmony with the world that he had created.

One night, as abruptly as he had left the palace in his father's city all those years ago, he gathered together his paltry belongings, and without a word, left.

His intention had been to return to his father's city, but he could not - instead he wandered, into landscapes over the hills and far away, and tried to forget.'

ACT III

He was awakened, by the sound of laughter!

ACT III

Scene i: The Innocents Meadow

"Perhaps you are thinking he needn't have left?"

The artist frowned. "Was he sure - that she was not there?" It seemed a reasonable question to ask, but the king carried on as if he hadn't heard: "That perhaps he'd made a place, perfect enough for her?"

That word again: 'perfect'; it jarred on the artist – it had done ever since the king had brought it up, but particularly now: her assumption had been exactly as the king suggested, but she hated to admit it. She recoiled even more when the king said: "If the artist is not perfect, how then can the artist make a perfect thing?"

"But – no-one is perfect!" she responded, defensively.

"No-one? But – we're surrounded by perfect people. Everywhere you look, you see them, no? Perfect strangers – we say it all the time." The king smiled his increasingly irritating smile, adding: "Perhaps our imperfections only reveal themselves when we get to know each other? Should we all remain strangers then? And the things these perfect strangers make, might they then be perfect?"

The king was once again getting on her nerves.

"We can't all be strangers...," she argued.

"Perhaps it would be better if we were...? Or perhaps it would be better if we were not here at all?" Before the artist could offer an instinctive rebuke, the king said:

"Tell me – do you think we are here for good, or for ill?"

"Well...good, surely?"

"Surely, yes ...." He waved his thin hand loosely around the room: "But perhaps it is all ...for ill."

"No, no. No..."

"You believe that goodness prevails?"

"Why yes...I think so, yes..."

"What if goodness prevailing, is of itself, an ill?"

"But...how could that be so?"

"It may be."

"How? Goodness is not an ill...how can you believe that?"

"Look around. Look at what we do – everything we do, comes at a cost. And if everything we do costs, how can that be goodness?"

The artist didn't know what to say. The king's face was hidden in the darkness, but she had no doubt he was watching her. She was grateful she couldn't see him, and made no move to light the braziers – she feared that she would not like what she saw, feared too that she could no longer picture the king, in reality or in fiction, as the king she admired. The portrait slipped further and further to the bottom of the canvas.

"It is a dilemma, no? I suspect it is best not to think too hard on it...if you do, you cannot help but wonder..."

"Wonder?"

"Wonder if there is a better place than this...better than the good or the bad..."

The king had descended again into his state of saddened solitude – he muttered: "...if we destroy, whenever we create..."

He fell silent until the artist again prompted him to resume his account.

"So – she wasn't in the slums then?"

"Shall we see?" the king replied. The artist waited – but the king, insistently, repeated himself: "Shall we see?"

Momentarily, clouds parted and moonlight broke into the bedchamber – the king's eyes were on her, looking at her closely and clearly with intention, but she could not determine what he meant. She nodded, dumbly, somewhat irritated - the king paused momentarily; it was enough for the artist to perceive that something had passed between them, an opportunity, lost – there was dissatisfaction in his gaze, disappointment too, and something else...she couldn't quite decide.

The moonlight disappeared, and in the darkness, the king continued......

'For years the prince wandered; some trick of his mind might have revealed the truth of it: that he did not wander aimlessly, but searched for the girl, hosting an unspoken hope that perhaps she had found her way back to the safety of the white plain. Though he recognised, vaguely, landscapes he and the girl might have traversed those many years ago, he could not find a trustworthy route back - had he even the capacity to admit that that was indeed his quest.

His hair grew, longer, and became speckled with grey, his face, bearded and grey too – but other than these explicit and recognisable signs of age, he retained his youthful physique, and with it, his princely posture, except for a slight ache in his back. He walked, unhurried, and effectively unhindered; his body became lean, his face, chiselled if somewhat drawn, and his eyes, sharpened: his vision did not dim, as might be expected, but rather became fixed, and clarified, as if able to discard automatically, unnecessary sights, focussed perpetually in its adopted aspect of loss, accepted, and hopeful longing.

He was dressed only in a long plain robe, fashioned from the cape he had once worn so proudly; its colours had faded to a single hue of ochre, and its texture, once of a soft luxurious velvet, had lost its sheen and become transformed to something almost resembling cotton. He carried nothing other than a rough satchel, in which he kept some charcoal and pencils, and also, the faded and tattered blindfold. This was the sum of his possessions: his feet were bare – the soles of his feet having hardened themselves sufficiently by the rigours of his years wandering.

It was perhaps inevitable, wandering at length so aimlessly, that eventually he found himself back, once again, in his father's city - or rather, what was left of it.

A significant amount of time had passed, time enough for nature to re-claim what had been taken: where the city once stood, a foundling and enormous meadow now grew. On the morning that the prince stumbled upon it, he did not at first even recognise where he was.

Sprouting plentifully between the remnants of broken discarded stones, rubble, and bent twisted steel, all of it seasoned with infinite grains of shattered glass, were plants and shrubs of all kinds, spindly and light, swaying easily in the breeze; it was like a rippling sea, a whispering meadow of reeds, summer flowers, poppies, dandelions and daisies stretching away in every direction.

Some vaguely recognisable structures protruded, prescient enough to confirm that this was indeed the same city: the royal palace, devoid of its crowning dome; here and there a crumbling temple and more profusely: abandoned taverns, like ragged limbs, a foot perhaps, left unnaturally detached from a body obliterated; and the lines of the streets remained discernible, though their purpose less so, like a poorly guest that has stayed too long, and doesn't know that it is long past time to leave, nor has the capacity to do so.

Otherwise there was little else to suggest that, where the meadow grew, there had stood a vast and incredible city.

Only in the far, far distance, where the mountains rose up, was there sign of human habitation - all along the horizon, trails of smoke trickled upwards, from what must have been innumerable chimneys – it were as if the mountains were imbibing on copious, and conspicuously rich pungent tobaccos. Indeed, the fragrance from the smoke blended with the sweet odour from the meadow flowers, to become not unlike the sickly overpowering scent the prince recalled, that accompanied ceremonies held in his father's great houses of worship. It was a memory, like so many others, that filled the prince with a yearning for his past; the memory warmed him, it infused him with a curious comfort: distracted, he set down his satchel – for the first time for years, he felt relieved: there was no activity pressing on the prince, no responsibility or instruction; there was no need to wander.

And so...he rested.

Later that morning, lazily he explored the empty, whispering meadow. He washed in pools of rainwater gathered in convenient hollows in weathered stones left remnant from some fine construction, and after lunching on rich wild strawberries and blackberries, he lay down again in the long grasses to sleep. Petals of pretty flowers twisted across his vision, bees hummed and butterflies floated aimlessly between them as dandelion seeds drifted casually by; the prince then fell into an easy slumber.

He slept until late in the afternoon, when he was awakened by the sound of laughter.

It was the first thing he was aware of, the first thing he heard: laughter, soft, and gentle laughter, the laughter of what could only be, children. Then he heard voices, too – lots of voices, chattering with childish enthusiasm.

A boy's face appeared over his. He stared at the prince, and then turned and ran away, shouting: "The king's alive!"

King? The prince was confused. He rubbed his eyes, and began to sit up – and then small hands were pulling on him, small cold hands. Another boy's face appeared, then another. More small hands pulled him, pulling him to his feet. Standing, the prince saw that there were three or four of them, five, then six of them, bright and clean faced but pale little boys - they were shouting: "The king's alive! The king's alive!!!"

At first the prince could not understand who they were calling to - but then, from out of the meadow, he saw tens, maybe hundreds of children even, suddenly running towards him. Children of all ages and sizes!

They danced ecstatically around him, their arms linked, shouting: "The king's alive! The king's alive!" One voice rose above the others, proclaiming: "Long live the king!" and as if on cue, the children knelt – and for the most part, they almost completely disappeared into the long reeds! It was comical, and the prince could not help but smile. However, despite the persistence of their penitence, he felt obliged to correct them.

"I...I am not a king," he apologised.

The children said nothing.

"I am not a king...," he repeated.

One child looked up, a little boy, then another.

"I'm sorry..."

"But...you are a king," insisted, quietly, another.

"I'm not...I am a prince," the prince said, trying to be conciliatory. It didn't work. More cries followed: "No, no - you are, you are. You are OUR King...!"

One little girl, as pale as all the others, hesitantly, stood up. "We made you a crown...and a throne..." she said, pointing to a pile of stones and boxes, clearly rather hastily erected, but shaped enough to be recognisable as a seat. Upon it was a ring of rose petals.

She knelt, crestfallen; many of the children whimpered as the prince, again, insisted he was not a king. Then one boy began to cry, then another, and suddenly they all began to cry – !

The prince, appalled, held up his hand: "OK," he said. "OK – I am your king, if you say I am."

Instantly the children stopped crying; cheering, they jumped up and danced enthusiastically around him, and led him to the 'throne': he had to sit down carefully so that it would not collapse: the boxes were made of thin panels of wood, hardly stronger than thick card; they crumpled slightly under his weight. Nonetheless, the 'throne' held. The children then acted out a coronation in his honour, ceremoniously placing the 'crown' of rose petals on his head, and parading in front of him, bringing him gifts of berries and flowers, which they piled around his bare feet.

As they came up to him, each one more beautiful than the last, dressed in the cleanest and most delicate of light fabrics, they smiled, smiles as bright as stars; they giggled as they deposited their tribute; the prince graciously thanked them. He did so, honestly honoured – he had never seen such children as these, as innocently imbued; he could not imagine how they came to be there, and for some reason he did not want to ask. Their demeanour was so unusually composed, and surreal because of it, he hardly trusted himself that indeed their presence was in fact real. They behaved so kindly to each other, and they moved with such delicacy, their only incumbency being the little hard boxes that hung on string around their necks, or swung uncomfortably from their shoulders; they all carried them but their purpose, other than to construct a 'throne', was unknown to the prince. It did not even appear as if they could be opened.

The 'coronation' lasted until the night set in; the mountains lit up like Christmas trees, thousands and thousands of tiny lights flickered and flashed, on and off in the distance. The prince built a large fire, and the children gathered around, many sitting on the boxes that they carried. They supped on berries, and afterwards played games, running and chasing each other around the fire, or off into the shadows of the meadow. The night wore on, and the prince struggled to stay awake – the children giggled, and laughed, noisily, but despite this, he fell asleep, and when he awoke the children were gone.

That day the prince wandered, disconsolate, through the

meadow – it had been a long time since he had seen or spoken to anyone. He had been content to do so, content to live out his days as such - but the company of the children had been wonderful. He had to admit, he now regretted the time he had spent, alone.

He searched through the meadow, hoping that perhaps some of the children might still be there, but in his heart he knew they would not: the meadow was silent, apart from its own gentle whispering, sweetly and not unlike that of the children, but wordless and without form.

Late in the day, becoming tired, the prince sat on his 'throne' - or the remains of it, for the boxes too were gone - and drifted off again into an easy gentle slumber.

He was awakened, by the sound of laughter!

At first he thought he was dreaming – but small hands grabbed him, pulling him up. Those same childlike voices were shouting: "Long live the king!" The prince smiled as he looked about, at the same few boys who had wakened him the day before, and at other children too, boys and girls, perhaps ten or twelve or more, and then, from out of the meadow, hundreds and then hundreds and hundreds more of them!

"See, I told you," one boy insisted to one of the many newcomers. He pointed to the prince: "Our king!" he said proudly.

The prince bowed graciously in acknowledgment of his station. Together, they re-enacted the coronation, and as the evening closed in, the prince again built a fire. They sat around, they sang, and danced, the 'king' ensconced happily on his 'throne'. At times he was pulled to his feet, dragged and thrown about, and thrown then to the ground. They tumbled over him, and demanded that he chase them through the meadow, despite the darkness. The prince feared somewhat for their safety – the meadow was littered with the remnants of the city, and often they stumbled, fell and cut themselves; but they never bled, nor were they caused pain by their accidents. It might have given the prince cause to wonder why, but he was just grateful for it; carefree and without abandon they chased the prince and each other - the prince felt like a child himself! But he was of course, much older than they were and the games exhausted him. He tried his best to stay awake – but as the night wore on, he was overcome with tiredness and once again fell asleep to the sound of children laughing. In the morning, when he awoke, it was to silence – the children were gone.

But the prince was not saddened as before: he predicted that they would be back, and true enough, late in afternoon, as the sun began to set, from out of the meadow, the children reappeared. It was as if the meadow itself served them up.

That night, they re-enacted the 'coronation', they played as they had the night before, and in the morning - the children were gone.

During that day and the next, the prince waited patiently the return of the beautiful children - and return they did: every evening, as the sun set, they appeared, happily drifting out of the meadow, more and more and more of them.

So it went on: throughout the day, for hours on end, the prince would lie comfortably in the meadow, looking up at the flowers, at the sky, at the clouds, and at his own hands. Regularly, he dozed, and then drifted off to sleep......he lost track of time, as he slipped between consciousness and dreaming, as he wondered at the shape of everything, of every measurement and every proportion, he dwelled upon the fundamentals of existence, and upon too, his past. Perhaps it was because of his age that his mind turned so religiously to his history. Perhaps it was because he was home, at last, and after so many years absent, that he spent his hours, musing sadly and reflecting on his childhood: his youth had been so safe, and happily spent in the company of his father, his mother, and his grandparents. They had taught him about the world, and shown him all the simple things in it; he recalled the long walks with his grandfather in particular, who explained the workings of the planets, the orbits of the moons and suns, the names of the gods, and who revealed to him the light from the moon, the power of water-falls, and showed him which flower was which, which leaf fell from which tree, and which leaf might soothe stings from insidious nettles that grew alongside the paths that they frequented. If the prince drew his hand through many of those same flowers, he could not help but picture his family, their faces, their voices, and despite some harsher memories, he felt the loss of his family recede, and gradually he was warmed by the recollections.

But like a candle that burns down eventually to nothing, the memories of his family faded, the images lost their colour, and their distinctness, and with it, their power to infer - but the same could not be said of the prince's memories of the girl. If anything, the image of her face ingrained itself into his, like a stone in his heart: her red hair, her pale features, her eyes, her beautiful, beautiful eyes. As he had wandered he had been able to force his mind to think on other things, to imagine *other worlds, and invent fables and tales that avoided having to think too hard on her. But in the solitude of the meadow, as if induced by its somnambulant whispering, the memories flooded back. He therefore welcomed the distraction that the evening brought in the form of the children.*

The children although they played, did little else. It worried the prince. They were so unprepared, really. On occasion it rained, it was cold – yet the children had nothing else to wear it seemed, other than their light silky clothes. There was no shelter for them anywhere, and though they did not seem to mind inclement weather, the prince could see they shivered, and that they were made ill by their sneezing and coughing. Like the cuts and bruises they sustained, their illnesses did not seem to trouble them; nevertheless, the prince decided they should be better protected.

It brought some purpose to his day, and helped him ignore the nagging concerns that lingered in his mind concerning the girl. Bending some willow and more supple branches from the many poplars that peppered the meadow, the prince made some small rudimentary shelters. He covered them in leaves and flowers, and inside on the ground he made a covering of twigs and reeds. He was delighted that the children, when next they came, played in the shelters – he made more shelters, more and more of them, from other things left lying around: bits and pieces of timber, rope, metal, even glass. Every day he made more - he wished he could improve upon the things he built, he felt that they were never entirely good enough - but the delight the children showed spurred him on. That, and the hope that they might not abandon him - but like vampires fearful of the dawn, as the sun began to rise on the horizon, the children would gather their laden boxes and scurry back to the mountains.

Left alone, the prince set about building even more shelters, each one more elaborate than the last, hoping that his efforts might entice the children to stay – but they didn't. He tried to keep awake, longer into the night, and instead of playing games with the children, he tried to enlist their help. He made building a game, he even encouraged them to build things with their boxes: they built walls, and little rooms, and towers, trying to outdo each other, to see how high they could be built – and then howled cheerfully when they collapsed! Once they decided to box their 'king' in – he stood with his arms poking through 'windows' of their hastily and rather clumsily constructed 'room', and they ran around pulling on his fingers as he tried to grab them!

The prince tried to build with everything, but the more he built, the sadder he became – certainly that was how it seemed to the children – their 'king' though, did not notice. He was as consumed with this task, as he had been when he drew on walls of the slums......

All the time, as the prince worked with his hands, laying stones and building walls, and making roofs and floors and windows and doors, he never stopped wondering who they were, these children, where they lived, and why it was so necessary for them to return to the mountains, why they came to the meadow in the first place. One evening, after he had set alight the fire, he sat with one of the slightly older children, a girl with dark hair, and even darker eyes; eyes that were as dark as coal. He asked of her: why do you leave?

"It is not safe for us...," she replied, aimlessly pleating her long hair. The prince assumed that she meant it was not safe, the place they came from – but if that was the slums, then how so? "Not safe?" he asked.

"No..."

"But why is it not safe?"

"I don't know...no-one knows. We just have to leave......"

"But it is safe, during the day...?"

The girl looked confused. "No, no...well, sort of. It's safer than here."

The prince was shocked – for what harm could come to them in the meadow? The girl explained: "We might get lost..."

In the meadow, in the daytime? Now the prince was confused. "But you could get lost at night?" he said.

The girl burst out laughing. It attracted the attention of one of the others, a little boy, very like the girl, they could have been brother and sister - and when the girl explained what the prince had said, he too laughed. The prince didn't understand.

"Get lost at night?" they giggled. "You can't get lost at night! Everyone knows you can't get lost...in the dark!"

The prince still did not understand – but he let it go. Instead, he asked: "What is it like, this place that you go to?" He expected the girl to describe the slums as he remembered them – the place renewed, re-made, delightful and full of warmth - but what she said did not entirely align with his expectations. Somehow, it didn't seem quite accurate as to *how he recalled the slums, nor how the children behaved there.*

"It is fantastic," she said. "We can do what we like! We can make what we like, and break what we like..." The little boy joined in, equally as enthusiastic: "We can climb as high as we like, and run wherever we want..." They went on and on..."and we can do this...and we can do that..."

"It's just great," the little boy finally concluded, and the girl nodded. But something in their description still confused the prince. It seemed to be a much darker, grimmer place, and certainly they made no mention of any of the more beautiful aspects of the slums, as they were when the prince had left.

Despite this, the prince had no wish to visit the slums, no more than he had any compunction to visit any of the more recognisable remnants of the city. (Only on one occasion had he returned to the royal palace, but it was ruined, and depressingly empty.. He found some of his discarded belongings there, and some semblance of his regal past convinced him to collect his sword, which he had left unsheathed, and lying on the ground. Its blade was rusted and blunt, but he had taken it anyway.) He was content in the meadow, building shelters and playing with the children. He looked appealingly at the two sitting opposite him.

"If I could make a place, safe for you here, do you think you could stay?" he asked.

Suddenly the girl seemed worried – she looked fearfully at the mountains. The boy looked dubious too. "I don't know what you mean...," she said.

"If I could make the meadow...perhaps, more like...you know, where you are from?"

"But how could you?"

"Well, if perhaps I could see for myself, perhaps if I were to come with you-"

"No, no...you musn't come! You musn't!"

"But why not?"

"No-"

"But...just to see, for myself...?-"

"No – please, no." She was clearly very upset. The prince promised as asked: "OK," he said, reassuringly. But he had already made up his mind: he would see for himself, this wonderful place, which, if so wonderful necessitated the children having to abandon it every night...?'

But was it a flower? And how could it be - how could anything grow here?

Scene ii: The Peacock in the Ruins

'Early the following morning the prince set out in the direction of the nearest mountains. He took his sword – for some reason he felt the need, perhaps out of some precautionary instinct, perhaps to remind him of his princely status; it hung heavy on his hip, and jarred uncomfortably against his thigh as he walked.

The distance was further than it looked, and as the day wore on his legs began to ache; his age had caught up with him more than he realised. He persisted – but despite coming closer to the mountains they seemed to shrink further and further away – and then, all of a sudden, they were rising up in front of him, more enormous than appeared either natural or possible! He came closer still, until it became clear that they were not the same mountains upon which the slums had stood; they were not mountains at all, certainly not mountains recognisable as such: they were mountains...but mountains of ruins!

Black shattered walls of destroyed buildings towered high into the sky, they teetered overhead, defying gravity, slender and un-supported. Smoke trickled sadly between them – smoke, that the prince had thought rose from chimneys, instead, rising from smouldering ashes, and fires that burned all around; a stale sickly odour mingled with their acid and foul choking stench. Underfoot the ground was hot, and in places, blistering; charred timbers lay criss-crossed upon broken stones, bricks and rubble, here and there embellished by some broken yet recognisable shred of furniture or torn and burnt fabric.

Shocked, the prince could only stare. Were these the same slums that he had left, so delightfully transformed? The scarred and crumbling walls, their windows left hollow like holes in a skull, stared accusingly back at the prince, but gave no clue as to their origin, so stripped were they of their surface.

He had to know - with his eyes burning and his hand clutched across his mouth, the prince clambered through the ruins, looking for some sign of recognition, some sign of life - but it was impossible. There was nothing left, nothing other than the jagged broken walls and piles and piles of rubble and debris that obliterated everything - even where the streets might have been.

Exhausted, the prince eventually stopped to rest. He sat atop a pile of rubble - above, the shell of a tall building stood, without floors or roof, and open to the sky. A light rain, blackened by soot and dust, fell on him.

All of a sudden, a tiny figure flitted between a door-way, and then another! Further away, other figures appeared, jumping over the rubble, and disappearing again into the ruins. Children's voices echoed, giggling ecstatically and manically. Some stones tumbled down from somewhere overhead, the prince spun around, and then, a small child collided suddenly, right into him!

He looked down into the dark, dark eyes of the girl he had talked to – was it just the previous night? – at the fireside. He thought it was her; but she had been clean, and healthy, and happy...this one was dirty - filthy actually - her face was streaked in grime, her clothes ragged and blood stained.

She glared at him as he caught hold of her. Her eyes blazed into his. "You said you wouldn't come...," she said, almost snarling. Then she looked away, at once angry and apparently ashamed.

The prince shook his head. He couldn't believe this was the same girl. "What...happened to you?"

Mutely the girl shook her head; her tangled and matted hair fell across her face.

"What happened here? What happened to you?" the prince repeated. He tried to ask it as kindly as he could, but he was horrified, at the ruins, and at the girl too, struggling so furiously against his grip. "Let me go!" she hissed.

"But – ?" He looked at the girl, appealing for her help. But she just glared at him.

"You're no king," she said, bitterly.

It was not what the prince expected her to say. The girl, resigned that she could not break his grip, spat on the ground.

"No," admitted the prince, shaking his head, confused. "No, you know I'm not. My father-"

"Your father is dead."

The prince recognised the voice immediately – the creature! The shock of it caused him to relax his hold on the girl, and she took the opportunity, to pull out of his grip and scuttle away. For a second, the prince was reminded of the girl in the saucer....she had been dressed in *rags too...*

The creature repeated: "Your father is dead...," adding: "so, that makes you king, no?" It was nowhere to be seen, yet the creature's voice was clear and loud in the prince's ear. "Over here," it said. The prince looked, but all he could see were the charred remains, above and around him. He looked, again, and then he saw...a flower, a golden flower, like an eye, waving slightly in the air. But was it a flower? And how could it be - how could anything grow here? But then there was another flower, and then another...and then, stepping gingerly and gracefully through a window, the creature appeared: a glorious golden peacock! Its crystalline feathers, its 'flowers', were spread open and wide, and made crisp little clunking noises as it walked.

"Your father is dead," the creature reiterated, nonchalantly.

"How-?"

"How? How do you think – he died of a broken heart. You broke it, of course. But I wouldn't worry – comes to us all. Better to have your heart broken, than not to have it used at all, don't you think? And if he didn't care about you, he couldn't have died that way...take comfort in that, no? - take heart!" The creature laughed, a high squeaky laugh, and the prince felt a fury rise in him – he tried to run at the creature, to get hold of it, but he staggered and fell headfirst into the rubble.

"Now, now...that will never do. You're hardly being kingly in front of your subjects."

Subjects? The prince, his hands scratched and his face blackened, blinking saw that some children had gathered; cautiously, they peered at the prince, their pale dirty faces lit up like small grubby moons, silently watching. For a second, the prince thought he recognised the children, as the same children who had taunted him long, long ago - but how could that be?

He stood and tried to shake the dust off him. The creature had disappeared.

"Where are you!" the prince shouted.

"Right here," the creature replied politely, its words echoing from every direction. The prince spun, around and around.

"Here!" the creature sighed, impatiently.

Looking up, the prince saw the creature perched, cross legged in an open window. It was fixing its nails, and preening one of its long feathers. Its other feathers clattered against the stone of the wall. Some smudges of dust marred its otherwise glittering hide: it sparkled in the sunlight.

"I've had a bit of a make-over. What do you think?" It held a nail out in front of itself, admired it for a second, and then wiggled its other talons at the prince, smiling. To all intents and purposes, it was a peacock, it had the beak of a peacock, but its face was almost like that of a fox, and when it smiled, it bared teeth, gleaming as white as polished ivory.

If it hadn't been for the voice, the creature was unrecognisable – it was stunning, and yet it still had the most ridiculous long taloned toes, and equally as long nails, one of which was clearly broken.

"Oh, this place," it tutted, coughing slightly as a waft of smoke blew in its face. It waved the smoke away with an irritated shake of its tail feathers, and smiled again at the prince.

"Where is everyone?" the prince asked.

"Everyone?   – why, they are - underground!" The creature giggled. It slipped of its perch and floated down beside the prince. Strutting around him, it pulled on the prince's robe with its small beak, as if inspecting an unnecessary purchase.

"Come looking for your drippy girl-friend, have you?"

"No-"

"Now, now – be honest. Sure you have."

"No - I came... for them." He nodded towards the children.

"Really? Well, that was very noble of you."

The prince ignored the sarcasm.

"What do you mean – underground?" he asked. The creature, in turn, ignored him. "So – you think you can still save her?"

"I told you – I didn't come for her."

"Really...?" It picked again at the prince's robe. "You're older..." it observed, and added with a sneer: "...but no wiser!"

Again, the prince tried to overlook the creature's jibe. Suddenly though, the creature drew its face close up to his. "You think you can save her!?" it hissed. "Do you really think so? You couldn't save – them!" The creature twisted its long neck to face the gathered children. Some recoiled, fearfully. It turned its sharp mean gaze back at the prince. Its feathers bristled. "You...you, idiot," it said, derisively. It may look different, the prince thought, but aspects of the creature's erratic manner were clearly the same. He felt obliged to defend himself: "But-"

228

"But – what? Bet you think you did your best. You did your best? Your best wasn't good enough!"

Wasn't good enough? Images of the slums, made wonderful sprang into the prince's mind – but the stench from the ruins fogged his memory, confusing him. Were these slums and these ruins, truly, one and the same? Suddenly he felt desperately weary; he sat slowly down onto the rubble. "But, I did do my best..." He looked up at the creature, and at the children too. "I did..."

"Oh, don't start..." The creature clattered about on the rubble. "You just couldn't leave it alone, could you? Change this, change that – for what? For this? Look at it, look at it – ruins, ruins, can't you see? All that work, all that effort, and all that you made – was ruins!" The creature threw up its head and laughed. It floated back up into the air. "You did this. This is all your work! All of it! You're a king, and this is your kingdom: a king of infinite, empty space!" It laughed, even harder.

The prince couldn't understand what the creature meant. He struggled to take his eyes from the faces of the children who continued to stare blankly at him.

"They can't stay here...," he said quietly.

"But this is their home...your home. Our home! The home you made for us: home sweet home!"

"They can't stay..."

"Well, I doubt they'll leave - there's no place like home, you know. And anyway, where else would you suggest they go?"

"They could ...they could stay with me."

"Stay with you...? Where?"

"In...my father's city...?..."

Almost immediately, a cloud seemed to descend on the peacock creature. Its golden hue dissolved into a dark, dark green. It floated back down to where the prince sat, and whispered harshly, close into his face: "You are insane, aren't you? And what will happen to them there, do you think? You'll make some garden for them, or some palace or some other great city?" It shook its head. "Pathetic...," it said.

"But they can't live there, as it is....and they can't live here..."

"They are better off, here, now, than anywhere else."

"No."

"No? At least here, they know what here is. They know what this is, and this." The creature picked up pieces of broken rock and glass, and threw them back down again. "This is, what it is – what other fantasy could you make, better than this one?"

"But – there must be something better, than this..."

"Like your father's city?"

"Yes..."

"But your father is dead!" the creature screamed at the prince. "Dead! Don't you understand? Dead!"

The prince, stunned, fell pale. "Dead...?" he muttered.

"Yes: dead." The creature, all of a sudden, abandoned its anger; and said, kindly: "What did you think?"

The prince stared at the creature, and vaguely, shook his head.

"You didn't think, did you?" The creature sighed, then fluttered back up to its perch in the window, and began preening itself again.

The children didn't move, nor did the prince. They just stared at the prince – and the prince in return stared back, at their eyes, vacant and helpless. Finally he hung his head. "I did my best," he said.

The creature sniggered. "There you go again, idiot....I give up."

For a while they said nothing. But then the creature said: "Well, ok, I have to admit – your best wasn't bad, I suppose."

The prince looked up, surprised at the creature's compliment. It shook its head though, smiling sadly and indicating the ruins all about them: "But your best is as good as it gets..."

Again, and for a while longer they said nothing. Darkness began to fall. The prince hoped the children would leave, that they would return to the meadow – but somehow he doubted it. He could hear them, in the dark, breathing, ever so softly. Throughout the night, great flashes appeared in the sky, and for no apparent reason some of the ruins collapsed. In the morning, there didn't seem to be so many children.

For the remainder of the day, nothing much happened – the peacock creature preened itself, endlessly, sitting high on its perch; the children hid motionless in the shadows, as the prince sat, immobile on the rubble, his head in his hands. The things the creature had said – were they true? Was this the best he could do? Was this, all this ruination, the result, the consequence even, of his efforts? And was it true, that these children, were destined, indeed, doomed to stay in this terrible place?

'I did my best,' he told himself, over and over: 'I did my best – can I, or can't I, do any better?' The question plagued him, it defeated him, and he would have stayed there indefinitely if the creature hadn't *interrupted his desperate and pointless musings.*

That night, as the moon rose overhead, he heard the creature sigh. "Still got weepy drawers on your mind, have you?"

The prince was inclined to deny it – but the creature carried on before he had the opportunity: "OK - I can take you to her...if you want."

The prince wasn't sure if he'd heard the creature correctly.

"Your drippy girl-friend. I can take you to her."

"Where...?"

The creature shook its head. "No, no," it said. "I can't tell you that. But I'll take you, if you want. I'll take you...but if I take you, I can't bring you back."

The prince nodded almost immediately, but the creature slowly, repeated itself: "I can't bring you back," it said, pointedly.

Mutely, the prince nodded. "Come on...," the creature clucked, and clipped away. The prince followed. He couldn't bring himself to look at the children who silently watched them go.'

The artist could not help herself. Horrified, she said angrily: "He just left them? How could he do that?" She stared accusingly at the king. "How?" she demanded.

The king said nothing; eventually the artist turned away. Her anger boiled inside her - she grabbed her brushes and began to paint – suddenly it came easier. Away went the soft delicate lines of the sketches, the bold and regal colours. She painted over what she had done with dark thick lines, lines that did not allow for any kindliness whatsoever; mean lines for a mean face.

Stubbornly she painted, and did not look up once; not once. Throughout the night, the king lay prone and silent as she frantically swept her brush thrashing brutally across the canvas. She wanted it finished, finished and done, so she could leave. It was with some frustration that the king began the account once again – she tried to ignore him, and painted furiously as he spoke.

She did not notice that the king had been crying. Nor did she notice that she painted in complete darkness......

A hazy mist clung to the ground, like clouds that had deigned to bring down to earth, the distilled secrets of their existence.

Scene iii: The Valley Beyond

'When they reached the edge of the ruins, the prince turned: suddenly, he was flooded with regret.

"I want to go back," he said. The creature shook its head, disparagingly.

"But of course you do...," it sneered, dismissively.

"I want to go back." The prince was adamant. "Take me back," he demanded.

"I'd love to...but I can't. See?" It indicated behind, and there was nothing there, save for the peacocks feathers: eyelets in their millions stared at the prince.

"I told you...you can't go back. You can only go forwards..."

"But I have to go back!" the prince said. He pushed at the colossal wall of feathers, but they did not budge.

"This way," the creature said.

Regretfully the prince turned. The creature tutted: "Not that way!" It tutted again. "You are such an idiot," it said. "This way!" It nudged the prince - its feathers were everywhere. The prince was confused. "Go on!" the creature insisted. Still confused, the prince pushed against the feathers. They barely moved. "Go on!" the creature shouted. "Go on!" The prince pushed harder, and suddenly the feathers parted and he tumbled through them!

Like sometimes in a dream, scenes shift from location to location without reason or logic, in an instant the prince was transported - to the most beautiful place he had ever seen.

Getting to his feet, he found he was standing on one side of a valley, of the most lush and glorious green; it spread itself flatly down in front of him, broadening out to meet a lake that glittered with a brilliance eternally charitable, and which reflected overhead a sky of the most intense and unbearable blue. He had to shade his eyes, so brightly did the sun shine and sparkle off the waters' serene surface; some birds twittered sweetly overhead, but otherwise it was silent, as majestically silent as the magnificent forest of trees that stood, impossibly tall and *slender on the far side of the valley, a forest that disappeared into an inviting darkness, and that sloped away above and behind as well.*

A hazy mist clung to the ground, like clouds that had deigned to bring down to earth, the distilled secrets of their existence. They parted willingly as the prince took a step forward - and then stopped.

"Where am I?" he wondered aloud.

He had expected the creature to answer, but it did not. He was alone. It was only his own voice that echoed back to him from across the valley - but his voice was changed, it sounded metallic, and strange, as if recorded. The words too were changed: 'Where are you?' *they said. The prince was confused. "Here?" he said.* 'Hear,' *his 'other' voice answered, and for a split second the valley disappeared, and in its stead, was the white saucer in the plain! It was only for a second, and so briefly that the prince could hardly believe it happened at all. But somehow, the valley, yes, the valley was familiar. Its shape, its form...like a saucer......the prince felt an anxiety rise up inside him. The girl...what about the girl?*

"Where...is she?" he asked, nervously.

'Here...she is,' *his 'other' voice replied.*

"Where?"

'There.'

The king looked, and finally saw – in the distance, on the valley floor, the vaguest of reflections. It was difficult to discern exactly where it began and where it ended, but, yes - yes, it was there: a blimp in the landscape, as if nature was slightly out of sync.

He moved around a little to be sure. Yes, there was no question...it was there: a box...a box of mirrors: the Mirror Machine.

He stood, transfixed for a second, and then tramped slowly, almost hypnotised, down the side of valley. The valley floor swam more deeply in the mist – it swirled in eddies about him as he came closer to the Mirror Machine. If it had been 'broken' before, it was no longer: reflections of the landscape glowed sharp and clear back at the prince, as did his own reflection, mystified and fearful.

How could this be?

He swallowed hard, and then reached out to touch the machine, to convince himself that what he was seeing was, in fact, true – its' cool surface yielded hard against his palm. He walked all around it, its corners snapping the landscape around as he did so – it was difficult to discern what was real and what was reflected. His own image too, revealed itself to him, in parts sometimes, and sometimes whole.

He became disorientated, and the malevolence that he had once felt emanating from the machine, suddenly overwhelmed him.

He almost whimpered: "But – I destroyed you!"

'But I destroyed – you!' *his 'other' voice echoed back.*

And then he heard: weeping, weeping, distant, and hollow, as if coming from inside a long, long tunnel. He pressed his ear up against the machine – the weeping was coming from inside...!

It was not in rage that the prince then swung his sword, but in desperation; he had to free her – he swung hard, as hard as his tired limbs would allow - but his sword simply went through the Mirror Machine! It did not shatter as he had expected; he swung, again, as hard as he could, his blunt and rusted weapon – surely the mirror must shatter! But it did not. Instead, slivers of mirror slipped cleanly down, and fell at the prince's feet - it was as if he were slicing through the landscape itself!

He swung again and again, and his sword sliced through the mountains, it sliced through the trees, through the lake, through the mist, even through the sky! Long smooth shards of mirror, austere and antiseptically liberated, coloured in shades of green and blue fell all about the prince; each one, hosting within its surface a sliver of the landscape, piled up to the prince's knees, piled up to his waist – and in their place gashes of white appeared, as if each slash was revealing a blank canvas!

Relentless, the prince swung and swung, until eventually, the landscape was gone! All around was white, except for the prince's own reflection, as large as life, sad, exhausted and dejectedly looking back at him.

There was no sign of the girl.

He rested his head against his own, reflected on the cool mirrored surface, his sword hanging loosely in his hand. Deep from within, he could still hear weeping, distant, but undiminished in its woe.

"I destroyed you...," he said again, his uncertainty plainly evident in the utterance.

'I destroyed you...,' *dispassionately, his 'other' voice repeated. It provoked the prince then to anger: he shouted: "I will destroy you!", and catching his breath, he lifted his sword and swung: off came his own head! He swung again: off came his arms! Again, and off came his torso, his legs, his feet!*

He swung and swung, and as antiseptically lacerated as the

235

landscape beforehand, his body, in tiny bits, lay captured in shards of mirrored glass.

Finally, the prince, wearied from his efforts, fell down. He lay, gulping for breath, his sword lying prone beside him.

The weeping continued, but jaggedly, interrupted - broken – the prince lolled in the mirrored fragments, as sharp, broken and shattered as the pitiful weeping.

"Where are you? Where are you?" he called out, weakly, in a gasp of desperation

But the weeping just continued, and then, there was a whirring sound, a click, and the weeping stopped.

And with it, so did gravity ......

Instantly, the prince was drifting in a pitch white sky, peppered by black stars; the shards of mirror, like satellites, floated by, orbiting him.

He touched them with his fingertips and they melted away, they formed themselves into clusters, and fell away again, they attached themselves to him, clung to him, hugged him, crawled over him, they poured out of his fingers, from out of his toes, from out of his mouth, and his eyes. Becoming lines, they spun out - and wrapped themselves tightly around him, they tied him up and then spiralled away again; he twisted, he turned, in hurdles and whirls he fell ; whether he fell, up or down he could not tell, he was spinning in the white sea of blackened stars and shards of sparkling mirror, of:

orange and ......

yellow and .....

purple and ....

green and ...

blue and ..

red and .

...then:

Faster and faster, the kaleidoscope of colours span!

Whispering, and laughing, colours caressed the prince, they fluttered through his hair...and became soft and gently, shapes; they formed, they disappeared again, strange, indescribable forms......and such patterns were revealed, in colours too strange to name!

And - suddenly! With an ungainly and painful:

'THUMP!', the prince crashed, senseless, back onto the meadow!

Seconds later, like frozen rain, the shards of mirror clattered down all about him......'

It drifted as if willingly subservient to the ebb and flow of the tides, rather than to the perfunctory forces of gravity and inertia.

Scene iv: The Maker in the Mirror

The last thing the prince might have expected was to be licked sloppily across the face. With his head aching, carefully he put up his hands, expecting to push the dog off him – but it wasn't a dog. He sat up and opened his eyes; whatever it was had floated quickly away. Absently, it floated back towards him: a creature, like a horse, but emaciated and with the colouring of a zebra. Its mane was made of long, twisting strands of luminous fibres, blurring in and out; the whole creature floated, upright, conversely - it should have stood upon all fours; it drifted as if willingly subservient to the ebb and flow of the tides, rather than to the perfunctory forces of gravity and inertia.

More like a sea creature than beast or fowl, the zebra fish settled its two hind legs benignly on the dry land of the meadow, poised like an uninvited, but lauded guest nonetheless; large dark and intelligent eyes regarded the prince, apparently with affection. When it spoke, its' voice, though gentle, sweet and almost feminine, was familiar – it was the creature, most certainly – but it was obviously bereft if its insolence and irascible inconsistency.

"Did you really think she would be there?" it asked, politely as it rummaged one of its watery hooves through the shards of mirror.

The prince was inclined to argue, but in truth he had to agree: "No," he admitted. The creature nodded its horse like head appreciatively, the tendrils of its long mane swirling about as if performing some extraordinary ballet; its tail swished as dreamily as a feather blown by the breeze. It went back to aimlessly shifting the shards about.

"The children will be back soon," it said.

"The children...?" The prince was surprised.

"Yes – the children," confirmed the creature.

The prince, shamefully, looked away. "They...they think of me as their king." He said it as if it were a confession, and at the same time, an acceptable admission of failure, spoken in confidence to this creature that was all of a sudden, so...approachable, unlike the creatures beforehand – it would surely both acknowledge and forgive the prince, his shortcomings.

But if the prince had hoped for support of his abdication of responsibility, he was wrong. The creature, instead, asked: "But, are you not, their king?"

"No...no, my father is king."

"But your father is dead?"

The prince, at the abruptness of the utterance, was hurt by the words - but the creature held no malice in its big dark eyes. It trailed some of its flittering fibres kindly over the prince's face.

"You are, presumably, the rightful king now?" it added, respectfully.

Just for an instant, the prince felt a surge of joyful acceptance sweep through him – but then it was gone. Despondently, he looked away and hung his head. He picked up his rusted sword. It was bent, and covered in ragged gouges. "I don't think I can fix this," he said. He dropped the sword, and distractedly lifted up some of the shards of mirror. He tried to piece some of them together. "I don't think I can fix any of this...," he said, sadly.

The creature tapped him lightly on the shoulder.

"The children-?"

The prince, letting the pieces of mirror fall, held out his hands in subjugation. "I cannot help them...," he said.

"But they do need help, do they not?"

"Yes," the prince agreed, "yes, yes, they do – but I cannot help them. I did my best, and my best resulted – in all this." He waved his hand around, at the meadow, at the remains of the city, at the mountains of smouldering ruins in the distance.

Again, the creature trailed its fibres across the king's face.

"Well, if not you, who then?"

Gently, it pulled the prince's head up. It said kindly: "Is it not better to do something, than to do nothing?" Its colouring of black and white stripes shifted gradually their tones, one to the other. The prince said nothing; he remained slumped, sitting on the ground, his rusted sword dangling once again from his hand.

The zebra fish creature, suddenly, with one of its lolling slippery fibrous tongues, slapped the prince across the face!

The prince looked back, startled. Pulling the sword from the prince's hand, with another tendril the creature waved a shard of the mirrored glass at him: it floated dreamily in front of the prince's eyes; the

240

creature lifted up more of the shards - each one held a reflection of the landscape or the prince's own body. They merged in and out of each other, each image, each reflection, appearing as if to float one through the other.

"This material ... is interesting, is it not?" said the creature.

The prince was entranced, as the creature repeated itself: "I said: it is an interesting material...what if you could make anything with it? Make anything you like - anything, perhaps, that you cared to imagine?"

The creature dropped one tiny shard lightly into the prince's palm. Reflecting on its surface was a leaf.

"What would you have me make out of this, for example?" it said.

"Make?" the prince asked.

"Yes, make...what would you have me make, out of this leaf?"

The prince was confused, he shook his head – but the creature nodded encouragingly.

"What would you wish a leaf to be?" it said.

The prince shook his head again. Hesitantly, he finally suggested: "Eh – a forest?"

With a snap of its tendril, like a whip, the zebra fish threw the shard to the prince's feet – there was a 'CRACK!', a flash of light, and there, in its place was a tiny, tiny forest! The prince could hardly believe what he was seeing – he squinted down to look. Though miniscule, it was in every way, without question, a forest! In awe, he looked up at the creature.

"You didn't tell me what size you wanted," it said, smiling.

The prince stared at the creature, and back again at the tiny forest. He picked up another shard of mirror. Turning it gently between his fingers, he said slowly: "What kind of material is this?"

"I suspect it is a material that does not yet exist...," explained the zebra fish creature.

But the prince hardly heard what the creature said – he continued to stare deep into the shard as if it were the most precious thing he had ever seen.

"And you can make...anything with it?" he whispered. "Anything...?"

"Yes – anything. I should think so."

The prince felt that same surge of joy sweep through him, and with it a passion unlike any ever known. Keenly, he asked: "Could it make - a shelter?"

"A shelter? - for sure," the creature replied.

"A house?"

"A house – most certainly a house."

"A city?"

"A city? Why not?" The creature smiled again. "And if you were to make a city, what would this city of yours be like?" it asked.

Enthused, the prince began to speak, to tell the creature of the city that he had imagined, whilst he had wandered, all those years ago – a city that would provide for everyone, that would be comfortable, and above all else: safe. "I know I would be defended," the prince confided. "If I found myself to be lost, I would be content to be lost, knowing that I would be found - I would know that I would arrive, or if continuing, know where I was going. It would be a city - that would raise spirits beyond the accustomed, it would inspire, it would make all who lived, able to be more, and it would comfort when any failed. It would house - us, all of us, and it would allow for us, us, its people, to be enriched without recourse to false expectation. It would secure for us, the balance, of the desire for the things we have, and have not, and satisfy us - this impossible contradiction: it would be a city, radiant, a fantastic reality, fixed and perpetually changing, as we change with it."

Breathlessly the prince expounded on his vision, and then told the creature, of everything he had tried to make before - and in that instant, at the memory of his father's city, wrecked, of the slums, transformed, then destroyed, his passion deserted him. Everything he had made had become ruined...deflated, he sat back down – but the creature waved its tendrils at him, and lifted him gently back up.

"One thing at a time," it suggested. "Tell me, in a word, what do you need this city to be?"

The prince sighed, and muttered something. The creature lifted his head..."What was that?" it asked. "I did not hear..."

"Perfect...," the prince repeated. "It needs to be perfect."

"Well, let's see...what would a perfect city be like?"

The prince shook his head again – almost reluctantly he said: "It would need to be...full...commodious..."

"Yes, yes, I understand...and is that all?"

"No, no - It would need to be...secure...firm..."

242

The prince's voice grew stronger.

"Yes, I see ...and...?"

The prince paused, and then replied, his voice, though trembling, certain: "It would need to be...beautiful...it would need to be...delightful," he said.

The zebra fish creature thanked him. "Yes, of course," it said, and it shook its watery mane. With a quizzical nod, it presumed: "...and you wouldn't want this city to be subject to the vagaries of nature, would you? Forever at the mercy of the extremities of recalcitrant seasons? You wouldn't want it drowned in needless tidal waves, or to fall into the cracks in the earth from some senseless earthquake, or buried in ash from some pointless eruption? You wouldn't want that, would you? You wouldn't want it susceptible to such mindless folly or disaster?"

Categorically: "No", the prince concurred. He smiled, hesitantly. The creature smiled openly back.

"Well, then - we have no need these." And with that, the creature gathered up all the shards that held reflections of the landscape, and with a wave of its tendrils, and with a 'SNAP', whipped them to the ground; they vanished in multiple flashes, with 'CRACKS!' of green and blue and red and orange and purple and yellow, and all the other colours of the rainbow! The prince couldn't help himself – he clapped with almost childish enthusiasm!

In turn, the creature stretched its tendrils out warmly to the prince, and wrapped them loosely around him.

"Shall we make a city that is better than nature...?" it whispered, seductively into the prince's ear. "Shall we? Shall we make a city that can love, rather than a city that needs to be loved?"

"Yes, yes," the prince willingly conceded. "But how...how can we?"

"You don't need to ask, nor wonder: 'how?' It is easy - you need only wish it, and it will be so." The creature, with more tendrils, lifted the remaining shards. "And we have everything we need...," it added. It held out a shard; reflected on it was the prince's eyes.

"So what kind of city would you wish me to make with these?" it said.

The prince hesitated.

"Tell me," the creature prompted. "Tell me."

After another moment's hesitation, the prince said, softly:

243

"Take my eyes...and make a city full of reflection, reflections without inflection and transparent and have nothing to left to hide; take my eyes and make a city, without windows: without deception, without lies!"

"And what kind of city would you wish me to make with these?" The creature held out another shard, and on it was reflected the prince's ears.

He said: "Take my ears...and make a city full of note, notes that are harmonious, are forever tender and never out of tune; take my ears and make a city, without doors: without discord, without fears!"

"And what kind of city would you wish me to make with this?" The creature held out another shard, and on it was reflected the prince's nose.

He said: "Take my nose...and make a city full of growth, growths that are perfumed, that never rot, nor waste, nor foul, erode; take my nose and make a city, without decorations: without decay, without decompose!"

"And what kind of city would you wish me to make with this?" The creature held out another shard and on it was reflected the prince's mouth.

He said: "Take my mouth...and make a city full of breath, breaths that are immortal, as deep as every ocean, and as clean as rain; take my mouth and make a city, without roofs: without disease, without drought!"

"And what kind of city would you wish me to make with these?" The creature held out another shard, and on it was reflected the prince's arms.

He said: "Take my arms...and make a city full of embrace, embraces that refute empty spaces in between, and put nothing out of reach; take my arms and make a city, without walls: without annulment, without alarms!"

"And what kind of city would you wish me to make with these?" The creature held out another shard, and on it was reflected the prince's hands.

He said: "Take my hands...and make a city full of welcome, welcomes that are hearty, hale, and most important: long - and always pleased to meet; take my hands and make a city, without streets: without duplicity, without misunderstands!"

244

"And what kind of city would you wish me to make with these?"
The creature held out another shard, and on it was reflected the prince's legs.

He said: *"Take my legs...and make a city full of fact, facts that are just so, doubtlessly secure, doubt denied and doubly twice as sure; take my legs and make a city, without columns: without bearing, without begs!"*

"And what kind of city would you wish me to make with these?"
The creature held out another shard, and on it was reflected the prince's feet.

He said: *"Take my feet...and make a city full of memory, memories that are mobilised, freed to rise from friction and walk away from any bitter strife; take my feet and make a city, without foundations: without dissension, without defeat!"*

"And what kind of city would you wish me to make with these?"
The creature held out another shard, and on it was reflected the prince's lungs.

He said: *"Take my lungs...and make a city full of smile, smiles that are sincere, and cannot be retracted, by any race or creed or gender or colour, or any freakish rogue; take my lungs and make a city, without cathedrals: without territories, without tongues!"*

"And what kind of city would you wish me to make with this?"
The creature held out another shard, and on it was reflected the prince's stomach.

He said: *"Take my stomach...and make a city full of passion, passions that are fulsome, enriched to swallow poverty, plague, possession, or any other possible pollution; take my stomach and make a city, without palaces: without corruption, without luck!"*

"And what kind of city would you wish me to make with this?"
The creature held out another shard and on it was reflected the prince's brain.

He said: *"Take my brain...and make a city full of wonder, wonders that are wonderful: wonders to behold: do not destruct, do not construct, do not instruct; take my brain and make a city, without universities: without claims, without insane!"*

"And what kind of city would you wish me to make with these?"
The creature held out another shard and on it was reflected the prince's lips.

He said: "Take my lips...and make a city full of kiss, kisses that are invincible, that linger and do not refuse, remorse, repeat, or repeal; take my lips and make a city, without courts: without evidence, without eclipse!"

The tendrils of the zebra fish spun round, slowly, and then faster and faster - the shards sparkled like a firecracker - and then slowed, and stopped. The creature picked up one of three remaining shards.

"And what kind of city would you wish to make with this?" On the shard was reflected the prince's mind.

The prince paused for a second, then said: "Take my mind...and make a city full of thought, thoughts that never necessitate, without words, without pictures, without references; take my mind and make a city, without squares: without define, without confined!"

The creature picked up the penultimate shard. "And what kind of city would you wish to make out of this?" On it was reflected the prince's soul.

The prince paused, again, and for quite for a while. Then he said: "Take my soul...and make a city full of one, ones together, not in pairs - where there is no life, and therefore, death is lost; take my soul and make a city, without homes: without rock, without roll!"

The creature smiled. It lifted the final shard, and handed it to the prince: "And tell me - what do you wish to make with this?" it said.

On the shard was reflected the prince's heart. He took it and turned it between his fingers – the shard throbbed, warm and soft. Quietly he said: "Take my heart...and make a city full of love, love...and that is all: take my heart and make a city, without corners: without others, without...apart." He held on to the shard, briefly, before handing it back.

The creature's tendrils then grew, swayed, turned and spun and like a curtain across the world, they closed, and then parted. With a tremendous: 'CRACK!', the creature cast the shards to the ground, each one exploded in a cavalcade of noise and light, a display of fireworks that accumulated one upon the other until the prince and indeed the world was obscured by the intensity of it!

When at last it was over, when at last every shard had been transformed by its brilliant consummation, when at last the zebra fish creature lowered its innumerable tendrils – there: was the city.

It floated, hovering above the meadow......ablaze with a light as if made of air, and breathing, with air as if made of light.

A city made, as if day and night, and black and white had combined to make it so......
    "Is this what we meant?" the creature asked.
    But the prince could not answer – for his eyes were unable to comprehend the beauty, unable to accommodate the absolute perfection of a city that glowed, as commodious, firm and delightful as he had wished it, made real in front of him.'

"I don't understand any of this," the artist muttered. The king said nothing – "I don't understand," she repeated. Paint splattered across the canvas.

    She turned and glowered at the king, whose indistinct face was barely recognisable in the gloom of the early morning light: "It doesn't make any sense," she insisted. In frustration she threw more paint at the canvas.

    The king, in a quiet voice, said: "Some things don't."

    "Don't! Don't what!?" the artist exclaimed angrily. She'd had enough of the king's cryptic comments. "Don't what!?" she demanded again.

    Paint splashed everywhere.

    "Some things don't make - sense," the king said, eventually. "Some things make no sense whatsoever."

    "Like this..." She waved her hand around, at her painting, at the palace, at the king. She glared at the king.

    "Like this tale?" the king offered.

    "Yes, yes! It's nonsense!" Suddenly aware of her status, she regretted her outburst. "I'm sorry," she apologised. "I'm sorry...my king." She went to kneel – but the king held out his hand. Confused, the artist hesitated – but the king nodded, she took it – and the king patted the back of her paint stained fingers.

    "What do you do, when nothing makes any sense?" the king said kindly to her. "You could be forgiven for doing nothing, could you not?"

    The artist, still deeply ashamed, hung her head.

"But what then?" the king asked.

The artist stayed silent. Kindly yet, the king asked her again: "What then?"

Eventually the artist looked up. "Do...something?" she said, quietly.

"Yes – do something, anything...perhaps, do everything."

The king nodded towards the portrait, covered in every colour imaginable.

He smiled.

"Sometimes you just have to try everything you can – and maybe then, sense will come?"

Doubtfully, the artist nodded. She hung her head again.

The king lifted her face up. Looking into her tired eyes, he said: "Shall we see?"

The artist stared, mute – as the king repeated himself: "Shall we see?" he insisted.

"I don't understand," she replied.

"Shall we see?"

The king's voice had dropped to a whisper, and suddenly, once more: sadness overwhelmed him. Tears formed in his eyes, and in that instant, the artist understood, as the king – *her* king, a king so strong, so wise, so regally assured; so much in every way, attributed with everything a king should be - pleading, almost begging, thinly whispered again:

"Shall we see?"

"Yes," she said, "yes!"

Trembling, and struggling to hold back her own tears, she reached out, and put her other hand gently over his; in a voice as calm as she could muster, reassuringly, and with as much conviction as she could, she repeated: "Yes – yes, we shall. We shall see."

It was some time before the king stopped crying, and was able to resume.

When he did, his colour was brighter, his eyes, clearer, his voice, stronger.

Much, much stronger.

As each ruin fell, a black mist appeared, consolidating into strands of fibres as if pulled out from the very depths of the earth;

Scene v: The Ashes of Love

'So blinded was he, the prince had to wait for the children to come, to hold his hand as he stepped up from the meadow onto the city. At first he thought they had lifted him, his whole body onto its surface – it felt like thousands of tiny hands held him. But the children's delighted voices scattered away, like notes fading in the wind, and he realised that what he stood upon was a surface, unique, unknown, and unbelievable. The soles of his bare feet were perfectly supported, the surface moulding to the shape of his sole, to its every contour; and with every step, propelling him easily along.

He followed no direction, but rather, allowed himself to be guided through the city – occasionally hands touched him, helping him, but on the whole he felt as if he was following some sort of invisible thread which steered him willingly forwards. Vague shapes, and tones, and colours that he did not recognise washed in front of his blurred vision. They were indistinguishable, but marked out nonetheless, perfectly as if measured by some harmonic scale, familiar but long, long forgotten.

As he walked, children's voices swam by him, laughing – he called out to them: what is it like? But he could not fully understand their replies, only that their voices were pitched to a sound more delightful than anything the prince had ever heard. He might have been disorientated and made dizzy by it all, by the strange sights and unusual sounds, but he wasn't. He felt surfaces press kindly in on him, he drifted with them, and when his legs tired, a seat formed beneath him, and he sat comfortably down.

Children skipped hazily by. He could hardly see them, they were little more than indistinct shapes, shadows even, but he heard them clearly, all the time laughing. He called to them again: what is it like? But he did not need their answers – he could sense their pleasure, their joy, and it so filled his heart he thought it might burst. Some semblance of his memory invaded his mind, interrupting his delight; he thought, momentarily, that he waited for the night to come – the expectation that the children would leave, briefly haunted him. But they did not – night did not come, nor day.

251

The passage of time seemed to have lost its capacity to harm, to age, to forget – and, its capacity to render darkness: the city was made of a radiance that pervaded everything! The prince, despite his inhibited sight, could sense the truth of it: there might be days, there might be nights, but there would be no diminishment of light.

He sat for a while, and listened to the city breathe in and out around him: later it became colder, and the city shrank to cover him as if it were a beautiful coat, and when it became warmer, the city spread itself wide, and cool breezes washed over him.

He sat for a while longer, and discovered that no two days were the same, and that in no two days was the city the same, and yet it was the city still.

He sat for a while longer yet, resting against a surface, a surface that he knew, held within it the power to hear and to forgive – for it was not a victim of gravity. It floated, as if drawing the ground upwards, as opposed to resting obligatory on it, one thing on top of another; suppliant, the surface consoled him, even of ills he knew not that he had. If he fell, he knew this surface would catch him – though he doubted that any would ever fall in this city. There would be no need, no need whatsoever - he called out: are there are no cathedrals, no palaces, no universities, no courts? No-one answered, but he did not need to hear. He knew it to be true – even though he could not see, he could see in his mind: structures of unquestionable purpose, their forms perfect to their function, and as such, formless.

He sat for a while longer, much longer yet, waiting for the flames to begin, the destruction - for it must surely be so, for there must be want - he called out: is there no gold here, no diamonds or coins or value of any kind? His voice disappeared as if his breath had turned into air.

He sat for a while longer, much, much longer yet. All the time, the children came and went, the shapes and tones and colours too - at one point a child appeared, more clearly, in front of him. It was the small boy he had talked to at the fireside. He was smiling. The prince smiled back. His sister appeared beside him, also smiling. Neither was pale any more, but rosy cheeked and red faced. They ran off, holding hands - but before they disappeared into the haze, the prince called out to them.

"The corners...," he said. They stopped, and turned. He hesitated, and then asked: "What is it like, when you go round a corner?"

The little girl shook her head. "What - what is a...corner, my king?" she said, confused. The prince smiled. "Never mind," he said. Cheerfully, she pulled the boy away, and they ran off, laughing.

He sat for a while longer, even longer yet. His heart seemed to slow, to almost freeze between one beat and the next, and the hope that lay in the space blossomed, it swelled and filled the place where he sat. He knew that here, in this city, there would be no waste, no pain, no suffering, no loss... and that there would be no place for ruins here, not now nor would there ever be – we won't get fooled again, he thought, and no need to pray for it either; we will not make mistakes – we will not need to learn, nor wonder, of what went before and think nostalgically upon it; there would be no beauty found in ruins, for there would be none!

But then: the image of the ruins, smouldering on the horizon, stirred the prince's mind, and with it, the image of the girl, the girl from the plain, lost in the maze of the slums, abandoned there by his hand. The memory fell like a stone upon him. He sat for a while longer, and then could sit no more. His longing for her, his loss, his love, it overflowed – the desire to see her so overwhelmed him, it obliterated the knowledge that she was dead. She's dead, he knew it, but the loss troubled, and confounded his reason. Having created a city so full of perfection despite his previous failures – suddenly he had hope, but he would never know if he did not know, for certain.

He had to look for her.

The meadow felt strange beneath his feet when he once again stepped down upon it. It took a while for him to become re-accustomed to the earth – it was not helped that his vision was blurred, and remained so. He attributed it to the glow from the city - it seemed to have enveloped everything. It even seemed to speak to him.

"She's not there," the city said, in response to the prince's obvious intentions. Or was it the creature? It was hard to tell.

"I know," he replied. "But I must try - and anyway, my work is not done." He looked about for the creature...some shapes, which looked like the zebra fish, floated around in his head.

"Will you accompany me?" he asked.

"You don't need me for this," the creature - or was it the city? – said. It, the city, smiled, though the prince did not see it smile: his eyes were blurred.

The city creature nodded – "You are an idiot," it said, politely.

The prince took it as a compliment. He gathered the city up and dropped it into his satchel.

The journey to the ruins was long and arduous, and made worse that the ground held a resistance within it – but the prince, even allowing for his age, had endured worse. And he was inspired by his own resolve: to finish what he had started. He sensed the creature alongside him, neither helping, nor hindering. He was grateful for the latter.

Eventually, the ruins appeared – they rose up in the distance as they had before – but as the prince approached they faded, they became transparent, and shrank the nearer he came to them. They became smaller still, smaller and smaller and smaller: eventually the ruins sat at the prince's feet like ant hills, tiny, tiny ant hills, that with a gentle wave of his hand, indeed, even with a gentle breath, crumbled. As each ruin fell, a black mist appeared, consolidating into strands of fibres as if pulled out from the very depths of the earth: the tiny anthills, like the mountains, dissolved, and turned into a black poisonous mass: and the city of ruins rose up, and stood towering once again over the prince!

But they no longer smouldered – they were almost barren, cleaned of all rubble and debris - all that remained were the bare bones of the walls. Even the streets were distinguishable, but unmarked and clean as if they had been diligently swept.

For a second the prince faltered.

"Did you think it was going to be that easy?" the creature whispered in his ear.

The prince whispered back: "No." But his resolve was certain – he pulled the city from his satchel, clutching it glowing in his fist, he swept his hand against a wall – and the wall was torn down, silently, and disappeared. He did the same to the next, and the next – and with each corner that he turned, he hoped that she would be there. But his hope did not cause him to hesitate, he strode through the ruins, wiping away every ragged wall, and paused only when one last corner was left standing; one ruined remnant. Only then did he stop, and allow himself to wish: that she would be there waiting for him.

But as soon as he drew his hand trembling through the blackened ruin, he knew: "She's not there," he said to himself.

And he was correct. She was not there...and neither, any longer, were the ruins...

The journey back to the city was easy – for in fact the city had come with them, he and the creature both, whose shadowy figure was barely distinguishable in the city's impenetrable light. It blinded the prince – he tried to retreat from it, but there was nowhere else to go.

He stepped back onto the city's miniature undulating surface, and felt the city hug him his grief...for so much had been lost: his father, his father's city, his people, his hopes, his future, his princess...everything, lost.

He slept, and tried to dream his grief away.

He woke; a child's face appeared in front of his, then another, and then another. Small hands were gently shaking him. Gradually more children gathered round: a tiny voice asked: "Are you sad, my king?"

The prince, though still faint from his stupor, knew he had never felt before, such incomprehensible happiness. Such euphoria......

"Are you in pain?"

"Why, no..." The prince was confused.

"Why then, do you weep, my king?"

The prince put his hand to his cheek, and only then did he realise – it was by tears that he was blinded. They fell continually from his eyes, and apparently they had done so for some time – but since when? He could not be sure. Perhaps when he had first stepped onto the city? Had he wept at it, then, had he wept ever since? Apparently.

But he wasn't sad - he wept, though, none the less.

"We don't like it when you cry," the children said......and so their 'king' tried his best to hold back his tears, to protect the children, that they might not worry.

It was, however, impossible.

They cared for him, and they refused to leave him be. He tried to explain: "I cannot live in this city, this city that I have made. It is too...bright." But his words, he knew, were feeble, and did not properly convey how he truly felt. He did not want to leave - but he could not stay. He wandered through the city of his own making crying, pathetic - the embarrassing 'king', who continually weeps. It was shameful, and caused the 'king' to seek, continually, shelter, somewhere to hide away...but the city would not let him......

Later, the prince slept, and when next he awoke, he was in darkness.....and he knew that it was the city that had made it so.'

The time of night was unquestionably over, and yet its memory lingered, as if trying to recall something important, some secret, unsaid, but significant...in its place, in the purposeful, potent and blameless light of morning, the artist looked at the latest version of her portrait – beneath the kaleidoscope of colours, a mean, dispassionate face stared back at her. She glanced at the king and wondered how she could have thought that of him – and yet within the portrait she recognised, even as she slowly painted over what she had done, some small parts of that vicious strength remaining; an ugliness - that was actually quite beautiful. She made no effort to distinguish those lines from the lines she now painted, no attempt to thwart the unusual combination of colours that collided on the battered canvas. She painted, with an unbearably unexplainable ease.

The king's voice washed over her: "Do you believe that creating anything is better than creating nothing?"

"I suppose it depends...on what we create?" she replied, her own voice distant, her hand moving, unseen.

"What if we create...that which is beyond question? What if we create...nothing?"

The artist did not reply – she swept her brush blindly, this way and that, and then, like a deer suddenly conscious of an impending threat, she froze. For it seemed to her as if the portrait had spoken: 'Nothing' it said. 'Create nothing.'

"Nothing?" the artist mimicked, quietly.

"Yes, nothing," the king said.

The artist turned slowly to face him – but his face was not his real face, but seemed, instead, to be the face of the painting. "No thing...," he said, but the voice came from everywhere, and from nowhere.

She blinked, and rubbed her eyes. The king's face ran like watercolours in the rain. She rubbed her eyes again, and then the king was there, as he had always been, propped in his bed, sallow and frail.

He smiled.

The artist shook her head, slowly. She frowned, wondering 'who is this king?', and asked aloud: "Who is...this prince?"

The king did not stir, but instead, resumed the final instalment of his wondrous account.

They would talk, long into the day, their voices echoing
warmly into the dome that hung high overhead.

Scene vi: The Lions in the Maze

'In the darkness, the creature appeared - but no longer was it the grim and misshapen thing it had been, nor was it a random concoction of animals, either gruesome or gorgeous – it was in fact, now, quite the opposite: it was singularly, a lioness - though a long haired lioness, which imbued it with the regal aspect familiar to the male lion. Overall, it was most assuredly, in totality: female. Curiously perhaps, it was made entirely of concrete, and wore a suit of pearly white linen – but otherwise it was as magnificent an example of raw feline beauty as one could possibly imagine!

Every morning its graceful figure would announce itself by stealthily casting its shadow around the rotunda, as it climbed in through the great oculus above. Impossibly it would scale down the walls, and come and sit by the prince.

They would talk, long into the day, their voices echoing warmly into the dome that hung high overhead.

"You called me an idiot," charmingly the prince reproached the creature, one sunny morning. A fantastic shaft of sunlight sliced across the concave surface of the walls – otherwise the rotunda was set into dark recesses that harboured shapes which were about as distinct as forgotten memories.

"Yes, for indeed you are." The liony creature purred.

"Yes, indeed I am."

"And you, you abandoned me once, twice, three times even. I trusted you." It purred still, and licked behind its ear, without looking at the prince.

"You lie...," the prince laughed, and gently chided the creature. "You never trusted me."

"Well, yes, true, but then again, we all lie, don't we?"

"Yes..."

"'Everything I say is a lie'...have you heard that one?"

"Yes, yes I have. I think, it's a lie."

"Yes it is."

"Your maze is very fine......"

"You've seen it?"

259

"Many times. Many times I've flown over it."

"But how do you fly, without wings...?"

"Since when, does one need wings to fly?"

"You still talk nonsense......"

"Well, yes, but then again, who talks sense?"

And so their conversations would go, like the rotunda in which they sat, round and round, ending every time with the same observation on the creature's part: "Your mirrors need polishing..."

"Yes..." Obediently, the prince would gather up the blindfold from beside his simple bed, hardly that but just a conglomeration of rugs that lay on the floor of the vast circular chamber.

As the light began to fade, the creature would propose: "Shall we?", and the two of them, not as incongruous as one might expect, both aged, slow, steady but harbouring a lithe spirit, paired like complimentary colours, would step out from the great portico - the singular feature that marked the entrance to the great rotunda - onto the meadow.

In the far, far distance the city glowed bright and heavy on every horizon, and between the city and where the prince and the liony creature stood, was the maze. It surrounded the meadow; it marked out its furthest limits, to the north, south, east and west. The walk to the maze took some considerable time - the meadow was as expansive as ever – but it was a pleasant walk: the prince was not tired by it; no remnants of the ancient city made by the prince's father remained, the meadow was cleaned of any detritus. The prince could stroll casually through the swaying grasses, knowing that whichever direction he took, the walls of the maze would be there, impassively waiting.

They were magnificent – the walls of the maze: every one, mirrored, top to bottom, side to side, and the floor too, all of the maze, mirrored - and polished to perfection.

Reflection, reality, it was therefore difficult to tell, in fact everything reflected seemed real.....and though each reflection was a distortion, the distortion was...enviable. The landscape stretched into an infinite distance, the meadow appeared to go on, forever.

Only the reflections of the prince and the creature gave indication of place, or of scale - yet even as they came closer, as their reflections grew larger, one could be forgiven for predicting that they were the anomaly, and that they would simply disappear into their own reflected image......

Such was the faultless quality of the maze; it would have inspired amazement, even if it had been crafted by some sophisticated machine – but it had been built by hand, by the prince's own hand. It had taken eons to complete: the prince had gathered every shard of mirrored glass he could find – there had been so many, so, so many – he had cleaned them, cut them and fitted them together with unlimited care, seamlessly, that hardly a joint was discernible.

Actually it had been easy to do...because it had been necessary. He could not risk anyone finding him – any of the children, that is. They could not be allowed to worry, about their 'king' who wept, and he would no longer need to worry about them, they were safe now. Safe, in the city, that lay somewhere beyond the labyrinth of the mirrored maze...

He would, though, still seek from the creature, re-assurance: "The city?" he would ask.

"You have no need to worry. You are safe here." The liony creature's voice was soft, yet deep and re-assuring.

"And the children?"

"They are safe too..."

"All of them?"

"Yes – all of them."

"You are sure?"

"Aren't you?"

The prince did not need to reply. The creature, purring, answered for him: "Of course you're not. Doubt...it is a necessary evil. No point really, in telling you not to worry?"

"No," the prince concurred.

As soon as they reached the maze, the prince set to polishing. He took guidance from the creature, though he really did not require any: his hands could distinguish the slightest blemish. He did not need to see therefore, which was convenient – because he couldn't. One might assume it was because of his blindfold, but the blindfold made no difference to his sight: his tears fell endlessly, whether blindfolded or not. It simply made things more...manageable.

He polished - the light of the moon - or was it the glow from the city? - shone down upon them, the prince and the liony creature, both reflected innumerably in every direction.

He polished - until he ached. He would polish some more, and then, before the sun began to rise, he and the creature would stroll back to the rotunda. It stood proudly right in the middle of the meadow, whether of stone or concrete it was hard to tell. Its scale was deceptive – to the meadow it appeared to be benevolent, humble. And yet inside it was vast, empty but not hollow.

With a nod, the creature would take its leave of the prince at the entrance portico. Stepping into the cool, dark interior, the prince would gently remove his blindfold; he would sleep for a while – briefly only, for he would wake to the sight of the liony creature descending down from the bright round oculus, its distinctive shadow cast by the early morning sun.

They would talk, until eventually the creature would make its daily observation: "Your mirrors need polishing...", and at the creature's prompt: "Shall we...?" they would repeat their routine, their long walk through the meadow, to the shining maze.

Every night, the prince polished, and polished.

Diligent and attentive to his task, he would meander deep into the maze, but he would never get lost, and he would never go so far as to jeopardise returning to the rotunda before the dawn. The liony creature would accompany him, wherever he went, they would always walk together, silently back to the rotunda, the prince would sleep, be woken by the liony creature, they would talk, and then make their daily pilgrimage to the maze...and so the nights and days passed......

And gradually, the prince became content.

As he grew older, and as the years passed he permitted himself the luxury of acknowledging that it was true: he was, at last: completely content. He never once, thought about his past, his father, his father's city, his time spent in the ruins, his time spent wandering...

And he never once, thought about the girl.

But then......

Early one morning, the prince was woken, not by the shadow of the liony creature, but by the sound of weeping. Soft, sad weeping.

In a panic, he stumbled from his bed; his eyes blinded by the light, he staggered, all round the rotunda – but there was nobody; his old heart pounding, he retreated back into the shelter of the rotunda's darkness; he lay down, and stared at the oculus, desperate for the creature to appear.

When it did, he immediately told it, almost feverishly, of what he had heard.

But the creature simply purred, and said: "We only hear what we want to hear."

Somehow, by its purring the prince was comforted. He convinced himself that he'd imagined the weeping, that it had simply been: a dream.

Nevertheless, from then on, his polishing became considerably more intent.

He knew he had no need, his maze was impenetrable, and none could ever pervade its endless reflections – but every night, he would linger longer in the maze, and he began to make further slight adjustments to its construction, some additional finishing touches, here and there – and as he worked, later and later into the night, he began to imagine all sorts of things:

Sometimes he thought he heard children, playing in the maze - but the maze was huge, sounds rebounded everywhere and were deceptive: perhaps he just imagined it......

Sometimes he thought that there were children sleeping, sheltered within the maze - he had to step lightly over them as he polished, feeling his way for fear of waking them: perhaps – but perhaps he just imagined it......

Sometimes he thought he felt a handprint impressed upon the surface of the maze. But it faded, never to be retrieved......

Sometimes he thought that there were no blemishes at all, and that he did not need to polish the maze, nor would he have to, ever again......but then...

Sometimes he thought he felt handprints everywhere on the mirrored surface...and that no matter how much he might polish, he would never be able to remove them... but these were simply, imaginings, and nothing more......he polished, regardless...

Sometimes he thought that he had polished the maze so much, it disappeared......but it never did, and he would return to the rotunda, confused, to sleep......and...

Sometimes, when he slept, he heard the girl, weeping, heard her delicate footfall; but it was just a dream, in his dream he would chase endlessly after her around the great rotunda - but he would never find her......

Sometimes, when he and the creature left in the evening, he thought he could see the ground around the rotunda pressed down, as if trodden on repeatedly......

Sometimes, when he and the creature returned from their nightly duty, he thought that the grasses around the rotunda were worn in the morning dew......

Sometimes, he thought he saw small footprints impressed upon the ground throughout the meadow......

Sometimes he thought he heard things, voices, saw...things...

Sometimes he thought he saw the girl......

But these were all imaginings, nothing more than that – it was just his imagination......and he imagined so, so many things.......:

Sometimes he imagined that the maze pressed in close around him, and he could never find his way out...he could not return, he could only ever go forwards......or stop......

Sometimes he imagined that the maze was the city......

Sometimes he imagined that he was the maze......

Sometimes he imagined that the maze was weeping......

Sometimes he imagined that the weeping would drown him, drown him in a sea of tears......

Sometimes he imagined that he was drowned already, drowned in the girl's tears...drowned, in her eyes......

And...

Sometimes he imagined that the girl waited for him around a corner......

Sometimes he imagined that the girl waited around every corner......

Sometimes he imagined that he was the girl......

Sometimes he imagined he was alone......

And then, one time, he imagined, that he imagined...

When the liony creature next appeared, it sat down next to the prince and said nothing.

"You don't need to keep telling me," the prince said, finally.

The creature smiled. "No?"
"No – I can do this by myself."
"You sure?"
"Yes - I'm sure."
The creature nodded, and as the prince turned away, crawled up the walls, and without even a backward glance, disappeared through the oculus.

That night, as the prince, for the first time, sat alone, polishing the mirrored surface, from around a corner appeared the girl.

The prince could not see her, and was aware of her presence, only when she took the blindfold from his eyes.

Overhead clouds parted, and in the moonlight they stared at each other, it was all they could do: they were frozen.

Down their cheeks, tracks of tears shone. They glittered in the moonlight, little by little they dried; no more tears - neither hers, nor his - followed.

Slowly, the girl smiled at the prince, that same smile which he had seen, momentarily before...the smile in the saucer, the smile reflected in the Mirror Machine. He felt his own face crack, his hand shake, dropping the soft cloth, the blindfold, he could no longer hold.

Reaching out, they put their hands gently together, and pulled each other into a perfect embrace: no longer two, but simply: one.

The corner, and all corners dissolved, as the black and white shades eddied around them, and then they also dissolved, evaporating like a last breath exhumed in the coldest fog; the creature fluttered away overhead, and disappeared, the children's laugher, faded too, the world around them, the maze, the mirrors, and every reflection – all faded, and vanished.

There was nothing left, save the city and the two figures, sheltered in each other's arms.

The echo of the curse, which had so long rung in the prince's head, echoed no more.

Hovering in the brilliant silence of the radiant city, the girl, her head nestled into the shoulder of her perfect prince, whispered, words like tears that fell, soft into the prince's ear:

"My dream…… has come true."'

Epilogue

The old king sighed and fell silent, his eyes closed and sunken, as if the recounting of his tale had exhausted him, more so, as if the telling of it had removed some very essence of his being. He appeared, again, saddened, and yet, somehow, also relieved. A weight seemed to have been lifted, and when he looked at the artist, she could hardly fail to notice a stark purity in the king's gaze. It bored into her, into her own incredulous gaze – for was that it? Was that the summation of the king's account, of this girl who wept round corners: that 'her prince had come'?

The artist was both mystified and disappointed: mentally she winced. There must be more to it than that, and so she asked: "What happened...to the prince, and the girl...?"

"Can't you guess...for of course, they both lived, happily ever after."

The artist could not tell if the king was joking. He held a smile in his words, though his face did not show it. She felt her disappointment deepen.

"Tell me," the king said: "Have you found your prince?"

"No – no, I don't want a prince..."

"No?"

"No."

"No – but that is what you wish for...that is what everyone wishes for." The artist shook her head, but the king insisted: "Prince, princess – it does not matter. We all want, one or the other."

"But...a prince ...?"

The king corrected her. "We all of us, want to be loved," he said.

The artist was inclined to disagree – but she couldn't. The simplicity of the king's statement, and the quiet authority with which he said it, refuted any argument. She held though, reservations, but again, it was as if the king had read her mind.

267

"Even then, being loved is easy. Loving, now, that is harder...for us all to love, we have to love ourselves, and how can we do that, truthfully, if we are none of us perfect?"

For the first time the artist could predict what it was the king intended. "Presumably...we have to love our faults?" she suggested.

"And if we love our faults...we have no faults. That, of course, may be a fault..." The king smiled. "Tricky, isn't it?" He shook his head. "We spend an inordinate amount of time wasted as a consequence of our differences, and yet, we all have so much in common. Even if we were to dispute every point, who could dispute this one thing: the desire to be loved? Don't we have for certain this one thing – and yet, how could we have been made, to exist so, wishing, all of us, for the one thing that we have no control over, the one thing that matters to us all more than anything, and yet it is as elusive as ...as knowing what is around a corner?"

He paused, and then said, quietly: "Yet who would wish, for a world without corners? I would that there were none...but then again, just think of what would be lost?"

The artist thought the king was being rhetorical – but he asked again: "In a world without corners, what would be lost?"

Without hesitation, she replied: "Hope. We would lose....hope."

"Yes, hope. Of course - we would lose hope. We hope, don't we...all of us, around corners? Perhaps, that is what they are for...for you never know-", and the artist finished the king's sentence for him: "You may find perfection, around a corner."

The king smiled, and before the artist could say anything further, said: "The court wishes to know, what are my wishes?"

"Yes – they ask me, every time I leave, whether you have spoken."

"And they want to know what, exactly?"

"You have no heir..."

"No, I have no heir...no hair either!"

She smiled, but still could not save herself from expediting the request of the Royal Court. "My king-" she began.

"I am not your king. I am nobody's king."

If his words suggested self-pity, his tone, negated it, as did the seriousness of his countenance.

"But...the Royal Court? They need to know, your wish-"

"My wish? My wishes have all come true...but for one: for you to finish my portrait."

At the mention of the portrait, the artist looked at her unfinished work. The ease with which she had painted the night before had evaporated.

"I still can't get it right...," she said.

"No ......you never will. Not if you continue to think of me as your king."

"But you are a king...my king..."

She dropped her head, fighting back tears. Gently the king reached out, and kindly stroked her red hair.

"I am not a king. I am a man. And what one man can do, any man can. Or woman." He lifted her face up, and smiling, winked. The artist couldn't help but smile back, as the king said: "Paint the man, not the king, that is what I ask, and that is all. Paint what you see."

"You've made it harder..."

"No, not really. Take your time, all the time in the world...and make as many mistakes as you like. The more the better...do not compare, do not reason...create." He smiled again, his kingly smile. "Remember, it is better to create something..."

"Than nothing ...," the artist said.

He patted her hand, nodding. "Yes, yes indeed...oh, and one more thing..."

Indicating for the artist to come closer, he whispered into her ear......

The artist sat for a long, long time, staring at the old king, whose last breath had hardly registered – his face showed no sign of change, but simply reposed, as if asleep.

In the evening, as the sun set, she went to the terrace that looked out over the great city. She stood, and stared, at the wonder of the city: a city without walls, without gates, without streets or squares – at a city of endless corners......lights gradually came on, peppering the view below like campfires randomly lit in a forest.

"Beautiful," she said. She looked back at the king who had created it.

Silently, and without prediction, she wept.

She could not help it – her tears fell, unhindered, and without levee. They might have drowned the city below, so corpulent were they, they might have submerged it and rendered it lost to the mists of fable – but for some invisible hand that captured every one. Those same hands led the artist to her easel. Mixing the salty liquid with her paints, she painted, blinded by tears as the words of the king rattled round and round in her head: "Have you ever wondered about corners?"

When finally the portrait was complete, she left it standing next to the king's bed, and left. She was met, as usual, by members of the Royal Court, the few remaining: they were evidently disheartened, and lost, without expectation – it was not surprising that the artist's announcement: that she had completed her commissioned task was met with unenthusiastic and disconsolate acknowledgement. She was not retained, and free to leave, and for a second, hesitated, her hand lingering on the soft metal of the great door handle that led to the city beyond. It would be so easy, so, so easy......

She turned.

"The king is dead," she said.

The knowledge was met with little more than slight nods, and a collective sigh. She was inclined to say nothing further: the king's legacy, entrusted to these defeated individuals? She could just leave, and keep the king's final wish secret – but loyalty forbade it. Loyalty, and trust.

She cleared her throat.

"He told me his final wish," she said.

At first nothing happened – then one of the court, frowning, asked her to repeat what she said.

"Before he died – he told me his final wish," she said again.

Suddenly they were all on their feet, clamouring about her. The court absentees were called, other notaries and scribes; word spread throughout the city, an excitement bordering on fever rippled through the streets. Every inhabitant gathered into the great debating chamber that sat in the centre of the city – it was packed, tight from floor to rafter, as the artist was ushered in, and led ceremoniously to the speaker's platform.

Expectantly everyone stood, nervous and wide eyed, as the artist was invited to tell them, to tell them all, of their beloved kings final wish.

'They're not going to like this', the artist thought. 'Oh well...'

She swallowed, and took a breath.

"He wants you to tear the city down," she said.

There was a stunned silence. Faces of the Royal Court were set, and aghast.

"He wants you to tear it down – and re-build it – "

"Re-build it?"

"Yes – re-build it. He wants you to rebuild it - better than it was."

"Better?"

"Yes – better."

For a while the silence extended, and if possible to imagine, deepened.

Then a voice from out of the crowd, said: "But – it is perfect. How can we make a city, better than this one?"

The artist smiled.

"That," she said, "is exactly the question..."

And with that she stepped from the platform, made her way through the assembled crowd, and disappeared.

And so it came to pass, that the great city was destroyed, and another built in its place. It has long since passed into oblivion, this city, and even those cities that have been built since, each one better than the last – they all exist only in fables and fairy tales. But perhaps the city, built in response to the king's final wish, persists in memory, more than any other as being unique, for its renown born primarily from the legend of its great gallery that housed the curious portrait.

To this day, many recall tales handed down from generation to generation, of a time when all the people of the world sought to visit the great gallery, the centrepiece of the city, to stare at the portrait of a once great king, a portrait few would argue, was the face of a king, but also the face of a man...or was it a woman? It was hard to tell.

It was a face, nonetheless, smiling, mysteriously, as if knowing, with absolute certainty, what lay around corners......

Post-Script:

The story of the girl who wept around corners, like all the stories the princess told her friends, held them in captivated rapture – that there could be such worlds, full of kings and princes and artists and trees and houses and cities and farms and heroes and villains and spaceships and aliens and pirates....the preface list was endless!

How she imagined such things from staring into the grey blank shadowy world below was unfathomable – of course, if they knew the truth, that their towers grew from the back of the ghost of an enormous winged mare, a Pegasus with unicorn crown, that had died too young, and that they were perpetually in flight, as the Pegasus, ignorant of its state, searched in blind hope from one wondrous land to another for her home, resting occasionally to drink from convenient streams that snaked confidently through barren landscapes, they might have shared less enthusiastically their respect for the princess. She had told them of this fantasy, and they nodded as much in accord as they did with every other tale she told. Her insistence of the truth of it did not negate their affection: she was wonderful, and they wished that they too, could dream, as she clearly could!

For her part, the princess wished she could sew better, dance better, talk better, but more so, that she could explain better. But she couldn't. "I can't explain," she would continually worry, and berate herself for her failure. She might have perished with the weight of it, but for realising, in a moment of clarity, what she had to do.

So one day she climbed to the top of the tallest tower and threw herself from it.

She fell, in the absolute certainty that the ghost of the winged horse below would catch her; that it would break her fall with its coat so soft, that it would in turn gently neigh, would nuzzle her, with affection and would let her cling to its pearly white mane, and carry her to worlds even beyond her capacity to imagine.

Stranger still that the world did so peacefully sleep, be-calmed and adrift, and one and all dreamt the one and same dream: the killer sweet dream of dreams!

THE REST OF THE WORLD

Once, upon a time, there was a coincidence - as unlikely a coincidence as a coincidence could likely ever be. For it so happened, that by some chance, the world, and everyone in it, went to their bed at precisely and for the same time: every sole person - man, woman, child and small babe, from every profession and every trade: every baker and maker, and carpetbag shaker, every faker and house decorator; every sky-diver, every driver, skiver, miser and made up disguiser; every kind giver, motor home liver and those who deliver; every sky watcher, every ball catcher and eager team coacher; everyone lame, shamed, chained or once famed; everyone near and far, far away, from every corner of the globe as it spun: from the north, from the south, from the west and the eastern rising sun; and also, each bug and wee and big beastie, on land, flying high in the sky or deep down in the sea; and also each plant, each tree and each seed from each pretty bright flower; and every ghost from within every machine; each and every known living thing, fell to rest, to sleep, all at exactly the one and identical hour.

Strange though it be to accept such a thing could once have occurred, it has to be told, true, and as true as a word: the world then fell silent, and nothing did move, nought fought, nor argued, whispered, nor wept, nor cried, lied nor defied, and none were confused or misused, whilst all of the creatures, the great and the small, slept, and they dreamt; and, boy, did they dream! Stranger still that the world did so peacefully sleep, becalmed and adrift, and one and all dreamt the one same dream: the killer sweet dream of dreams!

For everyone dreamt: that man became woman, and woman became man; every child became adult, and adult survived; and every black became white, every white became black; and every city, a house;

275

and a forbidding prison: a pale and greenhouse; and every train station a tumbling dice, a reward: a vice, and a poor transit camp became a street-map; every church became mission, a phrase: a transition, every castle set high on a hill became an illegal, and hid whiskey still; every roof slate became a green and sweet leaf, and every leaf became a full flower, and a flower: immortal; every sock became a cloud, every cloud became a hug; a shoe became a hat, a hat, got fat; a car became a horse, and a cart became ok to be put before it; every well became a tower, and a tower: a sky rocket; every grain of sand: a forest and a tree became a lung; every stone became a paper, and a paper became sharp scissors and then scissors became stone; every brick became a wall, a wall became a window and a window, an egg carton; an egg carton laid an egg, and an egg became a sausage, and a sausage became a pair; a movie: a bestseller and a plane became a plain, and the sunshine: reigned; and plain became rain, and plain became plane; a mirror: a masseur, and a debt: an avenue; right became right, and right became deaf, and entry signs, left; dark became key, to delete or return, and time became money, and money: a burn; every clock became a lamp, and a lamp became a candle, and a candle, once a glass, became the wind; thunder became wonder, and lightning became lighting; every line became a point, and a curve became a circle, a triangle met a sphere, and a sphere became a stair; up became now down, heaven became hell, and hell became a haven; a hall: a hotel lobby; a hero became loser, a loser a keen hobby, a mugger: a device, a terrorist, Christ, a chess piece: pizza slice; demon became angel, an angel only child; every fox became a hound, a hound became a mouse, a cat became a dog, and dog became a cat; and sea became as sand, sand became as rock, and rock became as air; fire became water, and water became solid, and solid became soft, notes became a silence, and silence became easy; red became blue, blue became green, night became day, summer: winter; every crowd became one, and one became none; every boy became a girl, and a girl became a boy, and death......became a lost, and found, and long forgotten, favourite, cute and cuddly toy.

276

When they awoke, when the world and everything in it, opened its eyes, yawned, and stretched, and blinked in the soft warming light of the early morning sun, every secret that had been, for forever, hidden and forbidden, was shamelessly revealed. None, not even one, was shunned: each was unveiled, and the most secret one of all, disclosed, and exposed, and deposed, and at last there were no rooms, for secrets - and sorrow was no more.

*No people were hurt as a consequence of this dream...no planes fell from the sky...how so, you may ask......? Well, in dreams, and only in dreams, anything, and everything is possible......

I finished your story Christopher:

THE COW THAT HAD NO SPOTS

Once upon a time there was a cow that had no spots. The cow was rather sad that she had no spots - apart from her rather curious distinction, the cow was the same as the other cows; but when she went to play with them, they all laughed at her: "What kind of cow are you, that has no spots?" they sneered, "re: moooooooohhhhh-ve yersel', spotless!" they jeered, rather meanly!

So she went to play with the horses; but they also laughed at her for having no spots: "Neeeeiiigggghhhh chance, spotless!" they jeered, rather haughtily!

So she went to play with the chickens; but they also laughed at her for having no spots: "Cluck off, spotless!" they jeered, rather rudely!

So she went to play with the pigs; but they also laughed at her for having no spots: "So oft it chances, that for some vicious mole of nature the stamp of one defect shall in general censure take corruption from that particular fault, spotless!" they jeered, quoting HAMlet *(Katies idea!)* rather pretentiously!

The cows, the horses, the chickens, the pigs: they all laughed at the cow - but as for the sheep? They didn't laugh, they didn't even giggle, or chuckle, snigger, snort or chortle; they didn't even smirk!

And why should that be? Perhaps because they too, like the cow, had no spots? But neither the pigs nor the chickens had spots. Perhaps it was because they, like the cow, were completely white? Perhaps…? Perhaps it was because they, like the cow, ate grass? Perhaps…?

Or perhaps the reason that the sheep did not laugh at the cow was because they were kind and considerate, not stupid, cruel, bigoted and ignorant - like the cows, horses, chickens and pigs!

Or, to put it another way, perhaps it was simply because the sheep were not: 'Baaaaahhhhhh-d!'

So the cow decided to ignore the other animals, and played with the sheep instead……she never went back to the chickens or the horses or the pigs, nor especially, to the cows.

She may have been one, but that didn't mean she had to act like one!

From then on she stayed with the sheep, and the sheep in turn effectively adopted her, so proud were they to have a cow as one of their own - and the cow, content to have found true friends, lived happily ever after (until shearing day of course!)

I have another story Christopher, I don't have the title yet, but I have the first line:

'Once upon a time, there was a little boy who loved everyone......'

Sweet dreams, wee man...

love you...

x

'My hope is constant in thee.'
        MacDonald of Clanranald Motto

Printed in Great Britain
by Amazon

20317348R00167